ember's fire

NORAH WILSON

SOMETHING SHINY
PRESS

Published by:
Norah Wilson / Something Shiny Press
P.O. Box 30046, Fredericton, NB E3B 0H8

Cover by Kim Killion, The Killion Group Inc.
Edited by Lori Gallagher
Book Design by Author E.M.S.

— one —

EMBER STANDISH *tap-tapped* the trunk of a leaning birch at that one particular bend where a tiny, unnamed spring fed into the Prince River, for no other reason than she'd double-tapped that tree dozens of times before. Though not in a very long while. Nearly ten years.

Picard's camp. That's where she was headed, and she was almost there—two miles from her starting point at the base of the mountain where she'd left her two brothers.

Her gut tightened at the thought of what awaited her there. *Who* awaited her.

For about the hundredth time, she thrust the thought away. It was a beautiful fall afternoon and she intended to enjoy it as long as she could.

She looked down at the gully in front of her. She could probably pick her way across the moss-slippery rocks without even getting her hiking boots wet, but where was the fun in that? Grinning, she reached up, wrapped gloved hands around the leaning birch and swung herself out and over the narrow stream, releasing her grasp to land lightly on the other side.

Nailed it!

Her smile widened.

This was rough terrain, but the challenge only invigorated

her. After a decade away, it was good to know she was still up for anything this land could dish out.

Ah, Ember Standish, you've still got it.

"Make that *Dr.* Ember Standish." Sometimes she had to remind herself.

Okay, she *liked* to remind herself. She'd put ten years and countless hours of classes, studying, and residency training between the woman she was now and the girl she'd been when last she made this hike along the Prince River.

Well, not technically a girl. She had been all of eighteen, waiting for Jace's arrival, her stomach jumping with nervousness and yes, hot anticipation.

He had been one year older…

She drew a deep breath, filling her lungs with the cool, fresh air. She wasn't a girl anymore. This time when she faced Jace Picard, she would do so as a woman. A successful, educated, confident woman.

Not that she'd ever lacked for confidence. Even as an adolescent—hell, even during those awkward pre-teen years—she'd been self-assured. She'd always done well academically. Spectacularly well, actually. And though she liked her eyelash curler and lip gloss as much as the next woman, she'd never been beauty queen material. Too many freckles for that, and her nose had that little bump in it. She'd inherited those things from her mother, Margaret Standish, along with her pale skin, red hair, and green eyes, and that was all right with her. Even when kids teased her about her carrot top, she'd never really wanted to change it. Well, there was that one time in undergrad when she'd gone through a white-streak phase…

She smiled at the memories. It would have been impossible to grow up in Margaret and Arden Standish's home without being confident. Ember knew she was always valued and respected. Safe. Loved.

She'd come to trust that feeling.

That had been her great mistake.

Jace Xavier Picard had been her great mistake.

She tramped on a few more minutes, pulling her gaze away from the river to her left and peering into the woods on her right. She was getting close. She knew it.

The late Wayne Picard—known by most everyone in Harkness, New Brunswick, as Old Man Picard—had chosen to locate his camp way back in off the river. The same folk also knew that if they should find themselves at the mercy of the elements while hunting or hiking or fiddleheading, they were welcome to take temporary shelter there, as long as they left the place as they found it. To that end, there was always a spare key stashed in the Export Tobacco tin nailed to the wall of the shed out back. The trick of it was the cabin wasn't exactly easy to find. Constructed of logs, it was naturally camouflaged in amongst the trees barely a corner of the building was visible from the river's edge. It was well off the beaten path, and that path wasn't very beaten to begin with.

A moment later, she spotted it. And caught her breath on an unexpectedly sharp pang.

Dammit! She'd had the better part of an hour to prepare herself to see him again. How could just the sight of the cabin get her heart pounding?

Forget that. How could the hurt feel so fresh after a freaking *decade*? She'd come back to Harkness dozens of times in the intervening years. Any pain she'd felt had become progressively more muted, time having layered the wound with protective scar tissue.

You never had to see him those other times. And you sure as hell never had to come out here.

That was it. The cabin itself. So many memories were attached to that place. Tender, hopeful, happy memories—all of them shattered by Jace's betrayal.

Ember swallowed. She would *not* let her mind go back there. She was not that starry eyed, head-over-heels young woman anymore. Bursting with trust? That was behind her.

She was a doctor. Had graduated in the top five percent of her class and had no less than a dozen offers on the table.

Her spirits buoyed at the thought. A hospital in Toronto was dangling a hefty signing bonus, though it didn't compare to what the brand new, state-of-the-art facility in Montana was offering. She hadn't ruled out Victoria or Calgary, either. Both of those offers were enticing, for different reasons.

Then there was Long Beach, California. Hannibal Thompson and Joanne Pine, a couple of med school buddies, were buying into Hannibal's parents' practice in the Golden State, allowing them to scale back their activities. There was room for one more partner in the booming family and obstetrics practice that catered to the area's wealthiest clientele. Hannibal and Joanne wanted that one more partner to be Ember.

The buy-in was huge, but she could swing it. Part of her university ride had been on scholarship, which kept the student loans somewhat under control. But even with that debt load, banks were anxious to extend new, ridiculously large lines of credit in view of her future earning potential. And it wasn't like she had to come up with it all up front. Her friends were prepared to take part of it in instalment payments, over the next five years. She'd had a look at the practice's financial statements, of course. It would be a sound investment. More than sound. It would be positively lucrative. She couldn't think about it without hearing a *ka-ching* in her head.

No, she hadn't gone into medicine for the money, but after being a poor student for so long the prospect of making some was appealing. So was the idea of working with Hannibal and Joanne.

And California was thousands of miles away. A lifetime away from Harkness. A lifetime away from this river. Harkness Mountain. These memories.

Old Man Picard's damned camp.

She drew a deep breath and started toward the cabin.

What would her dad think about her relocating to California? Her brothers, Scott and Titus? She'd been on the verge of raising the possibility earlier, as they'd sat together, munching on the world's best grilled cheese sandwiches. She'd yet to sign the contract—still had a week to mull it over—but she had pretty much decided. Telling her family would solidify the decision more than anything else would.

But just as she'd put down her sandwich and opened her mouth to ease into that discussion, the phone had rung and their dad had gone into the living room to answer it. Scott had taken the opportunity to grill Titus about whatever mysterious reason he had for calling the two of them home, but there'd been no time for that discussion either. Arden had returned to the kitchen with the search and rescue request.

Well, it wasn't an official search and rescue mission. The call had been from Faye Siliker, Ocean Siliker's mother. Mrs. Siliker thought her daughter might be up on Harkness Mountain and was worried enough to ask Arden to dispatch Titus to search for her. After what had happened to Ocean's best friend Lacey Douglas up there, Ember could understand Mrs. Siliker's concern. But at the same time, Ember knew Ocean. She was smart, resourceful. A Harkness girl. She'd be fine. And if she was up on the mountain in any kind of trouble, she'd be in good hands with Titus. He'd find her.

She grinned. Ocean had always had the biggest crush on Titus. Maybe this was the push her dim-witted brother needed. Maybe he'd be smart enough to ask her out.

What was it her father always said? *Some folks need a little push.*

But that wasn't the only call for Titus's assistance Arden had fielded. The pharmacist, Danny Parker, a long-time friend of her father's—had also called to ask a favor. Some fellow had sprained his ankle while hiking in the woods and managed to get himself to Old Man Picard's camp. From there, he'd used his cell phone to call the pharmacy for pain meds and a pressure bandage to treat the sprain. He'd further requested that the delivery person stop at his vehicle, grab his briefcase and hump it out to the cabin with the meds. Normally, Danny's teenage grandsons would have handled it, but both boys were out of town. Thus Danny had called Arden to ask Titus to do it.

Of course, once the call about Ocean came in, it took priority. A potentially lost hiker beat a courier mission every time. Titus, the strongest and most experienced of them, was a no-brainer for the potential mountain rescue job. That left Ember as the obvious choice for the sprain victim, given her medical training. But she'd had to fight for the privilege.

She bristled with the memory of the discussion that ensued when she announced she would deliver the supplies and treat the sprain. Her overprotective brothers hadn't liked that idea one bit. No way were they going to let their kid sister hike into the middle of nowhere to attend to some unknown guy.

Let her do it? Huh! No way were they going to stop her.

They'd still be arguing about it if their father hadn't stepped in to endorse Ember for the mission. Though if Titus and Scott had known who owned that sprained ankle, they might have bucked their father's decision. And frankly, if she'd known who it was, she might not have fought so hard for the job.

But when asked who the patient was, Arden had confessed that the name had slipped his mind. She'd been alarmed. *Something slipping Arden Standish's mind?* That was so unlike him. Immediately, she'd started fretting that that was why Titus had called her and Scott home. Was their father suffering from dementia? Early stages of Alzheimer's?

There'd been no time to talk about her father's health or anything else. She, Scott and Titus had headed out directly for the parking lot at the base of the mountain. There they'd found both the vehicle Ocean Siliker had been driving and the injured hiker's luxury SUV. Using the keyless entry code the pharmacist had relayed, Ember had retrieved the hiker's briefcase. It wasn't until she read the monogram on the case's brass plate as she was strapping it to her backpack that she realized it was Jace she was going to find in that cabin. Who else had the initials JXP?

She'd also realized instantly that there was nothing wrong with her father's memory. He'd conveniently "forgotten" the hiker's identity to give her one of those pushes he was so fond of.

Her face must have betrayed her, because her brothers had suddenly gotten keen for Scott to make the trek and Ember to wait in the truck. She'd vetoed that idea, reminding them their father had given the assignment to her because of her medical training. Sure, Scott knew first aid, but no one knew why the guy had twisted his ankle in the first place. Maybe he had an underlying medical condition that caused him to stumble or even faint, in which case it wouldn't be just a matter of icing down and wrapping a sprain. Besides, if Titus found Ocean injured, Scott was definitely the best option for backup. Not only was he physically stronger than Ember, he was a more experienced climber. Reluctantly, they'd had to agree.

She was less than fifty meters from the Picard camp when her cell buzzed. She stopped, pulled her phone from her sleeve pocket. A text from Scott.

Hey Kid.

She knew to keep the conversation short and sweet. Otherwise Scott would be grilling her on every step she'd taken, or was about to take.

Cabin's in sight. No worries. Then for good measure, she added, *Stop calling me Kid, Jerk.*

She slid the phone back into her pocket. Then, drawing a deep breath, she walked up to the cabin.

Warm yellow light spilled out from the small front window.

Despite herself, her heart fluttered in her chest. She'd

placed a light in that very window once herself, a long, long time ago. But it had been a candle, one tiny flame, not this bright, electric light...

She shook the memories away.

She was Ember Standish, M.D. All grown up, with *lots* of places to go. So much to do.

So over the past.

She was no longer in love with the captain of the high school boxing team—Coach O'Bryan's middleweight star. Carrying love notes in pencil cases, writing their initials—E&J—all over the place.

Three crows flew past, their cawing cries seeming to mock her. Then they were gone and there was nothing but the low whoosh of wind and distant murmur of the river. Ember dropped her pack at the door, glad to get the weight of it off her shoulders. She wanted to stretch her back before she knocked.

That and she wanted to compose herself before she walked in. A chance to slide into doctor mode. Objective, but not too detached. Professional.

She hefted her knapsack by the handle and knocked on the door. "Hello in there. It's Dr. Ember Standish. I'm here to help. Danny Parker sent me."

After a few heartbeats, she heard a flat, "Come in."

That voice. Low and velvety, it still made something quiver low in her belly. Thank God for the hour of forewarning! Otherwise she might have turned and fled.

Firming her lips, she opened the door and stepped inside.

The kitchen area was lit by the bulb over the sink—the one she'd seen from outside—but the rest of the cabin's interior was dimmer. Not so dim, though, that she didn't spot him instantly. He sat on one end of a double recliner love seat, his feet elevated.

Jace Picard. Her big mistake—the man she'd trusted.

She closed the door behind her, and walked toward him,

her eyes adjusting as she went. The cut of his jaw, that black hair, so dark against his complexion. That well-muscled body. The piercing blue of his eyes. It was all so achingly familiar.

The look in his eye, on the other hand, was not so familiar. She'd never seen that kind of coldness in his face.

She was pretty sure it matched the iciness in her own.

"So it *is* you." She dropped her bag on the floor. "You son of a bitch!"

− two −

JACE PICARD looked up at Ember Standish.

Under his scrutiny, she crossed her arms tightly in front of her, her face grim. Clearly she was not thrilled to see him. Of course, he didn't need the hostile body language to tell him that. The whole *son-of-a-bitch* remark pretty much gave it away.

But—damn it all to hell—she was more beautiful now than ever. She'd always been fit, but her lithe teenage form had given way to a woman's body. More lush and generous in some places, yet more angular and hard in others. Her face in particular looked thinner, as though life had honed and sharpened her features.

"I'd get up," he said, gesturing to his propped up ankle, "but under the circumstances..."

"You're forgiven." Her gaze raked over him. "For not getting up, I mean."

As if there had been any doubt. "Naturally."

She removed her jacket and turned to hang it in the small doorless closet like she always used to. As if nothing had changed up here.

Little had.

She unwound a bright red scarf from around her neck and slid it onto the hanger with her jacket. She always had loved scarves. This one looked to be expensive.

There was something else he noticed about that scarf: she wasn't threatening to wrap it around his neck. Which could only mean that Titus hadn't told her about the land deal yet.

Outerwear stashed, Ember turned back toward him and he was struck again by the changes in her.

A full decade. That's how long it had been since he'd seen her. Well, in the flesh. He'd seen pictures of her, though. *The Harkness Times*—which had actually made the leap to online five years ago—had run a few stories about her over the years. Announcements of scholarships. A picture of her at the family Christmas party a few years ago. Human interest stuff. The sort of small-town business that kept a little paper like the *Times* alive.

Then there were the updates from his stepfather, Wayne Picard. The old man had passed along every bit of gossip that came his way about that "smart-as-a-whip Standish girl" whenever Jace stopped in to visit. Which had been often, especially toward the end. Jace had nodded and smiled as, year after year, he was filled in about the life of Ember Standish.

The one who'd broken his heart.

The last time he'd actually laid eyes on her was ten years ago. Well, ten and change. July 2, specifically. He'd met her for breakfast in town that morning. Titus had dropped her off at the local diner. With a nod to Jace that was half warning/half even more warning, in case he didn't get it the first time, Ember's overprotective brother had driven off.

Jace and Ember had been dating a solid year by then. They'd fooled around, but they'd been holding off on going all the way until she was eighteen.

Old fashioned? Absolutely. But she'd wanted it that way, and he'd respected her too much—loved her too much—to push her beyond her comfort zone. They'd waited well on the side of the line she'd drawn. It was going to be the first time for both of them.

He still remembered what they'd eaten that morning. She'd had French toast with strawberry jam, while he'd worked his way through a western omelet. And as they'd sat at that corner booth with the metal napkin dispenser and wire basket full of condiments, she'd talked non-stop about their future. Not just about the night before them, but all of it. He'd held off university for a year to work with his stepfather in the family business. That year had made him even more sure he'd wanted to pursue a business degree, and he was planning to do it at the same university where Ember was set to do her pre-med. They'd be moving to Ottawa in the fall. That was to be the beginning—the *next* beginning—for them. They were young and in love and they had their whole lives ahead of them. Lives they planned to spend together.

Jace had sat grinning like a fool that morning as she'd talked. In his heart, he'd known he was the luckiest man in the world.

Also the most nervous one.

Not just about the sex. He was going to ask Ember to marry him. He had the ring. A narrow gold band with a small diamond. His stepfather had offered to give Jace the money to get her a ginormous rock, but Jace had declined. It would be enough for his Ember, and after university when he could afford to, he'd replace it with something more deserving of her.

And as he'd sat there happily listening to Ember's headfirst planning between jam-slathered French toast bites, he couldn't wait for the evening to come.

But that evening never came. When he'd reached the cabin, she wasn't there. He'd sat alone in the thick of the pines, growing more anxious by the moment as the sky grew darker. When she'd finally called his cell, he'd been so relieved. Until she'd unloaded on him about the pictures. It was the first he'd heard of them. Her voice was so tear-choked, he'd had a hard time grasping what she was saying. When he realized what she was accusing him of, he'd leapt to defend himself. She'd hung up, then hung up again when he'd called back. The next time he tried, the line was busy. Clearly she'd taken the phone off the hook.

Frantic, he'd raced back along the river, out to the parking lot. Then he'd sped to Ember's house. Arden had met him at the door, gruffly advising that Ember wasn't interested in speaking with him. With no alternative, he'd left, determined to come back the next day after she'd had a chance to cool off. Except when he'd turned up the next morning, she'd already left on the outgoing bus.

He'd gone home, determined to pack his bags and follow her. But then he'd spoken to Terry.

She'd broken his heart, utterly.

That was a long time ago, he admonished himself. *Back when you had a heart to break.*

Yet something jumped in his chest when she drew a breath, and said his name.

"Jacc…"

He lifted an eyebrow

"I know you're not my biggest fan, and I'm sure as hell not yours, but I really am here to help you. Can we at least try to be civil?"

Civil? That might be a stretch. But he nodded anyway. "Sure. I'd offer you some coffee, but I'm a little indisposed right now."

It had been a painful hop around the kitchen once he'd made it into the camp, lighting the old wood stove for warmth, plugging in the electric kettle, and digging the vodka, fresh lemon, and honey out of his pack. But the exertion had been worth it. He'd downed one hot toddy standing there at the counter, a medicinal-sized smash of vodka, hot water, fresh squeezed lemon and honey. Then he'd made another toddy—a stiffer one—to sip on before settling himself on one side of the reclining love seat.

"Right. The ankle." She crossed the short distance between them and bent to look at his feet. She had no trouble identifying the injured one, which was obviously swollen. Gently, she peeled his woolen sock back far enough to expose the ankle fully. She stopped when he winced.

She turned her green eyes up at him. "Sorry."

"It's okay."

"What happened?" she asked.

"Stupid. I was hiking along the river's edge, making my way up here. I slipped on a rock and turned my ankle, right where two birch trees lean out over the water."

"Where we used to swing over that little gully?"

"You remember."

"Yes," she said flatly. "I remember."

"Well, I've gained a few pounds since we used to swing like monkeys from those branches. In recent years, I've just picked my way across on foot, but the rocks turned out to be slipperier than they looked."

"I'll have to take your word for it. I swung across." She lowered her eyes to his swollen ankle again. She began to poke and prod. He sucked in a breath, but didn't flinch.

"So, why are you here, Ember?"

She glanced up, surprised. "I told you. Danny Parker called the house looking for a volunteer to hump this stuff out to you."

"I understood he was going to send one of his grandsons."

"Both boys are out of town for the Thanksgiving weekend, as it turns out, so he turned to Dad."

Jace watched her face. "And did you know Danny's parcel was for me? Did Arden?"

"Dad claimed the name slipped his mind, so I had no idea until I retrieved your briefcase." She tilted her head in the direction of her pack with the slim briefcase still strapped to it. "Not too many people with that monogram, I don't think."

So she'd found out it was him in the parking lot, by which

time it would have been too late for her to decline the job without losing face.

"I never would have called Danny and asked for this stuff if I'd known—"

"That you'd be facing me again?"

And there it was—the challenge in her voice. That bit of tell-it-like-it-is Ember Standish. He was still working out how to respond to that when she held up an apologetic hand.

"Sorry. That was uncalled for."

"No worries."

She bent her head to the task again, easing his sock the rest of the way off. Then she gently explored his foot and ankle. Her hands were warm, her touch capable as she performed her examination.

He cleared his throat. "I'm surprised Titus or Scott didn't make the trek out here."

She looked up. "How did you know Scott was home?"

His pulse—already elevated from her touch on his skin—quickened. "Thanksgiving weekend." He forced a shrug, as if the holiday itself was explanation enough. He hoped it was.

Ember studied him a moment. Then she got up and retrieved the pharmacy bag from her pack. She tore the wrapper off a fresh compression bandage and began wrapping it around the lower part of his foot. "Scott's back at the truck, in the parking lot. Titus had to hike up the mountain to help someone."

"Is someone hurt?" he asked sharply.

Until his stepfather got sick, Jace had spent most of his time in Fredericton, where he ran a consulting practice helping small businesses. But when Wayne was sidelined by illness, his role with WRP Holdings had grown. With Wayne's death, it had expanded even more. Which meant he was now spending more time in Harkness in a sparsely furnished, company-owned apartment, and less at his professionally decorated condo in Fredericton. But despite having been away so much, he still knew the locals. Well, most of them. The old families.

Wayne Picard had left the bulk of his sizable estate and business—sixty percent—to his biological son from his first marriage, Jace's half-brother, Terry Picard. The other forty percent of everything had gone to Jace.

WRP Holdings owned a lot of land and properties around the Prince Region. Terry was aiming to acquire even more. He was especially anxious to get his hands on the Standish land.

Jace felt his jaw tighten.

"Hurt?" Ember shook her head. "I don't think so. Lost, maybe."

It took him a split second to realize she was talking about the hiker on the mountain. He'd do well to keep his mind off that whole Standish farm thing.

"Glad to hear it," he said. "I'd feel bad if someone was hurt up there and I'd hauled away a legit doctor over a sprained ankle." She just looked up at him and back to his foot. He found himself wanting to see those eyes again. "A local or a tourist?"

"Local," she said, without looking up from her work. "Ocean Siliker. I understand she's home from New York for a bit."

He knew Ocean. She'd been a year behind him in school, as had Ember. Jace relaxed a little. She'd always struck him as a bit introspective, but level-headed and capable enough.

She pulled her backpack close and dug out a piece of foam and a pair of scissors. As he watched, she began cutting two U-shaped pieces out of the foam.

"You didn't get that at the pharmacy," he observed. "What's it for?"

She placed one under the left side of his ankle bone, with the open side up. "These will fill the hollows under your ankle bone, keeping fluid from building up there. It'll also give the ankle more stability."

With that, she put the foam piece down, grabbed the roll of bandage and began wrapping. Silently, he watched her circle the ball of his foot a couple of times, then loop it up behind the ankle and back down under the arch. She changed the position of his foot slightly to achieve a right angle. Pain shot through him, but he managed not to wince. Or so he thought.

"Sorry." She grimaced. "I know this doesn't feel great, but it'll help get the swelling down. That alone will make it feel better, as will the meds I'll give you in a minute."

"It's okay. Keep going." To distract himself, he said, "I can't believe Scott didn't volunteer to hike out here, even if he didn't know it was me laid up."

"I'm a doctor; I was the sensible choice." She positioned both foam pieces beneath his ankle bones and wrapped the bandage around to hold everything snugly in place, continuing with the figure eight pattern. "But he definitely would have insisted on coming with me, or more likely *instead* of me, had he known it was you." She looked up at Jace. "Dad conveniently forgot that it was you needing the help, and was quick to support me for the job. Which tells me he either didn't want you and Scott to cross paths, or that he *did* want you and me to."

He couldn't imagine why Arden would want to put either of the younger Standishs in his path, given the reaction they were likely to have to the news about the farm. But obviously he'd had no choice, what with Titus having to go search for Ocean. Again he cursed his inattention crossing that gully. This stupid ankle had forced Arden's hand. Jace hated that.

He and Arden had always gotten along. In fact, they were still on good terms. When Ember had up and left, Arden had refused to tell Jace where she'd gone, saying it was up to Ember whether or not she wanted him to know. But neither had he cast Jace as the villain for breaking his little girl's heart. In Arden's words, it took two to make a relationship work, so he figured it took two to scrap one.

Scott, who'd always been fiercely protective of Ember and thus the most likely to tear Jace's head off, had already left Harkness by then, thank God. Not that he was scared of going a round with him. Scott had the size on him; but Jace was a damn good boxer. He was just glad it hadn't come to that.

Titus, however, had had a few choice words for him, demanding to know what had happened. Jace had been tempted to tell Titus just what his sister had done, but he'd squelched the urge. There were just some things you didn't tell a girl's brother.

Clearly, Titus had gotten over his animosity. Or sufficiently over it to have approached Jace about WRP Holdings buying the farm. And now it was a done deal. All the paperwork had been signed. Though Arden and Titus had negotiated the right to stay until the end of the month, the actual transaction was set to take place after the holiday weekend. Tuesday at nine o'clock, as soon as the law offices opened.

Since Terry had put Jace in charge of all property acquisitions eight months ago so he could focus exclusively on the development end, Jace had overseen the purchase. It had been a struggle to keep his older brother from looking over his shoulder with this one, though. Terry'd had a hard on for that land for years, and now that it was within his grasp, he was having the devil of a time letting Jace do his job. He'd even called twice from Nassau where he was vacationing with his new girlfriend, trying to micromanage the deal.

Yeah. *Trying to.*

Ember's words cut into his thoughts. "Any allergies?"

"No."

"I thought you were allergic to lobster."

"Well, yes, lobster. But I didn't know we were dining."

She allowed a flicker of a smile. Barely. "When a medical professional asks you if you have any allergies, you tell them if you have any allergies. Not just the ones you think are relevant."

"Is my lobster allergy relevant?"

"Well, no, but that's not the point."

She'd finished wrapping his ankle. He wiggled his toes. "Huh. I still have circulation."

Her forehead lined with concern. "Does it feel too tight?"

"No, it's fine," he said. "I was kidding. Given how you feel about me, I thought you might be tempted to be a little...overzealous about it."

She closed her eyes a few seconds, but when she opened them, her expression was bland. "I'd never purposely hurt anyone," she said. "Even you."

"Thank God for the Hippocratic Oath, huh?"

Finally, she smiled as she looked at him, but it didn't reach her beautiful green eyes.

"I knew you'd do it, Ember. Succeed, I mean. Congratulations."

She didn't miss a beat. "Thank you. You know how much becoming a doctor meant to me. Especially after Mom's cancer came back. I worked hard and made it. And yes, I took that oath. But even without it, I wouldn't hurt you, Jace."

"But you did."

The words had slipped past his lips, but once out, he didn't regret them. And she knew what he meant. He could see it in her eyes.

He might have been the one who messed up initially, and messed up royally. Fine—he'd own that. But she was the one who'd never given him a chance to explain before running away. She was the one who'd let her anger goad her into doing something she could never take back. Her choices had carved out a piece of his heart as efficiently as any scalpel could have. She should have let him explain what had happened. Should have let him tell his side of the story.

There was more to what had happened that night than she'd seen in those damned pictures.

She stood, cleared her throat. Unzipping a side pocket of

her backpack, she pulled out a small bottle of pills and rattled them. "Danny sent Advil and Tylenol, but if you like, I've got something stronger here. Tramadol. It's a narcotic pain killer that my dentist prescribed after a recent root canal. If I start you out on that, it'll knock down the pain pretty fast. Later, you can take ibuprofen to help with the inflammation. Because they're metabolized differently, you can take them together without toxicity issues."

"If they can be taken together, why not give me both now?"

"We could, but believe me, it's better in the long run if we stagger them. You'll have more consistent pain control that way."

"Better how?"

"You probably should have a good six hours between doses. If you took both now, they'd both start to wear off, leaving you in quite a bit of pain before you could take the next dose. If we stagger the doses, you've always got fresh pain relief coming every three hours."

"So the narcotic now, the Advil in three hours?"

"Right. And three hours after that, you take Tramadol again. Then Advil three hours later and so on. Well, until you run out of Tramadol. There are only two more pills. After that, you can safely alternate the ibuprofen with Tylenol, which again is metabolized differently. Sound good?"

"You're the doctor."

She shook a white pill out of the container, then dug a bottle of water out of her pack. He held out his hand and she dropped the pill onto his palm.

"Thank you," he said, striving for the polite, grateful tone he'd use if she were an ER nurse dispensing relief, and tossed the tablet back.

"You're welcome." Her tone matched his for civility. She cracked the water bottle and handed it to him. Their fingers touched as he accepted it, and they both froze. Her eyes locked on his. In those few split-seconds, his heart leapt and started pounding.

Something still burned between them. Something impossible.

It was Ember who finally broke eye contact and pulled away.

"You're going to have to rest that foot, keep it elevated at least twenty-four hours. Forty-eight would be better. After that, you can start moving around more, but I wouldn't leave the cabin. You don't want to tackle that rough terrain until the ankle is more stable."

Well, if she could be cool about the electricity that had just arced between them, so could he. He hoped. "How long before I can walk out?"

She shrugged. "It could take a week. Maybe longer. It depends on the severity of the sprain."

A week or more? "No, that doesn't work for me. I've got business in town early Tuesday morning."

"I wouldn't recommend it. Seriously. And whatever you do, don't try to hike out alone."

Frustration made his words clipped. "What *would* you recommend?"

"Stay put," she said, ignoring the edge in his voice. "Or if you must go, get someone with a boat to come get you. In a few days' time, you could probably make it to the river's edge, with some assistance. Though it would have to be someone who knows the area well enough to find you." She drew a side table close to the end of the love seat and placed the Tramadol and the Advil on it, within easy reach.

"So that's it?" He capped the water and put it on the side table beside the pills.

"That's it. You now have the full benefit of my many years of medical training." Ember looked around, then bit down on her lower lip. "But I can't leave you like this…"

For a moment, he thought she'd meant something more.

"I'll stoke the fire and fill the wood box by the stove before I leave."

"Don't feel you have to."

"I'd do it for anyone. I'll fix you something to eat too." She looked at him in that no-arguing way. "I'm guessing you brought groceries?"

He pointed to his pack on the counter. "There are a few things in there. Eggs. Bread. Butter. Peanut butter and jam. There are also some canned goods in the cupboard. Nothing fancy or fresh. All non-perishable."

She nodded. "I'll fix something."

"You don't have to."

"I know. But I'm going to."

"Even though I'm a son of a bitch?"

She looked at him coolly. "Yeah, even though."

"Well, while you're feeling so generous, do you think you could help me get to the washroom?"

"God, of course. I'm sorry." She looked so contrite, he resisted the urge to needle her about missing an opportunity to punish him. He knew it wasn't maliciousness on her part. She'd just been completely focused on treating his injury. "I should have offered right away. I guess I make a better doctor than a nurse. Let's get you out to the outhouse."

"No need. We have a proper bathroom now." He nodded to the rear of the cabin. "The extra bedroom at the back."

Her eyebrows lifted. "Indoor plumbing? Does that mean you have potable water?"

"It does."

"Now there's an improvement a girl can appreciate." She moved in close. "Okay, let's get you up."

He flipped the lever to fold the foot support away. She helped him get to his feet, then tucked her shoulder under his arm on his injured side and slid her right arm around his back. He looped an arm over her shoulder. His ankle throbbed like a bitch just from standing up, but as he stood there with her strong body pressed to his, he suddenly didn't mind so much. God, her hair smelled good. *She* smelled good. To feel her solid warmth next to him, he could almost forget the pain.

Almost.

By the time he made it to the bathroom and back to the chair, his whole body had broken into a fine sweat. How could an ankle that wasn't even broken hurt so damned much?

He managed not to embarrass himself by yelping as she helped him settle back onto the chair. As soon as his foot was elevated again, she went to the small utility closet in the kitchen and came back with the mop bucket, which she plunked down beside the chair.

He lifted an inquiring eyebrow. "Okay, I admit that hurt more than I thought it was going to, but I'm not about to throw up."

"That's not what it's for. I just figured you might want to save yourself that trek to the bathroom for a while. At least until the ankle is a bit better."

Oh, God. Could he feel more useless? "I think I can manage the bathroom."

"Suit yourself," she said, but made no move to retrieve the bucket. "So, if the water pump works, I'm guessing there must be electricity to power those new appliances in the kitchen?"

"Yup. All the electricity we can use, courtesy of a windmill up on the ridge."

"That must have cost your father a pretty penny."

"It wasn't cheap." A novel, bird-friendly design, it had cost a small fortune, but Jace had paid for it, not his father. Since he was pretty much the only Picard still using the place with any regularity, he figured it was only right that he should foot the bill.

She looked around the rustic interior. "I like the improvements, but I'm glad Wayne had the good judgment not to modernize it entirely. High end cabinets and granite countertops just wouldn't have fit."

Since Jace had commissioned the changes, he supposed he could take that as a compliment. "Yeah, I guess it's not really rusticating if it isn't rustic, huh?"

"Exactly. Now let's see what you've got to make a meal from."

From his vantage point, he watched as she busied herself in the tiny kitchen area. Even with the addition of the refrigerator and the electric range, it wasn't exactly a chef's dream. The counter boasted a few covered canisters—tea bags, coffee, sugar, salt, and powdered coffee whitener—on the left side of the single sink. Heavy cast iron frying pans that had seen a good many trout over the years hung by hooks on the back wall. The shallow cupboards hid more heavy pots, some utensils, and an assortment of unmatched dishes.

She made herself at home.

He closed his eyes and listened to the gentle clatter of her working away. His ankle was feeling better already. The smell of butter melting in a pan wafted toward him, and he inhaled deeply, imagining the slow sizzle of it.

Slow? Could a sizzle be slow? He listened a moment longer and decided, yes, it could. It was really slow. Kind of nice.

He felt himself drifting, and that felt right. He could still feel pain in his ankle, but it was muted, not so sharp or urgent. He could feel the compression of the bandage too. The bandage Ember had applied so carefully, despite her deep aversion for him.

He went back to listening to the sizzle of whatever she'd put in the frying pan. Onion and garlic, from the smell of it.

Then he heard something foggy and funny.

It was Ember calling his name. He opened his eyes, and there she was holding the half-empty bottle of vodka, asking how much he'd had to drink.

Just a couple of decent toddies, not a half-bottle.

The answer formed in his mind, but he couldn't seem to

push it out. It was like someone found the gravity control and cranked it up. He was sinking, sinking into the cushions. Or maybe the cushions were rising up, buoying him against this super-gravity. His lids drifted closed.

Again, she asked him about the booze. *How much had he had? When did he have his last drink?* He tried once more to answer her, but the words stayed locked in his head. With a sigh, he surrendered to the weight and the welcoming darkness.

– three –

WAY TO GO, Dr. Standish. Give a man with God only knew how much alcohol in his system a freaking narcotic. Great start to your career.

She lifted his wrist and took his pulse. It was on the slow side, but steady. Still, she found herself holding her own breath as she counted his respirations. They were reassuringly normal…until she factored in that he was sleeping. Ventilation rates in a sleeping patient would normally be significantly more rapid and shallow than wakeful breathing. Jace's respirations were shallow, but not exactly rapid.

Crap.

She looked again at the bottle. A standard 750 mL fifth, it was now approximately half full. But unless his drinking habits had changed radically, she doubted he'd brought it with him. He'd never been much of a drinker. He'd probably found the bottle in the cupboard while searching for painkillers and drank some to take the edge off his pain. There were no empty bottles to be found, as a search of the trash disclosed. He certainly hadn't appeared intoxicated. The question was, how much had he drunk? Both narcotics and alcohol tended to slow breathing, through different processes, and when taken together, could be big trouble.

She bit her lip, counting the ways she'd screwed-up. She'd

asked him about allergies, but hadn't thought to ask if he'd had any alcohol. Stupid. True, he hadn't smelled of alcohol, even when she'd helped him to the bathroom. But this was vodka, not bourbon or scotch or any of the more aromatic stuff. He could have drunk quite a bit without smelling up the place. And he'd been in pain for hours. She should have at least considered the possibility he might have self-medicated with booze.

Then, instead of just giving him some of the ibuprofen, she'd handed him one of her Tramadols. A freaking narcotic!

Of course, ibuprofen and alcohol wasn't a good combination either, given the increased risk of a stomach bleed.

Inexcusable. That was the only word for it. She'd been anxious to finish up and get the hell out of there, yet her conscience demanded she ease his pain. If she were honest about it, she'd given him the narcotic more to expedite her departure than anything else. And if it weren't for the alcohol in his system, it would have worked. He'd be in good shape, pain-wise, but conscious. She could have whipped up a meal for him, stoked the fire, brought in extra wood, and left the meds within easy reach, along with a written schedule reminding him when to take the alternating doses.

But now she had to babysit him until he woke, to make sure he didn't suffer any harm from her mistake.

So much for a quick exit.

Her mind went back to worrying about the drug/alcohol combination. There were so many variables. How much had he drunk? When had he drunk it? Did he have anything on his stomach? How quickly would he metabolise it?

She looked at her watch. Okay, Danny had called looking for a runner about two hours ago. She'd had to scoot into town to fetch the stuff, then she'd sat down with her brothers for lunch. Add on the time for them to mobilize and get out to the parking lot, plus fifty minutes' hike through the woods. Yeah, at least two hours.

Chances were the first thing Jace did after calling the pharmacy was to start the fire so he wouldn't be cold as he waited. Then he'd have poured that drink. She glanced around. The only dish out of the cupboard was a coffee mug. She lifted it for closer inspection. It did smell slightly of alcohol, and was that a seed? Yes, a lemon seed. She'd seen a half a squeezed lemon in the garbage, and the other half sat out on the counter. She put the mug to her mouth and took the last sip of the clear fluid.

Definitely lemon in there, but lots of honey too. He must have made a hot toddy. That might not be so bad.

Of course, he might have had a couple of belts of straight vodka from that mug before he'd sat down with the toddy.

Argh. All this speculation was getting her nowhere. Only Jace could tell her how much he'd had to drink, and he wasn't currently talking. Maybe she could wake him…

She leaned over him to grasp his shoulders. They felt strong under her grip. Familiar. Warm. The urge to pull her hands away battled with the equally strong desire to leave them there. The latter won, but only because she needed him awake.

"Jace." She shook him gently. "Jace, can you hear me?"

He mumbled something mostly incoherent. But then she caught a few words: "Later…Angel."

Ember snatched her hands back from his shoulders as if they'd been singed.

Angel. She hadn't heard that particular endearment in forever. But it was no excuse to react like a scalded cat. She was a doctor, dammit.

She grasped his shoulders again and gave him another shake. "Jace, I need you to wake up," she commanded. "I need to know how much of that vodka you drank."

His eyes flickered open and he frowned. "Ember?"

"How many drinks of that vodka did you have, Jace? One? Two? A bunch?"

"Jus' two." His eyes drifted closed again and his frown smoothed. He was sleeping again.

Okay, two drinks. That wasn't so bad.

She checked his pulse again. Slow, but resting-slow—not dangerously slow. His respirations seemed a bit faster too. More like normal sleep-breathing.

He'd be okay. If she thought otherwise, she'd be on the phone organizing an evacuation. Still, she couldn't leave him. The least she could do was stay and monitor him until he woke naturally, make sure he was all right.

She sat down on the love seat beside him.

Medically speaking, he looked fine.

Aesthetically speaking? He looked more than fine. And because she could study him without him looking back, she did.

He was still so handsome. Even more handsome, if she was honest. Yes, the years had left their mark, but in a way that enhanced his masculinity. Even with his features relaxed in sleep, she could see there were new lines in his forehead, as though life had not been completely smooth sailing. Yet the lines bracketing his mouth and fanning out from his eyes had deepened, suggesting laughter.

She was inexplicably glad of that.

His thick, dark hair was cut shorter than he used to wear it. She wondered if it still curled when it hit his shoulder. Of course, it probably never got the chance these days. Judging by the expensive, precision cut, he probably stayed right on top of it.

She let her gaze roam over his reclined body. He'd filled out a little, but not too much. Just enough to save his six foot frame from looking gangly. Though when she was all of eighteen, she'd thought his slight nineteen-year-old frame was perfect. Heaven sent.

But now…now he looked like a man, not a boy.

She went back to studying his face. Eyes closed, his lashes

lay in a dark sweep against pale cheeks. She'd always loved his coloring, that contrast of black hair, pale skin and blue eyes. Her gaze went to his lips, barely open as he breathed, as if for a kiss. She remembered the last time she'd kissed those lips, when they'd parted outside the diner. That kiss had tasted like coffee and jam and innocence and young love.

But one of them hadn't been so innocent.

She propelled herself to her feet and moved away from the love seat.

She'd stay for a while to let the medication and alcohol wear off. Then she'd tend to that ankle again, give him some ibuprofen, stoke the fire a last time and cover him with a quilt so he didn't get hypothermic in his forced inactivity, then be on her way.

Ember looked out the window and her heart sank to see how dark it was outside. She glanced at her watch and groaned. Her body was still on Eastern Time. But this was Atlantic Time—a full hour later. And it was mid-October. Of course it was getting dark, especially in the woods. In another hour, it would be too dark to pick her way back over the rough trail.

Then, as if on cue, the wind picked up, making an eerie moaning sound in the trees.

Dammit. She was going to have to stay the night. In the cabin she hoped never to see again, with Jace-*freakin'*-Picard.

Suddenly, she laughed out loud. God, if Titus and Scott knew she was alone here with Jace and that she was staying the night, they'd be spitting bullets!

They were so overprotective. Scott especially, though he denied it. As if she didn't know he used to shadow her from a distance throughout their childhood and teen years, just to watch over her. Some nights she used to sneak out of the house via her bedroom window just to see if she could do it without him following her. She'd actually managed it a couple of times.

And yes, Scott had given Jace the brotherly *do not hurt her* speech when the two of them had gotten serious. Titus had too.

That was one of the reasons she hadn't told either of her brothers the whole story of why she'd run away so quickly that night. Yes, she could say it now—she'd *run away* rather than face Jace again.

Face him after she'd seen those pictures. That proof.

She'd been right here, in this very room, when she'd first laid eyes on the damnable things. It was around this time of the day too, but because it was summer, the sun had still been well up in the sky. She'd gotten here first— about an hour before Jace was supposed to arrive. But evidence of him having been there even earlier was everywhere. There were a dozen red roses in a makeshift vase and chocolate truffles— her to-die-for favorite. The small bed up in the loft had been made up with new satin sheets. Jace would have had to hike all the way out to the cabin with those things, then back down along the river again.

That long ago evening, Ember had sat down on the bed in the loft. Lay down. Stood up. Looked at her nervous self a dozen times in the full-length rectangular mirror on the back of the door. Would she look the same after? Would she be the same? Finally, she'd gone back down stairs in search of something to do to distract herself. That's when she'd remembered the envelope in her knapsack. It had been delivered to her house two days earlier, a large envelope addressed to Ms. Embre Standish. Beneath her name had been written a message in block letters—*For the birthday girl, do not open till you're 18. Ha Ha—Restricted material!* How she'd laughed when her Dad had handed it to her. Arden had pulled quite the face, but he'd said nothing.

She'd figured Jace was up to something. Who else could it have been from? Yeah, her name was misspelled, but she could see Jace doing that. She was always complaining about people writing it as the more common Amber instead of

Ember. It would be just like him to do something like that to mess with her.

In the end, she hadn't just waited for her birthday to rip the envelope open. She'd decided to wait for their special night, when she and Jace were alone together. That had been the plan, but then she'd got to wondering...

Finally, she'd torn the envelop open, upended it on the table, and the pictures had spilled out.

It had been like a dagger to her heart. Snapshot after snapshot of Jace in his bedroom at the Picards' house, sprawled on his bed with another woman. The very bed where she and Jace had occasionally fooled around—fully clothed, of course. But this woman wasn't fully clothed. She sat astride his hips, wearing just her black underwear. Or at least a black bra. With the sheets around her hips, it was impossible to say if she wore panties. But Ember had no trouble distinguishing Jace's face, eyes closed in bliss, or his hand on the woman's breast. A slightly older woman by the looks of it. Beautiful and more curvaceous than Ember's slight, teenage frame.

More pictures. The woman bent over Jace, kissing him. The black bra lying on the sheets beside them.

Even as Ember sat by Jace now, the memory still stung.

To her eighteen-year-old self, it had been devastating.

Jace sighed in his sleep and she checked his pulse and ventilation rate again. Pretty much the same as before. Nothing to panic over. He'd probably just sleep it off and be none the worse for wear.

She yawned and glanced up at the loft overhead. The bed up there would have been stripped of those satin sheets years ago, but she was guessing it would be a hell of a lot more comfortable than the love seat, even with its recliner feature. But that was a no go. She had to stay with Jace. Watch over him. He was her responsibility, thanks to her stupid mistake.

She climbed up into the loft, grabbed the Hudson's Bay blanket she found there, and scooted back down. Settling on the love seat, she reclined her side and pulled the blanket over herself. Then she glanced sideways at Jace. He wasn't shivering or anything, but she knew he was likely to be on the cool side from being so stationary. Grumbling to herself, she lifted the blanket and fanned it over both of them.

Then she dug her phone out and texted Scott. *Still w/ patient*, she typed. She paused, fingers hovering over the touchpad as she debated whether to tell him she was staying the night. She bit her lip. No, she'd break that news later, closer to full dark when travel would be problematic. Otherwise she might find Scott knocking at the cabin's door. She signed off with her usual *E* and hit send.

Instead of pocketing her iPhone, she selected an audiobook from her library, a hot new romantic suspense. In recent years, she hadn't had much time to read anything, and certainly not for pleasure. But with the explosion of audiobooks, she was now able to listen to voice actors read to her while she was commuting or exercising or doing housework. She often managed to read a book a week that way.

She thought about getting up to fetch her headphones from her backpack, but decided against it. She was too comfortable. The phone's external speakers would do, especially with Jace out like a light. She flipped up the foot support and settled back to listen.

An hour later, she stopped the audiobook and texted Scott to tell him that given the weather, she was staying the night with the patient. Her phone buzzed immediately with a call from her brother, but she let it go into voice mail. Then it buzzed to alert her to a text. As expected, he was madder than a wet hen. *Who is this patient?* She replied that patient confidentiality precluded her naming him, but that she could handle one gimped up guy, and to quit wringing his hands. After promising to check in with him in the morning, she'd signed off and re-started the audiobook. Lying back again, she let the narrator's sexy male voice carry her away.

– four –

"UNCLE ARDEN?"

Cordless phone pressed to his ear, Arden Standish leaned against the cupboard, looking around the familiar kitchen with a knot in his stomach. Titus's computer was tucked in a corner by the much-used microwave, beneath a shelf of never-used cookbooks. Margaret's aloe vera plant still sat on the windowsill. He looked at the china cabinet. His wife's Christmas dishes sat there still, shut behind glass. How he'd hate to see those go…

"Hello?" Scott said. "You still there?"

Arden blinked. "Sorry," he said into the phone. "Just thinking about… Well, you know how an old man's mind drifts."

"Yeah, right," Scott scoffed. "You're only sixty-five. There's nothing wrong with your mind. And you can still kick my butt at *Jeopardy*."

He chuckled. "Not on the movie questions."

"Especially on the movie questions."

"Been a while since we've played," Arden said. "Maybe we can have a rematch some night next week?" As soon as the words were out of his mouth, he regretted them. Scott was always in such a hurry to get away. He might be planning to be gone as soon as Thanksgiving was over. "No pressure, though. I know you have places to go, things to do."

"Yeah, but probably not before we fit in a *Jeopardy* or two, huh?"

"That'd be nice." He cleared his throat. "So you'll let me know if you need anything, right? The Jeep is all gassed up. Wouldn't take fifteen minutes for me to get out there."

"I will. Thanks, Uncle Arden. Night."

"Goodnight, Son."

Arden hung up. He would not be hearing from Scott. Not unless it was a bone fide, hell-breaking-loose emergency. He wouldn't want to worry the old man. Arden shook his head. That was Scott. Tough as nails. Protective of his family.

Even if that love was shown only in bits and pieces.

Arden smiled.

It wasn't just the family that had embraced Scott when he'd landed in Harkness all those years ago. The land had too. Maybe more than it had the other kids. More than Ember, certainly. Oh, she had no complaints, but the town had never seemed big enough for her. Titus had stayed around. He knew the work; did most of it by himself now. But oddly, it was Scott who *connected* with the land.

Their land.

The Standish homestead, bought by his moonshine-running mother and the love of her life, Edward Standish, over eighty years ago. When Arden had finally come along—a surprise for a middle-aged couple who'd reconciled themselves to being childless—he'd been born upstairs in this very house. Surprise number two came along a few years later, Booker Standish. As the eldest son, Arden had happily quit school at the age of sixteen to work the land with his aging parents. Booker had gone on to attend university, eventually settling in Minnesota.

So many good memories from his own childhood, and later with Margaret and their children. Titus learning how to drive the tractor—half-scared but determined to master the beast.

Scott running through the orchard with Axl, then a foolish pup, racing circles around him.

Then there was Ember.

A small chuckle rose from his throat. He used to catch lightning bugs with her on warm summer evenings. They'd put them in a Mason jar with nail-holes pounded through the tin lid. Afterward, he'd sit on the step with his brilliant and curious little girl as she studied the fireflies, turning the glass jar to watch them crawl and flit around inside.

Now his little girl was with Jace Picard.

He rubbed his temple. God, he hoped he'd done the right thing.

When it worked out that Ember would be the one taking the Parker and Ward's parcel out to a stranded Jace, he had taken a chance. He'd conveniently forgotten the name Danny Parker had given him.

The hell of it was, he didn't really even know what he was hoping for by sending Ember out there.

That she and Jace would somehow rekindle? Or failing that, at least talk out whatever had happened all those years ago. Make peace with it.

Or had he been hoping for something else? Something more selfish?

Dammit! An old man's foolish hopes...it was all gone!

He looked again at the china cabinet and sighed. Margaret's Christmas dishes—he'd start with those.

— five —

JACE'S DREAM was incredibly vivid.

Fantastically rich.

A little bit wild.

He dreamed of a beautiful woman with flaming red hair. She was standing in a floor-length red sheath dress that was slit enticingly high up the left leg. The bodice hugged her breasts and hips like a shimmery second skin.

It was Ember.

She walked toward him across a deserted, rain-slicked stretch of pavement, hips swaying seductively. Planes flew overhead in a star-studded sky. In the background he saw a building with a glassed-in box on top. An airport control tower. The flashing lights in the distance were beacons and the pavement Ember crossed was the tarmac. With the wind blowing through her hair, she walked on.

Jace closed in on her, swaggering forth in a tailored tuxedo. Despite the headache that nagged at him, he smiled and undid his bow tie, leaving it to hang loose. He stopped in front of her, smelling her scent, watching the light and dark play on her hair, seeing the smile on her face, arousal in her eyes. Then in a deep, manly, voice, dream-Ember opened her mouth and said: *"Chapter 11"*

Jace's eyes sprang open. What the hell?

Ember—the real Ember—stirred beside him on the love seat, face pressed into his shoulder beneath the Hudson's Bay blanket she must have retrieved from upstairs.

"Dax grasped Bella's bared shoulders gently. Despite the rapidly cooling evening air, her skin felt warm beneath his fingers. She was so alive in that flame-red dress. The look she gave him was both amused and challenging. She was practically daring him to kiss her. But he wouldn't, not until she wanted him to. No. Not until she begged him to."

Huh. An audiobook. That would account for the "dream" he'd been having. The voice droned on about Dax and Bella's encounter on the tarmac. He lifted his head and craned his neck to try to see his watch on the side table, but the movement sent a shard of pain ricocheting through his head. He closed his eyes against it, stifling a groan.

Poorly, apparently. Ember pulled away, then scrambled to sit up and shut off the narrator.

"How's the ankle?" she asked.

"A bit better, I think. It's this mother of a headache I could do without." He rubbed his temple. "Hell, I could do without the whole head right about now."

Ember got up to stand in front of him. She leaned to his right and grabbed his flashlight from beside the chair.

"Okay look into the light, please," she instructed.

Was she kidding? Just the thought of looking into that light made him want to vomit. "Is this one of those *kill me or cure me* scenarios?"

She bit her lip and lowered the flashlight. "I made a mistake."

He slanted her a look.

"Earlier this evening, I mean," she rushed to clarify. "Not years ago when we...parted company."

Yeah, it was getting more civil in here by the minute.

Dammit. What time was it? He turned his head again, this

time more cautiously, but his wristwatch was face down. If his head wasn't pounding, he'd sit up and reach for it.

He glanced at the woodstove. Judging by the temperature, the fire must have burned nearly out, so at least a few hours had passed...

Ember picked the watch up. After squinting to see the time for herself, she announced, "Half past midnight."

Her words were out of the blue, but just as uncannily timed as they'd always been.

He held out his hand for the watch. "I didn't ask."

She handed it to him. "No, but I knew you were about to."

"Oh really?" He slid the watch onto his wrist.

"Yes, really. You're so predictable. You always had to know the time."

He shrugged. "People change."

"Not so much on stuff like that."

"Really," he said. "Then you still carry it around?"

She tilted her head. "What?"

"A barrette for your hair."

He'd meant the remark as a one up, or at least an equalizer in some weird, challenging way he couldn't even explain. Yet as soon as the words were out, he felt the intimacy of them. How many times had he pulled a barrette from her hair to run his hands through its silkiness? How many times had she unclipped it herself and shaken it out, leaving it drifting and swirling around her shoulders like wildfire?

"Well, smartass," she said, "you'll notice I'm not wearing a barrette."

"Which means it's either in your jacket pocket or that backpack."

She sighed. "Okay, you got me. One in both."

He grinned and looked at his watch again. How had he managed to sleep until midnight? They'd been talking and then...dammit, he didn't even remember falling asleep. But obviously he had. And he'd stayed asleep for a good six hours.

Which begged the question, why was she still here?

Suddenly the wind gusted outside, elevating the droning sound he'd just begun to notice into a roar. It whistled eerily around the edges of the cabin and rattled the windows before subsiding again to the previous droning level.

He glanced up at Ember. "How long's the wind been up?"

"Since late afternoon."

"Is that why you're still here? Didn't want to fight the wind?"

She shrugged. "It was getting dark too. Not a good combination. Plus there was that thing about wanting to make sure I didn't accidentally medicate you into a coma."

Medicate him into a coma? What did that mean? He searched his memory again, but came up empty.

"Okay, enough stalling. Look into the light for me."

He looked up at her. "Must I?"

It was definitely Doctor Standish staring back. All business. "Just for a second."

He complied.

"Good." She lowered the flashlight. "Now follow my finger."

He stared up into her eyes.

"The finger, Jace. Not my face."

He dropped his gaze and followed her finger as she moved it slowly to his left. Then right. She nodded, apparently satisfied. "I'll give you some ibuprofen for that headache, but we really need to get something into your stomach first." She dug in that bottomless knapsack of hers again and produced an energy bar which she handed to him. Then she picked up the bottle of ibuprofen from the side table and shook two pills out.

He detested those bars, but with both head and ankle throbbing, he unwrapped one and ate it quickly, then accepted the pills and bottled water she offered. The warm water soothed his parched throat, so he drank some more of it.

She turned her attention to his injury. Her face was a mask

of intensity as she unwrapped the compress, but there was compassion there too. And when she touched his still-swollen ankle, he could feel the gentleness in her confident touch.

"Does that refrigerator have a freezer?" she asked.

The question struck him as funny. "Yup. A meat drawer and a vegetable crisper too. I can recommend it."

She rolled her eyes. "Ice is what I was getting at. It wouldn't hurt to apply some before we rewrap it."

"Ah, of course. And yes, there's ice." He knew that because there *hadn't* been ice when he arrived. It was the first thing he'd thought of to treat the ankle, once he realized there were no meds in any of the cabinets or cupboards. But all he'd found in the freezer was the empty tray. He'd refilled it.

He heard her open and close the small freezer compartment, then the rattle of ice cubes being dumped onto the counter. He smiled when he heard the water running in the kitchen sink and knew she was refilling the tray. That was the Ember he knew, always thinking ahead, planning for the future. There would never be empty ice cube trays under her watch. The freezer opened and closed again. After a few more rustling sounds, she returned with ice wrapped in a thin dishtowel.

She positioned herself at the end of his foot rest and lowered the ice pack onto his ankle. "Is that too heavy?" She glanced up at him. "I can take some ice out if the weight is causing pain."

It did hurt, but not much more than without the weight, and he knew the cold would more than compensate for it. The more ice, the better. "No, it's good."

She rearranged the pack slightly, tucking the bulky cubes in closer. "You really should keep a bag of frozen peas in the freezer. They make a great cold compress. Molds better to the injury."

"I'll take that under advisement, Doc. And I won't be caught without painkillers again."

His words hung there, both of them aware that the painkillers were what brought her out here.

He cleared his throat. "So, it's after midnight. Does that mean your brothers are going to burst through that door any minute and lay a thrashing on me?"

"Nope." She bent and rearranged the ice pack again.

"But they know you're out here with me for the night?"

"I let Scott know I was staying the night." She stood up again. "I just didn't reveal that you're the patient."

He lifted an eyebrow. "How'd you dodge that? I can't see Scott being very happy about you staying out in the woods with a strange man." For that matter, he didn't imagine Titus would be too pleased either.

"Patient confidentiality. Plus I reminded Scott that the patient was too gimped up to pose a threat to a kitten."

He grimaced. "Ouch, right in the ego. But true."

"How's the headache?"

"Actually, it's a lot better." Until she'd asked, he hadn't even realized that the pain was lifting. His ankle was feeling better too, but he knew that was probably mostly the ice. "I can't imagine what I did to deserve it, though."

Ember bit her lip. "I really am sorry about that."

"About what?"

"I shouldn't have given you those pills last night."

"What pills?"

Her face went still. "You don't remember?"

He looked up at her, a sinking feeling in the pit of his stomach. He really didn't remember much after she said she'd make something for supper.

"What happened?" He hated this stricken feeling of not knowing. Another reason why he limited himself to just one or two drinks—always. He'd learned that lesson once. "Oh shit, did I say any—"

"No! Nothing like that—at all." She drew a breath. "It's just that I had no idea that you'd been drinking. Especially so early in the day. But it should have occurred to me that—"

"I don't normally drink in the daytime," he said, feeling compelled to defend himself. "Hell, I don't drink much at *any* time. I don't usually even pack booze when I come out here, but this weekend I tossed that partial bottle of vodka in my backpack. And since I had the booze but I didn't have painkillers, I figured the *five o'clock somewhere* rule applied."

"Why this weekend then?"

He shrugged. "I'm not much for the holidays."

"Since your father died?"

"Yeah."

Sure. He'd go with that. It was partially true. But the real reason he'd packed a three-day backpack and headed out here was that he knew Ember would be in town. And having a drink or two while he sat the weekend out alone had seemed like a pretty good idea.

She moved to stand by the love seat, close to his shoulder. "I owe you an apology, Jace. I asked about allergies, but I also should have asked if you'd had any alcohol before I gave you that pill."

That was odd. "But I asked for the ibuprofen. The pharmacist sent it. Why would you feel bad about giving it to me?"

"I gave you one of my Tramadols." She watched his face carefully. "You really don't remember?"

"No, I don't remember any—" A sound bite flashed through his mind, a snippet of their conversation. He pushed again for the memory and was rewarded with a fragment. "Wait, was there something about a dentist?"

"Yes! That's right. My dentist gave them to me a while ago. It's a narcotic used to manage post-surgical pain. I thought it would knock your pain down faster."

A narcotic? "Well, that explains the memory loss, I guess." He dragged a hand over his face. "Anything else I need to know? Did I do or say anything?"

"No." She shook her head. "It was lights out pretty quick."

Well, that was a blessing, at least. "Thank you for telling me." He closed his eyes and pressed his thumb and forefinger to them. "You're a doctor, so I'm sure I don't have to tell you how stressful it is when you lose time."

She made a small noise. He glanced up to catch her expression. She looked positively stricken. Cold.

"Ember?"

"Are you saying this has happened before? The memory loss?"

"Just once," he said, meeting her eyes. "The morning after my nineteenth birthday."

"Jace, don't."

She moved to step back, but he grabbed her hand. This time, he'd make her listen. "You never let me explain. You never—"

"What's to explain? I thought we were waiting, I was wrong. You found someone else for the in between time."

"You still believe that?"

It was her turn to shrug.

He sighed. "I don't remember much about that night. I was a kid who drank too much and did something that I regretted with some woman I'd never even met before."

"Seriously, Jace, I don't need to hear anymore." She tugged her hand and he released it. "I saw the pictures, remember?"

Those fucking pictures. He still didn't know where they'd come from. "You're one up on me. I only saw the ashes of them."

Her throat moved convulsively. "I saw the ashes of everything else."

Her words rubbed him raw. She wasn't the only one who'd lost everything.

He wanted to leap to his feet. Wanted to pace the tiny cabin. But he was stuck in the damned chair. He found the

lever on the love seat and jammed the footrest down so he
could at least sit up. His ankle screamed a protest, but the flare
of pain seemed fitting.

She took a step back when he leaned forward. That made
him even angrier, but he reined the emotion in. He had a
chance now to tell his side, and this time she'd have to listen.
Unless she wanted to go out into the wind and rain in the
middle of the night, in the middle of nowhere.

"It's true," he said, deliberately relaxing back into the
cushions. "I have no memory of the night of my nineteenth
birthday, after about mid-evening. I woke up at home the next
day, cold and sick, with a hickey on my throat I didn't
remember getting."

"Ah, that was why you gave me the run-around for the next
week."

"I am not proud of that either. But I swear to God, I didn't
think there was any more to it."

She snorted. "Right. It was so inconsequential that you hid
from me until it healed."

His fingers tightened on the arm of the love seat. "I didn't
want you to think the worst. To hate me. And until you told
me about those pictures, I didn't believe anything more could
have happened. I mean, I don't remember who it was, what
she looked like. I don't remember anyone even catching my
eye. I don't remember a woman's lips on me or her skin or her
smell. And I sure as hell don't remember any of the stuff you
said you saw in those pictures."

The silence was heavy. Yet he felt a little lighter with it.
He'd been holding that in for a long time. The shame of
knowing something happened, yet having no memory of it.
How could he have lost control? Lost himself?

The worst of it was he would have sworn he'd never betray
Ember. Knew it in his bones. Back then, he'd never wanted
anyone else. He'd assumed any misconduct had been minor,
maybe a girl cornering him for a kiss in the back alley at the

bar or in a car. But from Ember's hysterical accusations on the phone that final night nearly a month later, there'd evidently been photographs. Compromising ones, taken in his bedroom. He'd tried to defend himself, but she'd all but jammed his words back down his throat. Being drunk was not a defence, she'd said. It was an excuse to do what he obviously wanted to do all along. By the time he trekked back out of the woods and reached her house, she'd refused to talk to him. And when he'd gone back the next day, she was gone.

Now that he'd finally gotten that off his chest, would she finally own up to the heartache she'd cause *him* all those years ago? No, not just running away, but for sleeping with his brother.

When Ember had left town, Jace had been determined to find her, come clean about everything. Hiding the hickey, the memory loss, the shame. He'd beg her forgiveness, do any penance she wanted. But then his older brother had come clean himself to Jace. He'd slept with Ember. The night she'd run from the camp, she'd run to him. Neither of them had meant for it to happen, Terry'd said. She'd been pissed at Jace over something. Somehow, when Terry tried to smooth things over for Jace, they'd wound up kissing. Then they kissed some more. When he realized what was happening, he tried to stop it, but she was so insistent, propelled by anger and a lust for revenge.

"I'm sorry, bro. She was your girl and I should have been stronger, but she was not about to be denied. You know how headstrong she can be."

He hadn't spoken to Terry for six months after that—not until the old man had forced a truce at their aunt's funeral. And Jace hadn't spoken to Ember until a few hours ago.

Now, after all this time, he'd confessed. Would she?

She didn't.

"You really don't remember the woman?" she asked.

Jace shook his head. "I don't remember anything. What she

looked like, what her name was. After you told me about the pictures, I asked Terry about it. He didn't know her either. Said she was just some chick I picked up in the bar and brought home. She was gone before I woke the next day."

God, he hated the way that sounded; the words practically stuck in his throat. He'd been with women since then, and some of them had been hookups, but that was mostly in his first year at university. He'd quickly decided one-night stands were not worth it. They just left him feeling like such a dick. He'd moved on to longer-term relationships, although most of them hadn't lasted much longer than six months.

"I know what she looked like." Her voice was matter-of-fact.

What was he supposed to say to that? How many times had he wished she hadn't destroyed those pictures?

About as many times as he was glad she had, he supposed.

"She wore bright red lipstick. In one picture, she was laughing as if you'd just whispered the funniest thing in the world into her ear." Ember closed her eyes as if the image she described was burned into her mind. "Her hair was blond and tightly curled. She was really pale—Goth pale—and had a spider tattoo on her shoulder."

An image flashed in his head. His mouth went dry and his headache roared back to life. "Was it a large spider?"

Ember's eyes flew open. "Yes, a red spider. A large one that looked like it was crawling toward her neck."

"A red spider…"

"I'm glad she was so *memorable*. You know, to help you narrow the possible pool down."

She spat the words at him like a mouthful of acid. They had to hurt her as much as they wounded him. But as soon as they found their mark, he let the pain go.

Because after all this time, something about that long-ago night had finally come into focus.

— six —

EMBER'S HEART missed a beat.

She was sure of it—one entire *lub dub*.

Her words had hurt him. She'd seen the telltale flash in his eyes, felt a small spurt of ugly victory. But he'd steeled that pain away quickly, another expression claiming his handsome features. His eyes had turned inward, sifting through memory fragments lost in the past.

Suddenly, she couldn't bear the discussion

"It's late." She pivoted and stalked away to put some space between them. Finding herself in the kitchen, she looked at the clock on the back wall. Nearly one o'clock in the morning. "Or early, depending on how you want to look at it. You must be starved. I'll make breakfast. Supper. Whatever."

"You don't have to do that."

Ah, but she did. Anything to be able to turn away and not look in those eyes right now. Jace wasn't the only one remembering the past. "I can hardly let my patient starve," she said briskly. "I'm already on shaky ground on the *do no harm* front, after the Tramadol thing. Let's see what we have to work with."

She scraped the cold, unappetizing looking onions from her first attempt at an omelet—the one she'd started before she realized he was high on booze and drugs—into the garbage.

After washing the skillet out, she put it back on the stove on a medium heat and dug the bottle of eggs out of the refrigerator. Yes, a *bottle*. Or rather, a Mason jar. A dozen eggs had been cracked and deposited into it. Pretty ingenious, actually. No cracked eggs seeping into your backpack.

Another trip to the fridge for cheese, butter, the unused half of the cooking onion, and some mushrooms. In the cupboards, she found a loaf of multi-grain bread, some small fingerling potatoes, some canned meats and canned milk. Nothing fancy. Your basic bachelor staples. But she could work with that.

"It won't be anything gourmet," she said. "But I'll whip up an omelet. Maybe some thin-sliced pan fries with—"

"Her name was Bridget. Bridget...something."

Ember stilled for a few seconds. Then, without a word, she went back to assembling the makings for their meal. The task kept her hands busy, but it did nothing to take her mind off of that night, that woman.

It was all she could do to stop herself from unleashing another sarcastic comment. *Bridget—such a pretty name for a man-stealing—*

She cut the thought off before she could finish it. The woman wasn't a *whore* or a *bitch* or any of the other misogynistic words that sprang to mind. And no one could *steal* a man who didn't want to be stolen. This Bridget person was just a woman who slept with a guy a decade ago.

She dug out a second skillet and put it on the other large burner. Opening the butter, she cut off a couple of hunks, and tossed some in each frying pan.

No, the onus had been on Jace—the one in the steady, supposedly committed relationship—to stay faithful.

She pulled out a cutting board and attacked the onion. A moment later, it was diced within an inch of its life.

What was the matter with her? Jace's betrayal shouldn't raise these feelings in her. Not after all this time. Why should she care?

Correction—why *did* she care?

Because it wouldn't be the first time you've doubted yourself over the years—doubted your decision to run like that, without giving him a chance to explain.

She'd hurled those tearful accusations at him over the phone, and when he'd tried to defend himself, she'd hung up on him. He'd tried to call back, but she'd taken the phone off the hook. When he'd come to the house, she'd refused to see him. And then she'd left early the next morning, before he could come back.

But if she was really honest with herself, she had to admit she'd wanted him to come after her—climb that highest mountain, race a white horse through the streets of Ottawa to find her, slay the dragon, *and win her back.*

Maybe she even resented that he hadn't.

But other than one conversation with her father, he'd done nothing to find her. And seriously, how hard would it have been? All he would have had to do was convince Arden he still loved her. Arden was such a softie, such a sucker for love. He'd have given it up.

But Jace hadn't pressed her father. He hadn't gone after her. The white horse had remained stabled, the suit of shining armour left standing in the closet.

He was supposed to have started at the University of Ottawa himself that fall. And yes, for that entire first month, she'd looked for him at every school event, at the few hockey games she'd attended, and on street corners. By October, she'd learned that he'd switched universities.

"That red spider tattoo was on her right shoulder, correct?"

"I think so." She'd spent years trying to erase that photo from her memory, but it came up easily. In her mind's eye, the tattoo was on the right side. But it had been ten years... Could she swear to that? She tried picturing it on the left, but couldn't. Then she realized why. In the photo where the woman had sat astride Jace, the photographer had clearly been on the right hand side of them, and that particular shot was the only one where the tattoo was fully visible. "Yeah, definitely the right shoulder."

His brow was furrowed as he dug for the memory. "And she was thin?"

"Way too thin. Except for up top. She appeared to be quite well endowed that way."

Jace's eyes seemed focused on something beyond the cabin's walls. "Yeah, Bridget. I'm sure that was her name."

"Do you know her?"

A muscle in his jaw leapt. "Apart from the biblical sense those photos would imply, no. I just...when you mentioned the tattoo, that name sort of leapt out of nowhere." He narrowed his eyes. "Do *you* know her?"

"No." I hank God. That would be adding insult to injury. But that name, *Bridget...* Why did it niggle at her? Why did it sound so familiar?

Ember looked down at the butter bubbling in the pans. Grabbing a small bottle of vegetable oil she'd found, she added some to one of them. As it heated, she sliced a couple of the small potatoes into thin, almost transparent medallions and put them into the hot oil. In the smaller pan, she tossed the diced onion into the bubbling butter. Then she poured four of the eggs into a bowl and beat them. When the onions started to look transparent, she added the eggs. For the next while, her mind was blessedly blank as she gave her complete attention to the meal. She removed the eggs from the heat before they had completely set, then focused on the fries. She'd sliced them so thinly, they were more like chips when they browned up. She removed them to some paper towel she'd found, then made toast.

She divided everything between two plates and carried them into the living room.

"There's some of Mrs. Budaker's raspberry jam in the front of my knapsack," he said, absently.

"She's selling jams and jellies at the market now, isn't she?"

"Yeah."

Ember placed their plates on the coffee table and went to retrieve the small bottle and a knife. Returning, she slathered a generous amount onto the toast, then placed his plate on his lap where he could reach it. Taking her own plate, she sat across from him on an upholstered chair. But as appealing as the meal looked, she couldn't stomach a bite.

Apparently, neither could Jace, who made no move to eat. From his fierce frown, she presumed he was trying to remember more.

She speared a piece of perfectly fried potato. "The pictures were taken in your bedroom."

He flinched like she'd slapped him. "Jesus, Ember. I know that."

She plunked her fork down. "Look, I'm not trying to be a jerk. I was trying to help, but I couldn't remember whether or not I'd told you that part."

"You did." He dragged a hand through his hair, leaving it standing up awkwardly. "Terry confirmed it. He said he caught a glimpse of her leaving our house by taxi early the next morning."

She gestured to his plate. "You should eat." She forced herself to take a bite of her toast.

He picked up his fork and ate some of the scrambled eggs and crispy potatoes. Then he put the utensil down.

"I don't understand. Terry took me out for a couple drinks—I'd just turned nineteen, finally legal to go to the bar. But I swear I only had a couple. That was it. We drove to the Purple Rocket in Crandler. I honestly...tonight was the first I remember any of this." He shook his head. "Blond hair. Stick thin. Bridget with a spider tattoo. Still not much for me to go on."

Bridget with a spider.

"Oh my God."

"What is it?" Jace asked.

"Bridget with a spider. I...I've seen that before."

His eyes followed her as she jumped up, plunked her plate on the coffee table and went to the firewood box by the back door. Yes, there it was! On the small shelf above the wood box sat the guest book. Nothing fancy or formal. Just a small spiral bound book that someone had left there years ago, after having written a *thank you* in it to Jace's stepdad for the use of the camp. It had caught on. Ember herself had signed it the first time she'd come up here with Jace. She'd put their initials within a wide heart once all those years ago. But she wasn't the only one who'd left an embellished personal message.

This time, she sat beside him on the love seat. She flipped through the pages, then stopped. "There," she said, stabbing a finger down onto the pad. "Bridget Northrup."

Jace pulled the book closer for a better look. "With a spider dotting the 'i'." He released his grip on the notebook. "So that's who I picked up in the bar."

Ember flipped back a few pages, scanning the other names. Suddenly, her brain was buzzing. "Unless..."

He looked at her. "Unless what?"

"Unless you didn't."

He dropped his gaze. "I think the pictures established that pretty firmly, didn't they?"

"Obviously she wound up in bed with you, but what if you didn't just pick her up randomly at the bar?" God, she couldn't believe she was even entertaining these thoughts.

He rubbed his temple as though his headache had come back. "What do you mean?"

"Maybe she wasn't as random as you think. Look at the names just below hers."

Jace leaned closer to read them. "Ross McDonald and Kendri Bloom. I know them. Friends of Terry's. They're married now. Kendri actually works at WRP in the Human Resources Department."

"And all three names are written in that distinctive aqua blue color."

"So?"

"So they were probably all here together, and used Kendri's or Bridget's pretty gel pen to sign the book."

"I still don't get it."

She bit her lip. "Maybe there's nothing to get. But it just seems that if Terry's good buddies Kendri and Ross were dating back then—which I think is safe to say given that their names are framed inside a pretty heart—and if Bridget-with-the-spider was here too, then she could have been with Terry."

"Maybe," Jace allowed. "Terry used to have quite a few female friends out here before my stepdad found out and put a stop to it." He picked up his phone from the end table. "Let's just see if we can find Bridget Northrup."

Within a few short minutes, he announced he'd found her. "According to this, she probably lives in Crandler," he said. "She's definitely a teacher there at Crandler Elementary."

His jaw tensed and Ember leaned in to see what was on the small screen. It was a tall, blond Miss Northrup shaking the hand of a proud fifth grader. *Local boy wins Provincial Essay Contest*—the caption read.

She looked away, hating the surge of jealousy. This was the woman who'd slept with Jace. But in looking away, her gaze fell on the guest book again. She studied the names, the hand-drawn heart with the shaded edges to give it a 3D look and the delicate curlicues at the point of it. Then Bridget's name, with the world's cutest spider forming the dot over the letter i. The date...

She sat up straighter. "Hey, look at this." She pushed the guest book in front of him. "Look at the date."

"Two weeks before my birthday." He looked up at her, wide-eyed. "Something's not right. If your speculation is correct and Bridget was Terry's guest-slash-lover up here that weekend, why would she be hooking up with me two weeks later? Unless she did it for revenge. I could maybe see that, given what an asshole Terry can be, but then why do it and not tell him? Terry said he never got a good look at her, only saw her briefly as she was getting in the cab the next day."

His words deflated her. "You're right. Not much point to revenge sex if your ex doesn't find out about it."

He made a choked noise and she looked over at him. He was looking back at her like she'd sprouted another head.

"Jace? Are you okay?"

"Sure. I'm dandy. Never better."

He didn't sound dandy, but *whatever*. If he had something to say, he could just say it. Or not. She wasn't going to pussyfoot around him.

She looked down at the guestbook again. "Maybe I was wrong about her being here with Terry. Maybe she was just a third wheel with Ross and Kendri."

"Maybe."

She picked up her plate and started pecking away at the food. It was cold, but she'd finally found her appetite.

After a few minutes, Jace started working on his plate too. He made short work of it, putting in on the end table when he'd finished.

"Thank you. That was very good."

"You're welcome."

They sat in silence for a few moments. Except it wasn't really silent. Outside, the roar of the wind in the trees was unceasing and rain pattered against the window. Though the cabin was still reasonably warm, the sound made Ember get to her feet, cross the room, and put some more wood in the fire. She pulled her shirt closer around her as she watched the flames dance through the ceramic glass door.

"I'm going to get to the bottom of this."

At Jace's words, she turned to face him.

"Whatever it takes, I'm going to find out once and for all what really happened that night."

Her chest tightened. Was *she* ready to know the truth? Oh, hell, what if she'd been wrong?

"Can you arrange a medical evacuation?"

A med-evac? She met his gaze. "Theoretically, I could, but I'm not going to. You don't need it, Jace. It's not a taxi service."

"I'll pay."

Spoken like a Picard. She crossed her arms over her chest. "It's not about that. What if someone really needed the service while it was tied up out here? Hell, what if Titus finds trouble in the mountain and needs it?"

His expression sharpened. "You're expecting trouble?"

"No one ever expects trouble. Lacey Douglas didn't." Poor Lacey. So young; such a tragedy. "But it has a way of finding people just the same."

He sat back, his expression grim.

"Jace, what's this really about? Why the urgency?"

"I have to know."

Despite herself, she felt for him. He looked so bleak sitting there.

"I want to know the truth about what happened that night just as much as you do." She went back to the love seat, perched on the front edge of the cushion so she could face him. Close enough so that he could reach out and touch her if he wanted to. And God help her, she wanted him to.

"The night I lost you..." He cleared his throat. "Ember. I'll never forgive myself. I'm not trying to shift the blame or get off the hook. I'm trying to find out what happened, *how* it happened. Why I lost you. How I could have messed things up so royally."

She looked down at her clasped hands. "We both lost."

His hand covered one of hers, his thumb grazing her knuckles. Her heart jumped, but she kept her gaze on their hands. Hers so small by contrast, his darker, the skin rougher.

He lifted his hand to her chin, tipping her face up to meet his eyes. She was prepared to see desire there and steeled herself against it. But she wasn't prepared to see it mixed with so much sorrow. So much pain. She had no defense against that.

He slid his hand behind her neck and pulled her toward him. She went willingly. Going up on one knee and placing a hand on his chest to support herself, she leaned into the kiss.

His mouth was warm and mobile beneath hers, familiar and strange at the same time. She pulled back after a moment to look at his face.

"Ember."

The hoarseness of his plea carried her back, erasing the years. She pressed her lips to his again, seeking that old, delicious friction. He gave it to her, and when his tongue sought admission moments later, she parted for him. The taste of him rocked her senses, flooding her with yearning. A yearning that only grew with his intimate exploration. But so did the sadness, the sense of loss.

She pulled back, looking into his face. Hand splayed on his chest, she felt the powerful pounding of his heart. "You have no idea how much I wanted that night with you."

Something flashed in his eyes and his face hardened. Before she could process the change, he closed a hand around her wrist and removed it from his chest, easing her away from him.

"I shouldn't have done that," he said, his voice as tight as his face.

She pulled back, smarting. How could he look so pissed off? So angry? She was the one who'd been betrayed.

And he'd been the one to call a halt to that kiss when it should have been her spurning him.

"Relax, Jace. We're adults." She pushed to her feet,

smoothing her jeans. "We stirred up some old memories. Nothing more."

"Right."

The silence stretched again.

She turned back to him. "You really want to find out what happened that night?"

"Yes."

"All of it?"

"All of it," he confirmed. There was a fierce determination in his eyes. And a warning in his words, "But Ember, if we start overturning stones…"

"Then we turn them all over," she agreed. "All secrets pulled out of the dark corners and placed on the table."

He hesitated. "Agreed."

He was hiding something. She could still read him.

"Okay, how am I going to get out of here?" He gestured to his foot. "I'm guessing hiking out is out of the question."

"It's not the worst sprain I've seen, but it would get a helluva lot worse if you tried to walk out of here on it, even with me helping you."

"What about by boat? Know anyone who can get in here for first light?"

First light? "You're not asking much, are you?"

He just looked at her, waiting for an answer.

Her mind flashed to a solution. A tall, dark, handsome, totally-just-a-friend solution. "Think we can get you down to the river?"

"Definitely."

"Then I know a guy who can get us out. For a price, of course."

That muscle in his jaw leapt. "Call him. I'll pay whatever he wants."

— seven —

JACE STOOD outside, leaning against the door to the closed-up camp, cell phone pressed to his ear. The wind whipped around him, hard and cold. He didn't care. *Let it.*

No answer. Again. He ended the call after the fifth ring and shoved the phone back into his pocket.

It was just about ten minutes to six, well before what Terry would consider a civilized hour, but Jace didn't give a damn. In fact, he'd been calling off and on all night. Yes, Terry was on holiday in the Bahamas, but he usually kept his phone on him. Maybe this new girlfriend—a good fifteen years younger than Terry—was wearing him out. Or maybe his big brother was sleeping off another late night of drinking and had set the phone to vibrate so he could sleep in.

Not that Terry would be hung over. At least, not for long. Whatever he took for his migraines did the job on those too. As hard as he partied, he seldom let it get in the way of work. He'd get up, swallow a pill, and keep right on going. Though at what cost to his liver, God only knew.

As for Jace's own poor, suffering head...

The ibuprofen had knocked the headache down for a while, but it had come roaring back. Ember had dozed off for a few hours, reclined beside him on the love seat. Rather than disturb her by thrashing and lurching around to get a dose of

Tylenol at the three hour mark, he'd just lain there until it was time for the next dose of Advil at dawn.

His head was finally starting to feel better, though. Just being outside had provided him with a measure of relief. He pulled in a deep breath. There was a quality to the air around here. The river, the mountain—this entire region of New Brunswick. Clean and clear. Heaven on Earth.

Wayne Picard had loved it here. His stepfather had invested hundreds of thousands of dollars in the last dozen years before his death into helping the aquaculture of the area. He loved the natural rhythms of the land, the river. Picking fiddleheads in the spring. Then it was brook trout and shad. Fly-fishing salmon from June right through August. Wayne wasn't much for big game hunting, but he'd loved bagging a few ducks and geese in the fall. The old man had wanted everyone to be able to enjoy nature and live in harmony with it. And he'd meant for WRP Holdings to follow that vision.

Jace shifted some of his weight from his left foot to his injured right foot to see how it felt, and was surprised by how well he tolerated it. Of course, Ember had iced it around five o'clock, then wrapped and braced it excellently. Maybe it was even starting to heal a little bit.

In the trees above him, crows began to caw into the blowing wind. How many dawns after sleepless nights had he stepped outside to be greeted with that very sound?

"Morning, boys," he murmured. "Good day to lie low, if you're looking for some free advice."

The birds scattered from the treetops as the wind whipped wildly around, and this time, Jace did brace himself. It was going to be a hell of a day. And a hell of a rough ride in that boat. That is, if her contact made good on his promise to meet them at the river's edge. He'd have to know the region very well to find the right spot to pull his boat out. Even Jace would be hard pressed to find it by water, and he'd been coming here since he was a kid. The river would be all white caps today too. That little bit of extra attention required by the rough water might make it harder for Ember's guy to find them.

Even on a choppy day like this one, the Prince River had a quality of home to it. A familiarity. Hell, the whole region had been built around it. But just like he respected Harkness Mountain, Jace never deluded himself about the dangers of the deep, swift-moving waters. Neither did Ember.

Ember.

She was the reason his night had been so sleepless. He'd fully expected her to crawl into the bed up in the loft for what was left of the night. Instead, she'd crashed on the recliner with him. But why?

Could she have wanted to be close in case he needed her? That didn't seem likely, since she'd helped him to the bathroom, tended to his ankle, and made sure he was comfortably settled before she'd slept.

Maybe she just hadn't wanted to go anywhere near that bed. The very bed he'd covered with rose petals all those years ago, in preparation for her eighteenth birthday, the date they'd set for consummating their love.

He'd read that in a book—the rose petal thing. Actually, it had been one of Ember's romance novels. He'd picked the paperback up and flipped it open to the crease in the middle. His first thought had been, *Did Ember's mother know she read this stuff?* But then he'd read on. It had been very…informative. He'd wanted to make the occasion as special as he could, as romantic as he could.

His lips thinned. Well, she wasn't the only one who'd avoided that bed. As many times as he'd retreated to this cabin, he'd given it a pass in favor of the recliner.

Suddenly impatient, he shifted his weight back onto his injured foot again. Not bad, but nowhere near healed.

Of all weekends for this to happen, for her to show up in his life again.

He hadn't told Ember about the sale of the property, even

though he'd had the chance. The longer he delayed breaking the news, the harder it was going to be. So why *was* he holding back?

Because you don't want her to bolt again.

For a moment the wind almost stilled, and a voice drifted up from the river—a man's voice.

"So, Red, tell me again why you and What's-His-Name are in such an all-fired hurry to head into town."

Red? Who the hell ever got away with calling Ember Red?

Apparently this guy did. Jace's lips thinned even further.

Ember made some reply, but Jace couldn't catch it. Her voice was naturally softer, and the wind had picked up once more.

Then he saw her coming through the trees toward him. Normally, he'd have heard the bushes rustling, but with the wind tossing the trees, such subtle sounds were drowned out.

She'd already carried both their overstuffed backpacks and his briefcase down to the river.

The latter was locked, secured with a bungee cord, and lashed tightly to his backpack. No way did he want it spilling its secrets. Not yet. If she knew what was inside that case, she'd skin him alive for having had her lug it up to the cabin in the first place.

And yeah, having to let her hump that stuff around rubbed him the wrong way. But he'd had no choice. He sure as hell couldn't carry it, gimped up like this. As much as he told himself that anyone with a sprained ankle would be in the same position, it still stung. He wasn't used to having to rely on anyone.

He'd done what he could inside to help with departure preparations. Between them, they'd made sure the fire in the stove was out and that all electrical appliances were unplugged. That meant repacking the perishable stuff and leaving the door to the unplugged fridge propped open. Ember had even packed up the garbage without him having to ask. That had pleased him more than it should have, to see she still had some country in her.

He watched her progress toward him. When she was about twenty feet away, she stopped, pulled out her phone, read something. Then her fingers flew as she input her own message. "This'll drive him crazy."

Him.

Brother?

Boyfriend?

The latter seemed unlikely—not the way she'd responded when he'd kissed her last night. Before he remembered about Terry and pulled away.

She slid her phone into a pocket of her coat and zipped it closed. When she resumed walking toward him, her face was completely sober again.

"Ready?" she asked.

He nodded. "The place is all locked up."

"I guess we're all set then," she said, but he noticed she patted her pockets searchingly.

"Forget something? Want to go in and look around?"

"Nah. If I did, it can't be too important. I've got all the critical stuff."

"Where's your Wild Man of Harkness Mountain? I thought I heard his voice."

"Ryker," she corrected. "His name is Ryker Groves. And he's waiting at the boat, like I asked him to. Because if he was here, he'd insist on helping you, if only so I didn't have to, and I know how much you'd hate that."

Her perception surprised him. Though he supposed it shouldn't. She always did seem to know what he was feeling, sometimes before he did. The fact that she still did pissed him off.

"For chrissakes, Ember, you don't have to *handle* me."

Her eyes widened. "I wasn't aware that I was."

"For the record, I couldn't give a shit who helps me, so long as I can make it to the river and get on with the search."

"Well, it's going to be *me* helping you, as we've already established. So, if you're quite ready, Mr. Cranky Pants, let's get this show on the road."

Mr. Cranky Pants? It wasn't enough that he felt so useless and dependent. Now he felt like a petulant child too. But to protest would only make him seem more…cranky.

"Okay, let's go." With a deep sigh, he pushed away from the wall, keeping most of his weight on his good leg.

Ember was beside him in a flash, sliding under his right arm and pulling his hand over her shoulder. Her movements were sure, clinical. She'd probably done this for lots of patients.

"Lean on me," she said. "Come on. Doctor's orders."

He did as she bade, letting her take some of his weight, but before they took a single step, she looked up at him. "Can we call a truce, Jace?"

"A truce?"

"Yeah, as in stop picking at each other." Her green eyes were earnest. "I need to know what happened that night just as much as you do—maybe more. That's why I'm going along with this…quest of yours."

"A truce until we find the truth?"

"Exactly."

"What about afterward?"

She bit her lip. For a second, it looked like she was going to say something, but someone else's words cut through the morning air.

"Oh, for the love of all things holy! Will you two get a move on? The Wild Man of Harkness Mountain has a job to do in town today."

Shit. Ryker Groves, standing just outside the tree line. Guess there must have been another lull in the wind.

"Yeah, well, considering how much I paid for this ride, I'm thinking you can wait for *What's-His-Name* to actually get to the boat."

"We're on our way," Ember called, whereupon Ryker turned and tramped back down toward the river. She looked up at Jace with a wide grin. "Your voice really carries."

"Apparently." In this light, with that wide smile on her face, she was hands down the most beautiful woman he'd ever seen. And with her tucked in tight to his side, he could feel her warmth and strength, smell her hair. Maybe this truce thing would be all right.

"Ready?" she asked.

He nodded and they started the hundred and fifty yard walk down to the water.

It was even more excruciating than he thought it would be. There sure as hell wasn't any room in his head for appreciating the smell of her shampoo. He very quickly learned that every step made his ankle throb harder than the last. Most of his focus was taken up trying not to gasp or groan with every movement. And once, despite the bracing job Ember had done, he managed to sort of twist the ankle. He did gasp then, but given that he wanted to vomit, he counted that small sound a victory. Ember noticed it, though, and insisted they pause a moment to let the pain settle down.

At his nod, they resumed. The thick trees became more sparsely spaced as they neared the river, and Jace could hear the rushing water. Then he saw him. Ryker Groves, standing on the shore.

He'd looked like a big lumberjack when Jace had seen him at the edge of the clearing minutes ago, but holy shit. He was freakin' *enormous*. He had to be six foot six, maybe six seven, and probably tipped the scales at two twenty or more. And not the refrigerator-shaped two twenty. The lean and muscular kind. Hell, the guy probably could have thrown Jace over his shoulder fireman style and walked him right out of the woods to his Escalade, let alone down to the river.

Ember did the introductions. "Ryker, this is Jace Picard. Jace, this is Ryker Groves, or as some of us call him, Seven Ten Sun."

Ryker snorted. "You're the only one who calls me that, Red."

Seven Ten Sun? Or was that Son? What did that mean? Was it a reference to his height? He was tall, but nowhere near seven foot ten.

Ryker must have read his thoughts, because he grinned, ridiculously perfect white teeth flashing in his darkly tanned, bearded face. "It's a long story."

"I'm sure." Clamping down on a surge of completely unwarranted jealousy, he gave Groves a nod. "Thanks for coming."

The big guy nodded back. "Hey, Ember calls, I come."

"Especially when there's a good commission in it, huh?" Ember teased.

"Don't tell him," Groves said, nodding toward Jace and lowering his voice confidingly, "but I'da come out here just to catch up with you."

She laughed. "We do have some catching up to do, huh? But I'm afraid it's going to have to wait. Jace and I have some business to take care of straight away."

"Good thing I'm a patient man, Red," he said. "Call me when you're free and we'll grab a beer, okay?"

"Okay."

He handed both Jace and Ember a yellow life vest. "Put that on, then we'll see about getting you boarded."

The boat was a fairly sizeable skiff. Groves had lashed it to the small floating dock, but it bobbed rhythmically with the wind-whipped waters. It took a moment—and some steadying help from both Ember and Groves—for Jace to clamber aboard. He sat on the bench in the center, as instructed. As

Groves steadied the craft, Ember climbed in, moving easily to the bow. Then Groves untied the boat and hopped into the craft, taking up position at the tiller.

The outboard roared to life and Groves guided them into the river. It took some expert manoeuvring to reverse direction in the white-caps, involving lots of spray smacking Jace in the face and dampening his jacket while they were at cross-currents. Up front, Ember took even more of the brunt, but she laughed in delight even as she clung to the gunwales. Strands of hair, luminous as fire in the diffused light of dawn, danced around her face.

They came about gradually until they were pointed into the current, and Groves opened the throttle. There was still some mist and spray to contend with, but at least they were on their way. One step closer to finding Bridget and solving the mystery. The knowledge allowed him to relax. Well, as much as a person with a throbbing ankle could relax while motoring into a headwind on the Prince River on a blustery day.

A number of large birds lifted from the trees on the far shore, claiming his attention. For a moment, he thought they were going to be treated to bald eagles fishing, but as he watched them soar, he realized they were turkey vultures. They could be hard to distinguish from a distance, but his stepfather had taught him how to tell the difference. Vultures held their wings in a slight V-shape as they soared, whereas an eagle's wings would be completely flat. He could hear Wayne now: "Just remember, V is for Vulture. Look at the outspread wings."

The kettle of vultures wheeled in unison and angled off over the trees.

The beauty of it all hit him afresh. Dammit! What Terry planned for the region was so contrary to their father's vision.

At the same time, he knew that if he'd been driving along the back roads instead of up the pristine river with its tidy lodges and hunting camps, he'd be struck just as hard by the rural poverty he saw. Homes and properties in need of repair. Rusted-out cars standing in yards. Too many citizens of the region had been out of work for too long. Jobs were needed here—in Crandler, in Harkness, in Tynsdale. All through the Prince Region.

Twenty minutes later, Groves pointed the boat toward a large new-looking place perched on the left bank of the river. As they drew closer, Jace realized it was a very nice house. So was the dock. Like the Picard wharf, it was a floating proposition, but that's where any resemblance ended. It was basically a floating boat slip with a roof on top to keep the boats out of the weather. Yes, boats, plural. The other was a flat-decked bass fishing boat. A four-seater. The man had some money and liked his outdoor pursuits.

"Can you park this thing already?" Ember said. "I have to pee like a racehorse."

"Doesn't that camp have a toilet?" Groves shot a quick look at Jace. "I could fix that for you, for a price. Install a small septic system and drain field."

"It has a toilet," Ember hastened to assure him. "I just neglected to use it before we left."

"In a little bit of a hurry, were you?"

"Yes," she said crisply. "And now I'm in even more of a hurry."

Groves laughed, but he tied the boat up and helped Ember out. Without a backward look, she hurried down the dock and up the stairs toward the wide house with its gleaming front wall of windows.

Groves secured the front end of the boat, hopped back in, and threw their backpacks onto the deck.

Then he looked at Jace. "If I steady her, can you get yourself onto the wharf? Or do you need me to help you?"

Jace waved him off. As much as his ankle hurt, he'd do this himself or die trying. "I can manage."

Groves nodded. "Okay, but for God's sake, be careful. If you take a fall, Red'll kill me."

As tempting as that sounded, it wouldn't be worth the aggravation to his injury. And as it turned out, getting out of the boat was easier than getting in had been. Still, beads of sweat had popped out around his hairline by the time he stood upright on the dock.

Groves went over to a giant covered storage bin, rummaged around for a moment and came with a baseball bat. He strode back toward Jace, gripping the bat part way up the handle with one hand and tapping the head of it into his left palm in a slow, rhythmic way. Jace's heart leapt. Immediately he went into boxer mode, his arms coming up. The guy was a giant, but if this whole thing was going south, he'd give him a run for his—

"Relax. I was just thinking you could use it like a cane to get upstairs." Groves gripped the bat by its knob and thumped the end of it on the deck to demonstrate. "Seems about the right height."

His words sounded helpful, but there was an unmistakeable warning in those dark eyes. He didn't have to say it out loud. *Hurt Ember and that ankle will be the least of your worries.*

"Thanks for the help." Jace met the other man's gaze unwaveringly as he took the Louisville Slugger from him. Then, propping the bat against his good leg to free both hands, he dug his wallet out. Quickly, he counted out a wad of bills and handed them to Groves. "Appreciate it."

Groves took the money. Without counting it, he transferred it into his own wallet, then slid it into his back pocket. "Anything for Ember."

"Yeah. I got that."

A grin flashed in that dark face, then it became serious. Groves marked him with a hard stare. "She was yours? Years ago?"

"Yes." His ankle throbbed like a bitch, the longer he stood upright. Jace leaned on the bat. It helped. "She told you?"

He shrugged. "I knew there was someone from her past. And I knew it was you the moment I saw the two of you together."

Jace felt that muscle tic in his jaw. "That was a long time ago."

"We've been friends for six years. Since I moved up from Arizona."

"You're a long way from home."

"Not anymore," Groves said. "Look, I don't know what you're looking for in tracking down this other woman."

Seriously? "Ember told you?"

"Don't worry. All she said was you needed to see this person from your past. That you both did." Jace's relief that she hadn't told him more dissolved when he continued. "Dude, I don't know what you're hoping to find in Crandler this weekend. And I don't know what happened between you and Red."

Sweet baby Jesus, why couldn't he have just left that ominous bat-thumping routine to speak for him? "No you don't," Jace said, hearing the irritation in his own voice and not giving a shit. "But something tells me I'm about to get some free advice on the matter."

"Don't hurt her. That's one heart that doesn't deserve to break ever again."

Jace felt like he'd been punched in the gut. He looked down at the briefcase strapped so tightly to his backpack. He wished he could tear that case loose and send it skipping across the water to sink in the Prince River. Because when she found out about the sale of her family home, her heart was going to break all over again.

Because of him.

– eight –

ARDEN STANDISH looked up from his newspaper at the sound of the knock on his door. His *kitchen door*, which meant family or friends. Of course, in Harkness, that was pretty much most of the town. Except he didn't need to pull back the curtain on the window to know which citizen of Harkness was knocking on his door at eight o'clock in the morning.

He set his coffee cup down and smoothed a hand over his whisker-free face—glad he'd taken the time to shave this morning.

"Door's open," he called. "Come on in."

Faye Siliker let herself into his kitchen bearing a large Tupperware container, the kind ladies used to transport cakes and pies.

"Good morning, Faye."

"Good morning to you, Arden." She greeted him with a smile. "I brought you a chocolate cake."

"That's too kind."

"Nonsense," she said briskly, crossing the roomy kitchen to deposit the container on the counter. "It's the least I could do to say thank you for your son saving my daughter."

"*Saving her?* From what I understand from Scott, everything's under control up there on the mountain."

"I'm sure it is. And if I know my Ocean, it just might be Titus who needs saving from her," she said dryly.

"I hope you're right."

They shared a chuckle.

He went to the counter and lifted the top off the cake carrier. Yup, chocolate cake, piled high with frosting. "Land sakes, woman, that looks deadly."

"Oh, no. Hardly any calories at all."

Please don't let it be vegan. "Really? How'd you manage that?"

"I made it with tofu, of course."

"Tofu chocolate cake." He covered his disappointment gamely. "Sounds delightful."

Faye snorted. "Arden Standish, you're the worst liar in all of Harkness."

Whoops. Guess he didn't cover his disappointment as well as he'd thought. "Am I?"

"Definitely. And clearly, I'm way better at lying than you are, judging by the expression on your face just now."

He brightened. "It's not really made from tofu?"

"Hell, no. I save that crap for when River's home. This is the real, wicked deal. You don't want to know how much butter and confectioner's sugar went into the butter cream icing alone."

"Oh, thank God." He glanced at the triple-layered work of art. "That would have been a crime." He looked up, catching her looking at the cake a little hungrily herself. "Now tell the truth—you just wanted an excuse to eat cake for breakfast, didn't you?"

She shrugged. "Who doesn't want an excuse to eat cake?"

"True," he conceded. "Take a seat, Faye, and I'll put the water on."

"Perfect. But I'll cut us a couple of slices before I sit."

She transferred the cake to the table, then rummaged in the utensil drawer for a knife and cake lifter. Meanwhile, he reached for the kettle and carried it to the sink to refill it. They worked companionably, the way only old friends could. Faye and Margaret had been close friends for many years before his wife died. Arden enjoyed Faye's company more and more as time distanced him from Margret's death. And he believed the feeling was mutual.

"What kind of tea would you like?" he asked.

"I'd love some of that chickweed tea, if you have any left."

"I'll check." He didn't have to check very hard. He'd picked up a package at the specialty tea shop last week when he'd been in Fredericton. Just in case Faye dropped by sometime, like she had a couple weeks ago, and a week before that.

When he came out of the pantry a minute later, the kettle had started to steam gently. Faye—quite adept at making herself at home in the Standish kitchen—had already set the table for two. But now she stood motionless, looking at the open china cabinet and the box at the end of the table with half of Margaret's Christmas dishes already packed.

"They're Ember's now," he said.

"Did she ask you to pack them for her? And does that mean she's decided where she wants to practice?"

"No. On both accounts."

Faye lowered herself into a chair. "It's true then. You're selling this place?"

The kettle whistled. Grateful for the interruption, he turned off the burner and proceeded to make the tea. Faye waited quietly, if not patiently.

He should have told her about the sale. Had meant to a handful of times. However, he could never bring himself to do so—not before the kids knew. That's what he told himself, anyhow. But there was more to his select silence on the matter. Way down deep inside, he hoped for a miracle.

Faye had served up thick slices of cake. He put the teapot on a woven hot pad in the centre of the table and took a seat. Neither of them reached for a fork.

"How'd you find out?" he asked.

"Scott told me. Well, you and Scott."

His eyebrows shot up. "But—"

"Relax," she said. "Scott didn't say anything. In fact, I'm guessing he doesn't know himself. I just put it together."

"Put it together from what?"

She lifted her shoulder in a shrug. "Scott mentioned that Titus had asked him and Ember to come home to talk something over. This on top of the fact that you've been acting strange lately. More quiet than usual. Then I come in and see you've been packing up Margret's—*Ember's*—Christmas dishes."

"The kids always said you were a sharp one."

"I repeat, you're a terrible liar. The kids thought I was a holy terror. But they *did* learn in my class." She shook her head. "Why, Arden? Why are you selling the homestead?"

He almost squirmed in his seat. "I'm old, Faye—"

"Oh, that's the biggest load of bullshit you've every dropped." With that eloquent pronouncement, Faye snatched up her fork and attacked the cake like she meant business.

Arden chuckled. "You never were one to mince words." He picked up his own fork and took a bite of the cake. It was just as rich and heavenly as he'd known it would be.

"You're not old, Arden. You're three years younger than I am."

"That's still too old to run this place alone."

"Then hire someone to give you a hand. It shouldn't be that—" Faye cocked her head. "Wait a minute...alone?"

This time, he did squirm in his seat. "It's Titus. He's spent his whole life here. Even when he went to university in Fredericton, he commuted to and from school nearly every weekend. And no sooner did he complete his degree when his mother got sick. He stepped up, took over running the farm. He even helped me take care of Margaret." He swallowed. It was hard, thinking about the sacrifices Titus had made. He'd been accepted into the RCMP cadet program and had been poised to fly out to Regina to start his training when Margaret's cancer came back. Without being asked, he'd made the decision to stay home to manage things, while Scott and Ember had gone off to chase their own dreams. But he didn't have to tell Faye any of that. She knew the history.

Arden cleared his throat. "He deserves his chance too. To get out into the world. When I made the offer to sell the farm—"

"You *offered* to sell it? Oh, Arden!"

He looked down at his plate. "I'd made him the same proposal before, more than a few times, and he always brushed it off. But—"

"But not this time," Faye said.

He took another bite of the cake. Chewed, swallowed. "Even after Titus took me up on it, I thought we'd have time. Selling a farming operation like this? I thought it would take months. Years. But Titus found a buyer right away."

"Who?"

He took another bite of cake to delay answering. She just waited.

"WRP Holdings."

"Oh, Arden, no. *WRP Holdings*? The Picards? What was Titus thinking?"

He felt like he'd just been punched in the gut. In the few weeks since the deal had been made, he'd heard more and more bad things about that company, and their new commander-in-chief, Terry Picard.

Sick, he put down his fork. "It was my decision, Faye. And he just wants his chance. His turn."

"At what?"

"Living, I guess."

She made no reply, just reached for the pot of well-steeped tea and poured for both of them.

"This place meant the world to the kids when they were

younger." He could feel her studying his face. He grabbed a napkin from the napkin holder—one with a Thanksgiving turkey burned into the wood that Ember had made in grade ten shop class. *Where would that go? Where would all the years of memories go?*

"Does Ember know?" she asked softly.

"Not yet," he said. "Losing this land will break her heart."

"Then don't lose it."

He looked at Faye's eyes—anxious, concerned, beautiful. Hopeful.

But it was too late.

— nine —

EMBER TIGHTENED her grip on the wheel. Her muscles were tense from crouching forward, peering through the curtain of rain.

They'd been driving for what seemed like forever, but they hadn't gotten very far. The rain and wind just would *not* quit. At times the visibility was so bad, she'd had no choice but to pull over onto the shoulder of the road and hope they didn't get rear-ended by another motorist.

She risked a quick glance over at Jace. His face was set in grim lines. Though he hadn't complained, she could tell his ankle was hurting and he had no way to elevate it effectively in the truck.

Yes, *truck*. They'd taken Ryker's GMC Sierra pickup, rather than backtrack to get Jace's vehicle. Ryker had loaned it to Ember for the weekend, saying he'd "make do" with his Infiniti. Yeah, some sacrifice. He loved that little sports car. But without even asking, he'd opened up the truck's cap, hauled out any tools he'd need over the weekend and tossed her the keys. That's when the rain had started. Hard. And as they discovered as they made their way south, it didn't seem about to let up any time soon.

"How's the ankle?" she asked.

"Fine," he lied. "How're your shoulders?"

"Fine." She forced those shoulders, which she'd unconsciously pulled up around her ears, to relax. Then another gust of wind caught the pickup and she had to fight to keep it between the lines, even at her greatly reduced speed. "Okay, I'm not fine. This is crazy. It'll take us forever to get there in this storm. I think we should find a motel and get off the road for a while."

"Agreed."

Once the decision was made, they passed sign after sign—*Closed for the Season. No Vacancy*. She was about to suggest they turn around and start back to Harkness when Jace sat up straighter.

"There. That's what we want."

Her eyes widened. "The Gnome Sweet Home?"

"Yup."

She turned her signal light on and braked as they approached the small motel. The tiny front yard was dotted with gnomes—and not just of the ordinary garden variety. There were high-hatted, big bellied Ninjas and dead-eyed zombies out there. Even an Elvis gnome. World's tackiest motel. She'd heard that the owner received gnomes from all over the world; Ember believed it. And the sign outside it read *Closed*, like many of the others.

She pulled into the parking lot of the place that had provided fodder for a million jokes over the years, staring in fascination. "I thought this place closed down years ago."

"It did."

"Then why are we stopping?"

"The old lady who owns the place still lives here, over the office. Rumor has it that if you're prepared to pay a premium, she'll find you a room. Off the books, of course."

"So, I guess we're about to test the veracity of that rumor." She put the vehicle in park and reached for the door release.

"Wait." He put a hand on her arm to stop her before she could hop out. "I'll do it."

She sent him a surprised look. "I don't mind doing it. Your ankle has to be killing you."

He cleared his throat. "How do I put this? Rumor also has it that Mrs. Dufour is more receptive to approaches from…um…people of the male persuasion."

Her eyebrows shot up. "You're going to *charm* her into giving us a room?"

"I'm going to try."

"Fine. But at least let me get you handier to the door so you don't have to hop so far."

She drove right up to the walkway. He climbed out of the truck and hobbled to the office. In just those few seconds, he got soaked. She watched through the passenger window as he rang the bell. A moment later, an old lady appeared. Ember wasn't close enough to the pair to even try to lip read, but the conversation looked…animated. Finally, ten minutes later, Jace produced his wallet. Five minutes after that, he limped back through the rain, a victorious smile on his face.

"The Picard charm worked, I see," she said as he climbed into the vehicle.

"She felt sorry for us." He ran a hand over his wet hair to slick it back off his face. "Officially, she doesn't have her motel license anymore, but…well, how could she say no to newlyweds?"

"*Newlyweds?*"

He grinned. "Hey, it worked, didn't it?"

She waggled her left hand. "We're not wearing wedding rings."

"That's because we just eloped."

She looked at him like he was crazy. "Like I'd ever elope!"

He pointed to the end of the row of rooms. "We've got room thirteen, around back."

"Of course. So passers-by don't figure out she has guests." She turned the key and the truck roared to life.

"Or anyone remotely connected to the provincial

government, the federal tax man, or the hospitality industry in general, I suspect."

She reversed the truck and headed in the direction he'd indicated, but her mind was racing. How many years had these units stood empty? Would the dust be millimetres thick? The bedding rotting?

She pulled up in front of room thirteen and killed the engine. "Key?" she asked? "I can run ahead and open the door."

"Don't have 'em yet. The proprietor, Mrs. Willa Dufour—who incidentally turned eighty-five and a half years old just yesterday, but doesn't look a day over seventy—is going to meet us here and open it up."

"Give the newlyweds the grand tour before she turns over the key?"

"Something like that."

A service door opened and their octogenarian host, clad in an oversized yellow raincoat that reached nearly to her ankles, stepped out into the weather. She was so small, Ember feared the wind might blow her away, but she was obviously stronger than she looked. Also, speedier. She made her way to their unit in no time flat.

Ember hopped out of the truck. She pulled her knapsack easily from behind the seat. His was harder to get out, with that damned briefcase lashed to it. Finally, one knapsack on each shoulder, she closed her door. Jace had climbed out too.

"Hang on a sec while I dump these and I'll come back to help you."

He waved her off. "I can make it myself. No need for us both to get soaked. Run for it!"

She dashed for the shelter of the wrap-around veranda. A dripping Jace made his way slowly to her. She winced, imagining how much that ankle must be throbbing after all the abuse it had suffered today.

They'd gone about this all wrong. They should have taken

the time to go back for Jace's vehicle. He could have sat in the back seat with his foot elevated. And they could have gone into the pharmacy in Harkness and rented some crutches. But when Ryker had ferried them to his place on the other side of the river, Jace hadn't wanted to backtrack and lose time. Letting her own desire for answers get in the way, she'd gone along with him. She shouldn't have. What kind of doctor was she?

For heaven's sake, it had been ten years. What difference would a few extra hours have made?

Jace made it to the dubious shelter of the narrow veranda at last, just ahead of Mrs. Dufour.

"Hello again, young man." The tiny woman looked Ember over. "And this must be your bride?"

"That's me." Ember forced a smile. "Thank you for renting us the room. We weren't looking forward to driving any further."

"I could hardly turn a new couple like you away, could I? It's raining pitchforks out here." She produced a key with a fluorescent red tag and opened the door, then led them into the room.

Ember put their knapsacks down on the threadbare carpet and looked around. It was no Hyatt Regency, that was for sure. But they were lucky to get anything.

She'd planned on them taking a room from the get-go, of course. She just thought they'd be closer to Crandler before they pulled off the highway.

And no, not for romantic reasons. For medical reasons. Jace needed to elevate that ankle. God only knew how long it would take to find Bridget Northrup, once they got started. It was the long weekend. She might not even be in town. Knowing Jace, he'd be on his feet the whole while if she didn't force him to stop and rest. Yes, he was making progress, but anti-inflammatories and the pressure bandage could only do so much, especially when he insisted on putting weight on it like he had just now. Rest and elevation were critical in these first few days or his Grade 1 sprain might graduate to a Grade 2, leaving the ligaments loose. He might wind up needing an air cast or a splint to stabilize it if he didn't take care of it now.

That was the reason—the *only* reason—she'd planned on taking a room.

She chewed her lip. He had kissed her back at the camp. And she'd kissed him right back. Which had to be the worst idea she'd had in...*ever*. Then he'd pulled away suddenly, completely. As if someone else had entered the room. Or some memory had.

"So what do you think, dear? Will this do?"

Mrs. Dufour's words pulled Ember back to the present.

"Oh yes. It's lovely."

The old lady cackled, then coughed, an unmistakable smoker's cough that went on and on.

"Oh, honey," she said, when she'd recovered, "even in its prime, I don't know that this place was ever *lovely*. But the last time I checked the hot water still worked." She moved further into the room. "Mind you that was a while ago. You might want to run it a while before you use it."

The old woman hit the switch on the wall.

"Oh good," she said. "Lights work."

Ember looked up at the single glowing bulb behind the dingy amber shade.

"Of course, the power could well go out in this wind." She fished in the pocket of her oversized raincoat and pulled out a flashlight which she handed to Ember. "Figured you should have one of these in case we lose our lights." She winked. "We could lose our heat too, but I don't expect that'll be a problem for you young 'uns."

"Yes. I mean, no. Not a problem."

Jace grinned, clearly enjoying Ember's discomfort.

"Well, I guess you've got everything you need, then." She headed toward the door. "Oh, there's no phone in these rooms anymore. Actually, I pulled them out long before they closed me—I mean, before I closed down. One less thing to worry about. But if you need anything, you just jog right up to the house. I sleep like a cat. I'll hear you before you knock on the door."

"Thank you." Ember's gaze went around the room again. The decor was dated but scrupulously clean. It had just one bed—a queen, thank God. Hopefully the bedding would be as fresh as the rest of the room. Two narrow, hard-backed orange chairs sat in the corners. The television was one of the old, bulky CRT types, and an old VHS player and huge remote sat next to it on the room's lone dresser, a piece of furniture that looked straight out of the eighties.

"The TV works. So does the VCR, but there's no cable," Mrs. Dufour said, her hand on the doorknob. "There are plenty of movies in the top drawer, though. And if nothing there catches your fancy, feel free to come up to the office. I've got lots more up there."

Oh God, *no cable? VHS movies?* If that was the case, it was a pretty safe bet there was no Wi-Fi. For Mrs. Dufour's benefit, she hid her dismay behind a bright smile. "It'll do wonderfully." She linked her arm in Jace's. "My husband and I are so grateful to have a place to stay."

Mrs. Dufour looked pleased. "Happy to be able to help, especially for a pair like you. Easy to see you're in love."

Ember had to clear her throat before she could reply. "Thank you so much, Mrs. Dufour."

"Yes, we appreciate you opening the place for us." Jace cast a look at Ember. "My wife and I will be quite comfortable here."

Mrs. Dufour was hardly out the door when Ember pulled away from Jace and went to the window. "Let's get some light in here."

The curtains rattled along the metal rod as she pulled the drawstring.

Room thirteen faced the Prince River. As rough and choppy as conditions had been this morning, they were much worse now, the wind churning the swollen river into endless whitecaps. She was glad she'd arranged the early dawn transport with Ryker. No way would she want to be out on that water now.

She thought of Titus and Ocean up on Harkness Mountain. She hoped they were all right. Dry at least. Hopefully they were holed up at the camp or the cave. If anyone could handle whatever the mountain dished out, Titus could.

The wind gusted, shaking the building and rattling the glass in its frame. Brrr. Temperature wise, it wasn't especially cold for October, but if a body got wet with that wind out there, it would be hypothermia city.

Come to think of it, it was pretty darned cold inside.

On cue, she heard the *tink tink tink* in the water pipes. Mrs. Dufour had left just enough heat on in these units to keep the pipes from freezing. Ember located the thermostat beside the door and cranked it up some. The tinking noise accelerated.

When she turned back around, Jace was sitting on the foot of the bed shivering.

"Crap!" She moved quickly to his side. "What was I thinking? You need to get out of those wet clothes and under the blankets. It'll likely be an hour or more before this room warms up."

"I'm all right."

"No, you're not. You're freezing. That ankle needs to be elevated, and you can't lie down on the bed in those wet clothes."

He muttered something, but he removed his soggy jacket and handed it to her. "Satisfied?"

"Now the boots and jeans." When he hesitated, she blew out an exasperated breath. "Jace, I'm a doctor. I'm not going to swoon at the sight of your naked legs. And the sooner you're out of those wet clothes, the sooner we can get on with treating your ankle."

"Anyone ever tell you you're bossy?"

"Pretty much every day since I learned to talk. Now get on with it."

He snorted, but stood up, released his belt, unzipped the jeans and pushed them down his thighs before sitting again. She knelt to remove his hiking shoes, then helped ease the jeans off, taking care with the injured foot. He shivered again.

She stood. "Can I get you to stand up one more time before we get you settled?"

He pushed to his feet again and she pulled the heavy coverlet off the bed. She handed it to him. "Wrap this around yourself and we'll get you settled on the bed. That way, I'll still be able to get at your ankle while you warm up."

When he'd wrapped the blanket around him, she guided him to the side of the bed. He looked a little grey around the gills as he sat down.

"On the count of three, I'll help you lift your legs. You pivot and lie back. Got it?"

He nodded.

She grasped his lower legs and on the count of three, got him horizontal.

"Now, let's get that foot elevated."

She went to the tiny closet and found one extra pillow. She used it and the one from her side of the bed to elevate his injured ankle. She wished she had ice, but just rest and elevation would make a big difference.

"How's the wrap job feel? Not too tight."

He shook his head. "It's fine. But is it time for another dose of something?"

That was about as close as he was going to come to admitting how much pain he was in, she supposed. She checked her watch. It was closer to two hours than three since he'd had the ibuprofen, but still a safe interval from his last dose. And maybe he could get off to sleep for a while. "You can have another dose of Tylenol now." She went to her knapsack, dug out the extra-strength Tylenol and a bottle of water.

He held out his hand for the pills and tossed them back, then accepted the water to wash them down with. He handed the half-full bottle back to her.

"I wish that were coffee. I'd have drained it."

"Would you like me to go see if Mrs. Dufour can scare up some coffee?"

"Nah. I'll be all right."

"You should sleep anyway, if you can." She adjusted the coverlet, tucking it loosely around his elevated foot.

"I feel like a caterpillar."

She grinned. "You look more like a burrito."

"I like my image better. Caterpillars turn into beautiful butterflies. We all know what burritos turn into."

She snorted a laugh. "True."

Taking the two chairs from the corner, she positioned them in front of the heater, then fetched his wet clothes and arranged them over the chairs' backs.

"What about you? You didn't sleep much either."

She turned and eyed the empty side of the bed. It did look inviting, even without a pillow.

As though he read her mind, he lifted his head and pulled his own pillow out. "Take this one. If I'm going to be stuck on my back, it'll wind up on the floor anyway. Gives me a crick in my neck."

"Really?"

"Really. Now lie down. I won't be able to sleep if you're going to be prowling."

She bit her lip. What could it hurt? It's not like they could accidentally get entangled. He was swaddled on top of the blankets and she would be under them.

"Why not?"

She shucked off her damp jeans, but kept her underwear, shirt and socks on. After placing her jeans on the seat of one of the chairs, she scooted back and crawled into the bed. Happily, the sheets were clean. Not a bit musty smelling. Mrs. Dufour had to be letting this room out semi-regularly for them to be so fresh.

She turned on her side facing Jace. "How's the ankle feeling?"

"Better." He turned his head to face her. "You were right about needing to elevate it. Thank you."

Oh, God. His dark head against the white sheets, that face, those eyes... Her chest constricted.

"Ember?" He lifted his head, concern in his eyes.

"It's nothing. A little indigestion from drinking that coffee on an empty stomach. It'll pass. But we were talking about *you*, mister. The first pharmacy we come to, we're renting you crutches. You can't keep putting weight on that ankle."

"Or what? It'll take longer to heal?"

"That too, but you could also aggravate it. You could wind up with it in an air cast for months on end."

"Sold. We'll get crutches."

"And when we get to Crandler, if we don't find Bridget right away, we may need to get a motel room there too. We'll need someplace to go periodically to elevate and ice that sprain, especially if we're going to be riding around in this truck. If we'd gone back for your car, you could at least be sitting in the back seat with your foot up while we drove."

"If we'd gone back to get my car, we wouldn't be here," he said dryly. "Not together, anyway. Your brother would have kicked my ass before he let you drive off with me. Or tried to."

He was right, of course. "Point taken."

"Speaking of which, do your brothers know you're here?"

"They know I'm with my 'patient'. Titus is still on the mountain, probably pinned down by the weather, so that should hold them for a while. He found Ocean, by the way."

"I figured he must have, but glad to hear it." Jace paused. "So I don't have to sleep with one eye open? No irate Standish man looking to go a few rounds?"

She laughed. "No. Now go to sleep."

"Yes, ma'am."

He dutifully closed his eyes and within minutes was sleeping.

She lay there listening to his respirations, watching his relaxed face. When she finally fell asleep, it was with an ache of loss and sadness in her chest.

– ten –

JACE GLANCED at his cell phone, then grimaced and placed it down on the table beside his mug of steaming coffee.

According to Google, there was one Bridget Northrup in the area. He'd called her listed number, leaving his name and a message asking her to call him back on his cell. Now he was going crazy waiting for his phone to ring. True, it had only been twenty minutes, but there were some things a man couldn't wait on.

Like discovering the truth after so many years.

He looked across the table at Ember. He'd put his menu down five minutes ago, but she was still reading hers. Or rather staring at it. Her eyes weren't flitting around the plastic, one-page breakfast menu of Chloe's Back Porch Diner.

Damned weather. Half the day was gone and he had nothing to show for it.

Back at the Gnome Sweet Home, he'd slept hard for over two hours, waking around noon. Ember was already up, and by the look of her, showered. It was still windy out, but the rain had stopped. She'd checked his ankle, pronounced the swelling improved, given him another dose of painkillers, and handed him his almost-dry clothes. He managed to dress himself, after which she'd helped him to the bathroom. He'd longed for a hot shower and a close shave, but given how much daylight they'd already burned, he settled for a quick wash-up. Then she'd slid under his right arm again and helped him out to the truck. He'd already prepaid for the use of the day room—in cash, with a nice bonus for Mrs. Dufour—but Ember had insisted they check out officially. Even though it was a distinctly *unofficial* stay, she thought they owed Mrs. Dufour the courtesy. She'd also insisted on doing it herself while he waited in the vehicle. Fifteen minutes after he'd woken up, they pulled out onto the highway, headed for Crandler.

He'd wanted to stop at the first greasy spoon they saw for a late breakfast when they hit town thirty minutes later, but Ember had had other ideas. The first order of business? Getting him crutches. He had mixed feelings about that, even as the pharmacist guided them through choosing the proper set. On the plus side, he now had more mobility, but there was also no reason for Ember to tuck herself under his arm.

Finally, they'd pulled up outside Chloe's. The hostess settled them into the last available booth, one of a long line of booths stretching along the west wall of the restaurant. Even with the wild weather, the diner was doing a brisk business.

He glanced at Ember, but she was still gazing at the menu.

Ignoring the rumbling of his stomach, he looked around. Far from a back porch, Chloe's was a sizeable diner fronting on Chandler's Main Street, tucked in between an antiques store and a coffee shop. The interior was nothing special. At best, it might be called cozy. But what it lacked in ambiance, it more than made up for with the quality of the food, not to mention the lumberjack-sized servings. It was hands down the best place for buttermilk biscuits in the entire Prince Region. Almost as good as Jace's mom used to make.

He took a sip of his coffee, stretched back a bit in the padded seat. How long had it been since he'd thought about his mother?

Jewel Cooper had died at thirty-two years of age, in a

car/bicycle accident that rocked the region. Jace had been fifteen at the time. By then, his mother had been married to Wayne Picard for almost five years. Five happy years, for all of them. She'd met Wayne at the bank where she worked, and after a year together, they'd tied the knot. Wayne had promptly adopted Jace, and it had taken no time at all for Jace—then ten years old—to start calling him Dad. Wayne had always been great to him, treating him like a son.

Not that Jace had a lot of experience with father/son relationships. He'd never known his own father. Didn't even know the guy's name. The few times he'd broached the subject with his mother, it seemed to make her sad, and he couldn't bear her sadness. He always figured she'd tell him when he was older, but then she'd died, taking the secret with her.

In the fourteen years since Jewel Picard's death, Wayne never came close to remarrying. When he died two months ago of complications from pneumonia, Terry and Jace were his sole beneficiaries. Control of WRP Holdings had gone to Terry, who'd inherited sixty percent ownership, compared to Jace's forty percent, an arrangement Jace had no trouble with. In fact, when he and Terry had gone to the lawyer's office for the reading of the will, Jace already knew about the sixty/forty deal. Wayne had talked a lot about his intentions. He'd also gifted Jace something before he died—he'd opened a joint account with a half million dollars in it, in case Jace should ever need it. Reading between the lines, Jace figured his stepfather meant *in case you need it to rein in your brother*. Their father had loved them both, but he wasn't blind to their faults.

He swallowed, surprised to find his throat was aching. It had been over two months, but sometimes he still had to remind himself the old man was gone. Jace couldn't have asked for a better dad. Wayne had always encouraged him. Made sure that whatever Terry had, Jace had just as much. Went to his boxing matches. And he'd always liked Ember. "Pretty and smart," he'd said of her. "Hang onto that one, Son."

If only he could have.

He picked up his coffee and took a drink to ease his throat.

Ember was still staring down at the glossy, laminated menu when their waiter—Bobby J, from his nametag—came to take their order. Make that *came back* to take their order. This was his second time around. The gangly kid didn't look a day over fifteen, with that barely there beard and the mom-pressed uniform shirt.

"Are you all set to order?" he asked.

"Almost." Ember shook her head slightly, as if that would shake her distraction away. "Just give me a sec."

While she decided, Jace went ahead and ordered. "I'll have two eggs, over easy, bacon, and two of Chloe's biscuits. And keep the coffee coming."

"Will do." Bobby J took his menu. "But if I get caught up and you can't wait, you're welcome to serve yourself." He nodded his head toward a row of coffee makers in the corner. "Refills are free." He looked hopefully at Ember. "Have we made a decision?"

"Yes. I'll go with the western omelet," Ember said.

"A couple buttermilk biscuits to go with that?" Bobby J. asked. "Chloe pulled some fresh ones out of the oven just a minute ago. The butter'll melt right into them."

Jace smiled inwardly. The kid was was a pro.

"I'll skip the biscuits, but I'd love a green tea." She handed the menu back and the waiter scurried off.

Jace regarded Ember across the table. Now that her menu was gone, her gaze had turned to the window and the trees outside, stripped now of half their leaves by the wind and rain. Her lovely face seemed slightly pinched with worry.

"Penny for your thoughts. Isn't that what you Standishs used to say?"

She cocked an eyebrow. "Make it ten and you have a deal."

"You guys still do that."

"Yeah."

But she didn't say anything else—at least not right away. Nothing about what was weighing so heavily on her mind. She just picked up her fork and started toying with it.

Was she thinking about Bridget Northrup? That was certainly a possibility. But the more he studied her, the more he thought there was something else.

"So, is our truce still in effect?"

She looked up, clearly surprised by the question. "I'm here, aren't I?"

"Well, if it still holds, you can tell me what's wrong."

Her gaze sharpened. "Who said anything was wrong?"

"You did."

"Excuse me?"

"Face it, Ember, I could always tell when something was bothering you."

"Seriously?" She made an inelegant snorting noise. "We haven't seen each other in *years*. What makes you think you know—"

"You still gaze away and chew the inside of your lip in that certain way. Look out windows, and lose your appetite."

She blinked. "I ordered an omelet."

"And skipped the fresh biscuits."

Her mouth tightened. "I've changed. I'm not that naive girl from the farm anymore."

"Of course you've changed. We both have. But somewhere inside, I'm still the same Jace and you're still the same Ember. A little older, and hopefully a lot wiser. But the point is, if something's on your mind, you can trust me."

Trust me.

She didn't have to say a thing; it was there in the way she looked at him.

He'd blown that privilege out of the water years ago. Too bad he couldn't remember doing it.

Suddenly those coffee pots in the corner seemed to be calling his name. He reached for his crutches and started to get up, but Ember's hand covered his.

He stopped.

"It's Titus," she said.

He propped the crutches against the empty seat to his left and sat back in his chair. She released his hand as soon as he subsided.

"You're worried about him up on the mountain?"

"Not really." Bobby J chose that moment to deliver her steeping tea and a promise that breakfast would be right up.

"So what is it?" he asked when the waiter left. "What's up with Titus?"

"I'm not sure. He called us home—Scott and me."

His heart rate leapt. "It's Thanksgiving weekend. Family time."

The words stuck in his throat. Most likely he'd be celebrating with a turkey sandwich and a Moosehead Dry, watching football by himself.

"Well, it hasn't been a very regular thing for our family in recent years," she said. "I've been too busy with med school and internship to make it home with any reliability, and we're lucky to tie Scott down to two or three days at Christmas. But Titus insisted—really insisted—that we both be home this weekend. I don't know why."

Jace swallowed. Fuck. He had a pretty good idea why.

The sale.

He had to tell her. "Ember, listen I—"

"Do you think it's Dad?"

He paused. "Arden?"

"Maybe Dad's sick," she said. "Maybe it's his heart. I mean, he's not exactly over the hill, but he's not a young man anymore either."

"I'm sure your father's fine. He looked okay the last time I saw him. And you're the doctor in the family, right?

Your father would consult you on anything medically related."

She shook her head. "I'd like to think so, but the Standish men can be stubborn."

"The *men*?"

He was rewarded with the flash of a smile, but then a strident female voice cut across his next words.

"Jace? Jace *Picard*?"

He looked up at the woman standing by their table, looking down at him disdainfully. "So it is you."

"What can I do for you?" He suspected that was where the polite conversation would end.

She planted her fists on her hips. "You can help me by getting the hell out of the Prince Region, you and your brother both. That's what!"

"Excuse me?" Ember stiffened in her chair. "I don't know who you are, but you're way out of line."

Jace put a hand over Ember's. "It's okay. I've got this."

He looked at the lady—if she were wound any tighter she'd blow right through the roof. He knew her. Budge Colpitts. One of the members of the region's environmental action committee, PR-PUSH—recently acquired enemies of WRP Holdings.

"You know where my office is, Mrs. Colpitts," he said firmly. "I've invited you several times to meet with me there."

She huffed. "Yeah, you and your company lawyer!"

He exhaled an exasperated breath. "You call and threaten to sue WRP Holdings, my brother and me *personally* over some alleged environmental infractions. Then you expect me not to call the company lawyers when you show up at my offices waving around documents I've never seen before, demanding I take action or there will be *hell to pay*." He kept his tone low and even, aware that all eyes in the place were on him. But he was even more aware that Ember's eyes were on him too.

"The whole region knows what you and your brother are

up too," Budge Colpitts said. "We're not going to let you get away with it!"

There was a smattering of applause.

Jace looked around the restaurant—at those with their heads lowered staring into their coffee cups, and unblinkingly meeting the glare of others. He noted a few weak smiles. A couple of apologetic ones. Budge seemed to have won the majority. But she couldn't leave it at that.

"And you..." She leaned in toward Ember. "You should be ashamed of yourself keeping company with this man."

Oh, man. Could she not see that was exactly the *wrong* thing to say to Ember Standish?

"I'm just fine with the company I keep," Ember said cooly. She reached over and wrapped both her hands around Jace's, smiling into his eyes. "More than fine, in fact."

He knew it was a mock display of intimacy, but it felt more real than anything he'd experienced in a long time.

Ember looked up at Budge. "Now you, on the other hand— someone who prefers grandstanding to communication, someone who would make a nasty, public scene in a family restaurant rather than have a civil meeting—*that's* the kind of company I could do without."

"Well, I can see there's no talking to you." Budge turned away and stalked off in an indignant huff. Ember didn't let go of Jace's hand until people went back to their meals and the din of the crowd rose again. He felt the absence of that warmth immediately.

"Thanks for the moral support," he said, "but you don't have to put yourself out there on my account. I can take care of myself."

"I'm sure you can, but I just can't abide that kind of rudeness." She leaned forward. "What was that about anyway?"

"That was Budge Colpitts. She's on the region's environmental action committee. They call themselves PR-PUSH."

"And she's mad at you why?"

He sighed. "Terry wants to take the company in a new direction."

"What direction?"

"He wants to get into hazardous waste storage and treatment."

She sat back abruptly. "You're kidding me."

"Unfortunately not." How could he tell her that his brother not only wanted to bring a large waste storage and treatment facility to the region, he wanted to bring it to Harkness. Specifically, to the Standish farm. But he had to tell her, and he had to do it now. His heart thundered. "Ember, there's something I have to—"

Then his damned cell phone rang.

It was Bridget Northrup.

— eleven —

EMBER PAID for their meals, adding a generous tip for Bobby. When Jace's call had come in, he'd gone outside to take it. Figuring he'd be antsy to get on the road as quickly as possible, she'd asked the young waiter to switch their meals to take out. He'd assured her he'd do his very best to expedite the order, and he'd come through.

Tucking her credit card away, she put her backpack down on the table beside their breakfasts—two eco-friendly take-out boxes packed in a big paper bag—and slid out of the booth. As she did, she felt the gaze of many other diners on her.

She couldn't blame Jace for taking the call outside, both for privacy and to get away from the din. And after Budge Colpitts's display, when Jace rose with the phone to his ear, all eyes had been on him again.

Not that being the cynosure had intimidated him. Not in least. He'd given them that face she remembered from his boxing days. That look of steel in his eyes, the hint of challenge in the set of his mouth.

Apparently some things hadn't changed. He'd still stand up to anyone.

What had he said? *Somewhere inside, I'm still the same Jace and you're still the same Ember.*

And that kiss. It had done the same old things to her, stirred up the same old feelings. And then some. She was no virginal eighteen-year-old anymore.

She grabbed her jacket from the hook on the side of the booth, pulled it on and zipped it. Shouldering the backpack, she grabbed the take-out bag in her other hand. Then she put the bag down again and patted her pockets.

Dammit. Her lucky red scarf. She was sure she'd had it on when she'd said goodbye to her brothers and set off for the cabin. Had she lost it along the way? Then she remembered that sense that she was forgetting something when they'd packed this morning to go meet Ryker at the river's edge.

She'd left it at the camp. Crap! She loved that scarf.

Okay, not the greatest loss in the world, Ember.

Right. She had more pressing matters to think about.

She picked up the take-out bag again and headed for the exit. She was almost out the door when someone tapped her on the shoulder. She stopped and turned, holding the door ajar, half expecting it to be Budge Colpitts again. Well, if she or anyone else wanted to give her a piece of their mind, take a parting shot about her association with Jace Picard, she was ready for them.

Except when she turned, she met a friendly male face. A familiar one, though she couldn't quite place it. The man was tall, well-muscled, middle-aged, and he was holding the hand of a little girl with lopsided, falling-out braids tied at the end with red elastics. She shot Ember a confident smile. Ember smiled back.

"My name's Janette," she said. "They tell me I look like a Janette, so you might have guessed that all ready."

Ember nodded. "Why, yes, I had. A very smart and awesome Janette."

It was the girl's turn to nod. "I know, right?"

"Sorry to bother you," the man said.

It clicked as soon as she heard his gravelly voice. "You're a friend of Dad's, aren't you? I've seen you out at the farm.

Mr..." She reached for his name, but her memory just wouldn't cough it up.

"Kirkpatrick." He smiled. "Stuart Kirkpatrick."

"Right, Mr. Kirkpatrick."

"Stuart, please."

The more he spoke the more she remembered him. "You've been to quite a few of our Christmas parties in the Far South Barn."

"Quite a few," he acknowledged.

"Didn't you used to bring those enormous chocolate chip cookies, big as the palm of your hand?" Oh, she was way too hungry to be thinking of those.

He smiled. "Guilty."

"Those cookies are the *best*!" Janette said. "But Grampy says I can only have half of one, 'cuz I'm small."

Ember's smile widened, imagining the little girl eating even half of one of those monster cookies. "Your grampy is a wise man."

Stuart's own smile slowly faded. "Listen, Ember," he said. "I saw you here with Jace Picard. About what Budge said...she was way out of line."

Ember looked around the busy restaurant. The head of the PR-PUSH, or whatever Jace had called it, had since left the premises. Too bad. She'd love for her to get an earful of this.

"I couldn't agree more. She was *completely* out of line. I've been away for a while, but I know Jace Picard. He's a good man. He'd never do anything to hurt this region or the people. He's his father's son."

"And a lucky lad he is," said a male voice at a nearby table.

"Lucky?" She glanced at the speaker, an old man. With his grizzled, patchy beard, skeletal face, and rheumy eyes, he made Mrs. Dufour look like a spring chicken. "How so?"

"Lucky to have landed a good-looking little gal like you." He nodded to her. "Man needs a good woman by his side."

"Amen to that, Charlie," someone muttered.

Practically everyone in Chloe's Back Porch was looking at her now, many nodding in approval. Ember felt the heat rise in her cheeks. Always lovely on a redhead.

"About what Budge said and folks' reaction...there's just a lot of tension," Stuart said. "Economically, it's hard times around the region. But nobody wants to see something come in that'll hurt the area down the road."

She was itching to get out the door to find out what Jace had learned, yet she couldn't walk away from these people whose concern was written so deeply in their lined faces.

"I know," she said.

"I hope Budge's outburst won't dissuade you from setting up practice here. I mean, if you were considering the area. Were you?"

In point of fact, she hadn't been. "I'm...I'm thinking over all my options."

"Well, I hope coming home is one of those options," Stuart said. "We badly need another doctor in the region."

Murmurs of agreement rose from those gathered. Even Janette.

Ember smiled. "Good to see you, Stuart."

He patted her shoulder warmly. "You too, Ember."

"Catch you later, Janette," Ember said.

"Later."

She pushed the door fully open and damned near banged into Jace in the entryway.

Her surprise was momentary. Of course he would take Bridget's call in the vestibule rather than outside in that howling wind. She'd locked Ryker's truck so that wasn't an option.

Jace stood there, leaning on his crutches, cell phone tucked away. Storm in his eyes. "I was just about to come back in."

"What did she—"

"Let's talk outside. In the truck."

He held the outer door open for her, a ridiculous act of

chivalry given that he was on crutches. She preceded him, but then held the door so he could exit more easily. They hurried across the parking lot, fighting the blustery wind and a few drops of rain. Ember opened the passenger side door. When he'd stowed his crutches behind the seat and climbed in, she passed him the takeout bag, then closed his door behind him. Circling the truck, she climbed in behind the wheel.

Before she'd even dealt with her seatbelt, she asked, "What did Bridget Northrup have to say?"

"Next to nothing." He jammed his own seatbelt into place with an audible click.

"She didn't remember that night either?"

He pulled a hand over the scruff on his face. "Didn't say that."

"Did she know who it was calling her?"

"Yeah. She remembered me." He met her gaze. "And she knows Terry quite well, as you guessed. Or rather knew him. It's been awhile since she's had contact."

Not that it was that difficult to put together. Terry was well known for sleeping around. Bridget-with-the-Spider Northrup was undoubtedly not the only girl he'd taken out to the camp.

"So what did she remember about that night?"

"She wouldn't talk about it over the phone."

Ember's jaw dropped. "Why?"

"She wants to meet us. In person. Tomorrow."

"*Us?*"

"Us." That telltale muscle ticked in his jaw. "I told her you were here with me."

"And she knows who I am? The old girlfriend?"

"Yeah." He faced forward, but she had the idea he wasn't really seeing the other cars in the parking lot or the trees dancing in the wind. "I was prepared to fight to have you present, so you could hear what she had to say unfiltered, but I didn't have to. She was adamant about you being there."

She swallowed. Bridget Northrup wanted to meet her?

Why? She would have thought she'd be the last person Bridget would want to see.

Things didn't seem quite so cut and dried as they had years ago.

The silence in the truck was so complete, the scattered, wind-driven raindrops hitting the roof sounded impossibly loud.

"She knows we broke up because of that night."

He turned to face her, looking so much like his teenage self. Her heart felt like it was being squeezed in her chest.

"And she knows how much I cared about you," he continued. "She—"

"Let's go see her right now."

"We can't," he said.

She frowned. "Why not?"

"She's going to see her aunt today. And I already asked— the visit can't be delayed. She's delivering something her aunt has been waiting on. So it has to be tomorrow, if that fits your schedule..."

"Oh, it fits," Ember said.

He smiled at her vehemence. "That's what I figured you'd say. So I told her we'd be there as early as we could."

"Good."

He turned his gaze forward again, allowing her to study his face in profile. His worried face.

Several seconds ticked by.

"What is it?" she asked softly. "I know something else is on your mind."

He hesitated. "You know what Budge Colpitts said inside? The hazardous waste stuff?"

She nodded.

"Terry wants to bring a facility to Harkness."

"To *Harkness*? No way! What would that do to the environment? Oh God, what'll it do to the town?"

"You mean what's left of the town."

Okay, that was fair. Like many areas of New Brunswick, Harkness's population was steadily dwindling with the exodus of citizens—mostly young adults—going west in search of jobs. It was an economic reality. But a hazardous waste treatment facility? Wayne Picard had been a strong believer in job creation, but not at such a potentially high cost to the environment.

"I understand we need jobs, but this…this is so wrong for Harkness."

"Agreed. And wrong for WRP Holdings too. Well, Dad's vision of it, anyway. But it's right for Terry."

"Is it right for *you*, Jace?"

She studied his face. What was it? That sudden hardening of his jaw, the shift in his eyes. Why such tension pouring in?

Ember's phone rang. She fished it out of her jacket and looked at the display. "I've gotta take this." She tapped to answer. "Dad, hi," she said brightly.

He was relieved to hear her voice; she could read it in his tone. And in his carefully worded inquiries about her well-being.

"I'm great, no worries." Conscious that Jace was listening to the exchange, she glanced over at him. "But Dad, you know that parcel Danny Parker needed delivered out to the old Picard camp? Well you'll never guess who the patient was. You know…the one whose name you forgot?"

— twelve —

APART FROM getting out of the truck to stand in the driving rain, all Jace could do was listen to Ember's conversation with her father. The same as he'd listened to her talking to the folks back at Chloe's diner.

Okay, there was a difference. She knew he could hear her conversation with Arden. Back there at the restaurant, she'd clearly had no idea he was on the other side of the slightly cracked door while she'd defended him.

Yes, defended him. And pretty vehemently. He was still trying to process that, coming as it had from a woman who'd called him a son of a bitch not twenty-four hours ago.

She sighed into the phone, drawing his attention.

"Dad, I'm a grown woman. We don't need to have that talk."

Jesus, what had *that* been in response too?

Ember smiled throughout the call—through the bucketloads of fatherly advice that Arden was obviously dishing out. Finally, she ended the call with a "Love you too. Goodnight, Dad."

At her loving tone, Jace felt that scraping inside. He couldn't help it.

Family. The Standishs were that kind of close-knit, caring family he admired. He'd always been happy that Ember had such a happy family life, but it was hard sometimes.

He used to dream about building a family. He swore if he ever got the chance to be a father, he'd be just as supportive and attentive as he knew Arden Standish had always been of his children. But these days, that was a big *if.* Oh, there were lots of women around who'd gladly walk down the aisle on the arm of a Picard man, and they probably wouldn't be too particular which one. That wasn't going to happen for Jace. He'd marry for love or not at all. If the parents didn't love each other, he didn't see how they could forge the kind of family he wanted.

Ember shoved her phone into her pocket and returned her attention to him.

"So, back to Bridget. What else can you tell me?"

"I can tell you my Google search results were behind the times. She's taken a year off from teaching to complete her master's in education. She's sublet her place in Crandler, and is staying with her fiance in Edmundston."

"Edmundston? What's she doing way up there? I mean, if she's doing her MEd, wouldn't she be in Fredericton?"

He shrugged. "Maybe she's doing it online."

"I suppose. Or maybe through a thesis option." She brushed a strand of wet hair back from her face. "So, how far away are we from Edmundston? Two hours?"

"A little longer, I think. But I haven't traveled that road in a while so I don't know what condition it's in."

"I guess we're going on a road trip, then."

Jace looked into Ember's eyes. God help him, he should tell her about the farm. But if he did, she'd never go with him to meet with Bridget. She wouldn't hang around for explanations. She'd kick him out of the truck and drive off. She sure as hell wouldn't go on a road trip with him.

He had to hold off telling her. He wanted her to be there when he finally heard the truth—whatever that turned out to be. No, he *needed* her there.

She was going to hate him all over again, but he'd cross that bridge when he came to it.

"Yes, a road trip. But by the look of things, we'd better wait until tomorrow to set out. This heavy weather is coming from the east, and I don't imagine it's going to ease up in a hurry."

As if acting on Jace's command, every light within sight of the parking lot of the small business complex went out. The flashing yellow arrow bulbs of the well-lit *Chloe's Back Porch* flickered to life momentarily, then died again. The traffic light at the nearby intersection was out too, and the wind gusted so hard, it rocked the truck.

"So, find a motel and get that ankle elevated again?" Ember said.

"Sounds like a plan."

"Then I'm going to get Ryker's truck back to him and rent a car. There's a rental car shop on the edge of town— Faulkner's. I'll stop in there."

"Makes sense. I know the place. We can pick up the rental, and I'll follow you out to Ryker's to return the truck."

She shook her head. "Not a great idea. You need to rest that ankle."

"I'm fine."

"And you're under my medical care now. So, like I said, I'll drive out to Ryker's in his truck. He'll drop me at Faulkner's and I'll pick up a rental."

"There's no need to —"

"Yeah, there *is* a need," she corrected. "He's my friend. I want to see him. Visit, have coffee, talk. Say thank you."

"How cozy," he drawled. *Ryker Groves.* He had no right to be jealous. Wouldn't be. Dammit—*wasn't.* "Sorry," he said. "That remark was uncalled for."

She shook her head. "This is strange for both of us, Jace. After all this time. Us. Spending time together. Being together. *Here.*"

He paused. Strange and more. He'd dreamed of this. Seeing her again. Talking. Being alone and close. "Here as in Crandler?" he asked.

"I meant close to everything finally being out on the table. All of it. Truth laid bare."

Jace's jaw tightened. *How bare?* Would she be willing to tell her end of things? And would it change things if she did?

Why had he let it change things then?

The thought hit him like a ton of bricks.

"Jace?"

He shuttered his expression. "You'll need a credit card, if you plan on renting a car."

"Got it on me."

"You hiked to the camp with your credit card?"

She shot him a look of waning patience. "I always pack my wallet, with ID. It's just habit, even if I'm headed out to the woods."

He nodded. "Of course."

"Breakfast." Ember gestured to the take-out sitting between them. "Let's get a motel, eat our breakfast there, then I'll give Ryker a call and make arrangements."

"Sounds good." Jace's appetite had deserted him, but he'd clean that take-out box completely before he'd let her see that. He said nothing as she drove, keeping his gaze trained out his window. The power outage and the increased wind seemed to galvanize people. They darted out into the storm to bring in patio furniture and anything else that wasn't tied down.

And inside the truck, maybe the two of them were getting ready for a storm of their own.

They drove by a church, closed up tight, the parking lot empty, but the sign outside invited. "Join us for the Ladies' Auxiliary Thanksgiving Feast!"

Thanksgiving weekend. A time for family, friends. Turkey and football.

Who'd have thought—in a million years—he'd be spending it here with Ember? Yes, here. This time and place. With those dark blanks in his memory—soon to be filled in by Bridget-with-the-Spider.

— thirteen —

AS HE'D warned her, Ryker hadn't yet made it home when Ember landed at his place. From their earlier phone conversation, she knew he was visiting his nephew for a bit, but he assured her he would leave the door unlocked. It was. She let herself in, locked the door behind her, dropped her knapsack in the foyer, and headed straight for the bathroom.

Well, he *had* told her to make herself at home.

Moments later, she stood under the ceiling-mounted rainfall shower head in his enormous marble shower, letting the hot water chase away the chill, grime and tension of the last twenty-four hours. When she finally persuaded herself she should get out, the bathroom was well and truly fogged up. She dried herself with a fresh, fluffy towel, then snagged Ryker's bathrobe from the peg on the back of the bathroom door. Wrapping it around herself, she cinched it. Then she wiped the steam from the mirror over the sink and laughed at her reflection. She looked like a child in a giant's clothing!

She gathered her own clothes and made her way to the laundry room, intending to throw them in the wash. She found some of Ryker's recently washed clothes in the washer, but when she went to transfer them to the dryer, she found the dryer full too. So she emptied the dryer, put Ryker's wet clothes in it, then threw her own clothes in the washer and started it. And bonus—there were socks in the load that had come out of the dryer. She folded the dry clothes, then snagged a pair of wool socks to wear. They were even more hilarious on her than the bathrobe, looking more like legwarmers than socks.

Making her way to his TV room, she grabbed the remote and stretched out on his couch. She found a *Firefly* marathon on the sci-fi channel and settled back to watch. After an episode, she hopped up to tend to the laundry, folding Ryker's stuff and putting her own clothes in the dryer.

Back on the couch, she somehow dozed off just as the *Our Mrs. Reynolds* episode came on, completely missing Mal in drag, swearing by his pretty floral bonnet to end the bad guy. Worse, she didn't even dream of space adventures with Nathan Fillion. Her dreams were haunted by Jace, who held her, kissed her, rekindled those long ago passions.

The sound of Ryker's key in the lock woke her just as the credits started to roll. She sat up, reached for the remote and clicked the TV off.

"Hey, Sleeping Beauty," he said. "Where's Prince Charming?"

She reached behind her, grabbed one of the small cushions and threw it at him. "That's for calling me a fairy tale princess, especially *that* one. Jerk."

"Jerk? Whoa, Red. My feelings are hurt."

She snorted. "Yeah, if you *had* feelings."

"Okay, you're right. You're the badass queen." He tossed the pillow back at her and she caught it on her lap. "Nice socks, by the way."

"Thank you." She grinned, dropping the fake antagonism.

If he had feelings? The guy had plenty of those. He'd just spent hours working on his nephew's computer. He was known for his solid construction skills. Few people knew that he was also brilliant with computers.

Even fewer people knew how kind he was under that big, gruff exterior.

"So did you get Alexander all fixed up?" she asked.

"Yeah, his laptop is fixed. I also hooked him up with a couple new games, and left his caregivers with some spare, charged-up batteries in case the power goes out."

"Thank goodness for computers, huh?"

"Absolutely. He watches movies. Plays lots of learning-based games. I'm trying to get him comfortable with Skype. His mom needs a break—needs a vacation. I'd love to send her south for a week or so this winter."

"And if Alexander could Skype with her, he'd be less anxious?"

"Probably, but I was thinking more about his mother. If Paisley could see him every day and know he was all right…"

"Would she go? I mean, knowing you're here taking care of things?"

He sighed. "Probably not."

He sat down in the recliner across from Ember, yawned and stretched his six foot seven inch frame. He pulled a hand along the back of his neck.

"Sorry to have gotten you up and on the river so early this morning," she said.

"No worries. Glad to help. And glad to fleece Picard's wallet."

She laughed at that. No doubt he had enjoyed taking Jace's money, but he'd have done it for free. Hell, he'd have come before dawn if she hadn't told him to hold off.

She wouldn't say so though—that whole feelings thing.

"Want a coffee?" Ryker asked.

"Sure, but let me get it."

"Mmm, I was hoping you'd say that."

She knew her way around his kitchen too.

She ground the coffee beans and started the drip maker. While it burbled and spat, she went to the laundry room, grabbed her clothes from the dryer and dressed. Then she retrieved her backpack and headed for the bathroom to brush her teeth and freshen her face.

As she finished her toilette, she was struck by the eyes looking back at her.

That skinny kid from Harkness was long gone, but something about her expression today reminded her of young Ember. Had seeing Jace again put that restless energy into her face? Maybe it was kissing him. She looked into her own eyes, seeing the banked heat there. Was it the possibility that she might have misjudged Jace all those years ago?

Dammit! She was a decade past that point in her life. She was a completely different person. A wiser one, she hoped.

If I knew then what I know now…

Ah, there it was, that familiar old preamble to the what-might-have-been thoughts.

But what if she *had* known then what she knew now? What if she could go back in time and be the woman she was today and not the girl of yesterday who opened those photos? Would things be different?

She'd still be angry. Hurt. And yes, those horrible pictures probably would have still landed in the old stove, ripped to shreds and lit on fire. But would she have been so quick to run in the night?

Jace was ten years older too. Would he go after her now?

She sighed at her reflection, then went back out to find Ryker standing at the kitchen island, coffee poured for both of them. He opened a cupboard behind him, took out a jar of organic honey and plunked it on the counter.

She eyed him. "You think I need an extra dose of sweetness today, huh?"

"Extra?" he said. "That would imply there was some in there to begin with."

"Jerk." She put some honey into her black coffee and stirred it. She must have stirred too long.

"Must have been a strange night, Red."

She looked up to meet his serious eyes. "We didn't have sex, if that's what you're wondering."

"I know."

She didn't know whether to be annoyed or impressed with his conviction. "How could you possibly know that?"

"Because I know you. When it comes to this guy, that old wound never quite healed. You'd be careful not to reopen it."

She shrugged, trying to sound blasé. "Everyone gets hurt."

"Yeah, they do. But some cuts are deeper than others. And it doesn't take years of medical school to see that."

Her mouth tightened. Why had she confided all of that to Ryker? How she and Jace had met, become friends, then more. How they were supposed to have taken their young love even further.

Of course, he'd confided things to her, too, that late night. The wine had flowed freely and so had the words. For both of them.

"I'll tell you something else I know," Ryker said.

"Man, I really want to see this crystal ball you've been peering into." She said it in a teasing tone, trying to lighten the mood. "It might help me make a decision about where to set up practice. You know, which offer to accept."

He ignored her not-so-subtle attempt to change the subject. "He's sorry, Ember."

She bit her lip, shook her head. "I know. But still…"

"And let me tell you something else."

Apparently, there was no deflecting him. "Fire away."

"You hurt him too."

She put her mug down on the granite counter. "He told you that?"

"He didn't have to. He still cares about you, Red."

— fourteen —

JACE LOOKED out over the Prince River. "So *this* is where the cool kids parked when we were in high school."

Ember laughed. "Must have been for the view."

"Yeah, right."

Hours earlier, she'd dropped Jace off at the Gnome Sweet Home again. They'd intended to take a room closer to Crandler, just to get out of the rain, but the power was out everywhere they checked. When the Gnome Sweet Home had come into view, they'd looked at each other and grinned. As luck would have it, Mrs. Dufour still had power and was happy to put them right back into room thirteen.

They were close enough to Harkness that they could easily have gone on to his apartment, but Jace was loath to suggest that. They stood a much better chance of steering clear of Ember's brothers, hidden away at the back of the motel. He also liked the idea of being with her on neutral ground.

So while she went to return Groves's truck and pick up a rental, he'd hung out in the room, watching *Jurassic Park*, the original, on VHS. Or rather he *tried* to watch *Jurassic Park*. Not even a young Laura Dern or velociraptors could take his mind off Ember, the sale, the truth to come.

Around three-thirty, she'd called from the road, asking what he'd like her to bring him for supper. He'd told her that after looking at room thirteen's walls for hours, what he'd really like was a change of scenery. So she'd driven straight back, helped him out to the rental car, and they'd gone together in search of takeout.

Now they were parked at Cupid's Point, about a mile off the highway, down a dirt road. It was little more than a worn-down patch of gravel big enough for a couple of cars, but it offered a fabulous view from high above the river. It also offered privacy. More than a few memories had been made in the back seats of old Chevys at the Point over the generations. Jace had brought Ember here many times, but no matter how heavy the petting got, they'd never taken it all the way. And not just because of her decision to wait until she was eighteen. But because he was going to make her first time—their first time—special.

Rose petals.

What had made her bring them here to this spot to eat their take-out food? He glanced over at her, noting how refreshed she looked after her visit with Groves.

Dammit, he was jealous. And yeah, he knew there was nothing romantic or sexual going on between Ember and Ryker. She'd flat out said they were just friends, and Jace believed her.

Also, Ryker was letting her share a motel room with him. Not that anyone *let* Ember Standish do anything. But no man in his right mind could stand to see her in such close proximity with another man—old boyfriend or not.

Was Ryker an old boyfriend too?

He gritted his teeth on that one. It was a possibility…

Ember reached for the brown paper bag and dug out the food, handing him first the burger, then the fries. She attacked her fries first, just as she always had.

He unwrapped his burger and ate a bite as he looked out over the wind-tossed Prince River. "Man, what a view. Good choice."

Of course, anything would be better than lying on that bed, looking up at the ceiling. But the view really was spectacular. The rain streaming down the windscreen leant the river and the landscape on the other side a certain softness, like an impressionist painting. The patter of raindrops on the car's roof added to the sense of intimacy.

"Sorry, it should have occurred to me that you'd be going a little stir-crazy in that room." She uncapped one of the bottles of water she'd brought and took a sip.

"If by stir-crazy you mean that I now know how many ceiling tiles there are in room thirteen, then yes, I'm officially stir-crazy. Hell, I can tell you how many *dots* are on each tile."

She laughed, then gave him an apologetic look. "Sorry. I figured you'd sleep at least part of the time."

"I did," he allowed. "Counting dots is almost as good as counting sheep."

"I'll bet."

They finished eating in silence. The burger was barely warm and the fries stone-cold, but in the confines of the car, with Ember? Best fast food he'd ever eaten.

She crumpled up her waste and stuffed it in the paper bag.

"You know, this place *does* look vaguely familiar..." She sent him an impish grin that hit him right in the libido.

Only with me. Never with anyone else.

The unexpected wave of possessiveness ripped through him. Without thinking about it, he leaned over, slid a hand behind her head and pulled her close so he could kiss the tantalizing white skin of her throat. She gasped, but didn't pull away. Instead, she lifted her chin, giving him better access.

She used to love that delicate nuzzling before he moved in for a kiss. Throat, ears, forehead, closed eyes, cheeks. He covered all that territory now, thrilling to how familiar, yet how strange, it felt. Then his mouth found hers at last, caressing, nibbling. She tilted her head to achieve a better angle, and when his tongue touched the seam of her lips, she opened for him on a soft sigh.

His heart was pounding a moment later when he lifted his head to look at her. Her mouth was slightly swollen, her eyes glowing with desire.

"My memories of this place are very much alive," he said, his breath stirring her hair. "I remember sitting here with a beautiful, fiery redhead, knowing I was the luckiest guy in the world."

She pulled back then, her eyes cooling. "We were so young back then. Young and innocent."

The sadness on her face wrecked him. "While we're strolling down memory lane, remember Constable Douglas catching us out here? Lacey Douglas's uncle?"

His words had the desired effect. Her eyes widened.

"Do I ever! I was mortified."

He smiled at the memory. The place had been deserted then too. But no sooner had they steamed up the windows when there was a *tap, tap* on the glass. "I was thrilled. Proud as a peacock."

"I remember. You grinned all the way home."

She was fully back on her own side of the car now and so was he. His fingers ached to reach for her hand, but he contented himself with looking at her.

"God, Ember you were the most beautiful thing that ever came out of Harkness. You still are." He shook his head at the memory. "Poor Scott. He had a full time job beating the boys back."

Her smile faded, and he knew just what she was thinking about. *That ass, Dundas Bloom.* He shouldn't have said anything.

"That Bloom boy spread those awful rumors about me in junior year, remember?" she said. "*Junior year*, for crying out loud. I'd barely even *heard* of some of the stuff he said I'd done. But the rumors got around to Scott and…"

"And Dundas Bloom soon learned to keep his filthy, lying mouth shut." He and Ember hadn't even started dating yet, but Jace had been tempted to give the bastard a thrashing. Scott had taken care of it before Jace had to. Which was just as well and a damned shame all at the same time. By then, Jace had been boxing for a couple of years, and Coach O'Bryan had strict rules. Zero tolerance for his boxers getting into fights. No second chances. Jace's stepfather, who'd directed him into the boxing program, would have been so disappointed. Yet if Scott hadn't stepped up, Jace would have. Gladly.

She reached for her water bottle, but made no move to drink from it. Just held it in her hands. "Well, that was a long time ago."

"Yeah, long time." Except he'd wager that it still angered her when she thought about it.

He reached for his own bottle of water and took a swig.

"I'm not a virgin anymore, if that's what you're wondering."

He almost choked in his effort to avoid spewing his mouthful of water. *Where had that come from?* For God's sake, she hadn't *left* Harkness a virgin. Pretty hard to come back in that state ten years later. How could she possibly imagine he'd think that?

Unless…did she imagine Terry would have kept his mouth shut about sleeping with her?

He realized she was watching him with concern. "Are you okay? Did that go down the wrong way?"

It sure had. The words, not the water.

"Why would I wonder that?" Tipping the bottle up, he drained it, then carefully screwed the cover back onto the empty bottle and put it back in the cup holder. "It's been ten years," he said flatly. "We're not kids anymore."

She blinked. "Well, I thought you might be curious too."

Too? She was curious about his love life? Or lack of it, lately. Whatever. He certainly did not want to hear about the men in her past, short of owning up to the night she spent with Terry. "I'm not really inter—"

"I had two boyfriends in med school, that's it," she said. "No one in undergrad."

Seemed like he was going to hear about it, whether he wanted to or not. "Too busy in undergrad?"

She sent him a reproving glance, then looked back down at the water bottle in her hands. "Mick was the first. Another med student—a year behind me. The other guy, Harrison, was a prof."

Fellow student didn't surprise him, but a *professor?* That sounded almost scandalous for Ember Standish. He wanted to ask if Arden knew about this? Scott or Titus? He thought better of it.

"So, serious relationships?"

"Semi-serious, I guess you'd say. Mick and I were together about six months before I realized a relationship just wasn't worth the time."

"And did this Mick share your epiphany?"

She grimaced. "Not so much. He didn't take the breakup graciously. But it just wasn't working. He was always wanting me to goof off and do fun stuff with him. And it was fun, at first. But then I started resenting the time he was taking." She shrugged. "I was just more serious about my studies than he was."

"Huh. I thought everyone in med school was a serious student."

"He had the brains for it, no question. And parents who pushed him. But he didn't really have the drive to be there."

"And this professor you had a fling with?" Jace couldn't help it. He pictured some older guy with a balding head and double chin and wanted to punch him in the face almost as badly as he had Dundas all those years ago. "Was he worth the time?"

"Harrison Broad was his name. He recruited me to be his

teaching assistant one semester. An undergraduate anatomy course," she said. "We hit it off. For a little while."

"What happened?"

"Med school happened. The TA experience was good, but it took time away. I should have known better than to get involved in a relationship on top of that. Like Mick, Harrison wanted more than I could give him. I refused to shortchange my studies for anyone."

"Good." He couldn't help it. He was proud of Ember, and dammit, despite himself, happy it hadn't worked out with either of those losers. Okay, a professor and a bright student probably didn't qualify as losers, per se. But if they were stupid enough to let Ember Standish get away... "They should have known better than to get between you and the books, huh?"

From the look on her face, he had no doubt she was remembering her rules for dating. Homework got done first— his as well as hers—after which she would go joyfully into his arms to kiss, laugh, talk. Dream.

"You think I worked hard in high school?" Ember said. "Double or triple that and you might get the picture."

"Bet you kicked ass."

"Yes and no." A shadow flitted in her eyes. "Undergrad was tough, especially with Mom dying. And Ottawa? I came to love it, but it was a hell of a long way from little old Harkness, New Brunswick, for a girl away from home for the first time."

They were supposed to have gone to Ottawa together.

She cleared her throat. "So, after Harrison, I avoided any more involvements. It was...for the best. I was one of the geek girls with her nose in the books at the library most every Saturday night."

"Most every?"

"Oh, there were a few times I let loose. I had some more adventurous friends."

He smiled at the sparkle in her eyes. He'd love to hear about those letting-loose times. But he'd also love to hear about the nights at the library. Mac and cheese dinner in the dorm. Her first patient of her residency. Her first success. And failure. Every moment of her life over the last few years. He would not have stood in her way.

Mick and Harrison had been fools. Idiots

"What about Ryker Groves?"

Two small lines formed in Ember's brow. "What about him?"

"So you and he never…?"

"Like I told you before, he's a friend. A good one. We catch a movie now and then. Have dinner or lunch whenever I'm in Harkness. He used to come up to Ottawa once in a while and we'd catch a Sens game together."

"Seven Ten Sun…what's the deal with that nickname?" Jace said. "Is that because of his height?"

She shook her head.

"Okay, so you call him that because you stayed up all night once to watch the sun rise at ten after seven."

"Good guess, but no. I was driving home for Christmas one year. It was a spur-of-the-moment thing. I'd actually planned to stay in Ontario for the holiday for once, but after my last exam, I changed my mind. I'd never missed a Christmas in Harkness, and when it came right down to it, it seemed wrong not to come home, you know? I got to thinking about Dad and Titus all alone, having to deal with the family Christmas party by themselves. Scott being…well, Scott, who knew if he'd be there to help out?"

What could he say to that? "It must be a hell of an undertaking."

"Massive," she agreed. "After Mom died, I didn't think it would keep going, but it did."

So he'd noticed. *Noticed?* More like he'd been *painfully aware*. Though he'd avoided attending the annual party, he hadn't been able to escape it. The *Harkness Times* always sent Glee Henderson to cover the event, and the digital pictures she took got posted online. Each year Jace swore he wouldn't access those pics. But every time—every freakin' year—he eventually gave in. After the first few years, he stopped pretending and logged onto the newspaper's site the very next day. First thing in the morning, he'd scroll through those Christmas snapshots looking for her. She hadn't missed many of them. And every year she looked more lovely to him.

"What would Christmas in Harkness be without the Standish party?" he said.

"Exactly. Anyway, after that last exam, I had a power nap, packed a few things. Then I jumped in my car and started driving. It was about six thirty in the morning, and I'd driven all night. I was exhausted—absolutely beat. I was running on coffee. All I wanted to do was go home and crash, and I was just about there. But things didn't go as planned."

"Let me guess," Jace said. "You got a flat tire?"

"You think I couldn't change a tire?" She cocked her head. "Have you forgotten the stories I told you about my grandmother and great aunts?"

He held up his hands in mock defence. "So it wasn't car trouble."

"Well it was, but Ryker's, not mine. His alternator quit."

"This would be about seven ten in the morning?"

She shot him an exasperated look. "Hey, are you telling this story or am I?"

"Sorry. Go on."

"I was almost to Harkness when I saw a car stopped by the side of the road, hood up. The driver flagged me down."

Jace's jaw tightened. "You stopped for a stranger?" He didn't add *one as big as Ryker*. "On a deserted road?"

"I'm a pretty good judge of character."

"From first sight? The guy's a *giant*. Have Scott and Titus heard this story?"

She sighed. "Can I finish?"

He reined himself in. "Be my guest."

"Anyway, I stopped and this huge guy runs around to the passenger side of my car. It had started snowing about half an hour before, and he was covered in snow. He looked like a freaking Yeti. So he jumps in and says, *Can you get me to Lightman House, fast?*"

Lightman House. Jace knew of it. A home for mentally handicapped teenagers.

"Why'd he want to go there in such a hurry?"

"His sixteen year old nephew, Alexander, was there."

Jace grew suddenly quiet.

"Alexander is well over six feet tall, but he has the mental capacity of a two-year-old. His mother—Ryker's sister—did all she could for him, raised him on her own for the most part after his father left. But there came a point where she just couldn't manage him at home and put him in the facility."

Jace's heart went out to the woman who'd had to relinquish her son. Six feet tall or not, he'd still be her baby…

"Alexander gets up every morning at six-zero-one."

"Not six o'clock? Six-oh-one?"

She nodded. "Yep. That precise…*six zero one*. He gets himself dressed and sits back down on his bed. He turns on his TV, but he won't come out of his room until ten after seven. Then he goes to the window behind the nurses' station to look outside to see if the sun's up yet or not. If it's winter and still dark out, he'll pull up a chair and wait for the sun to rise."

"He does that every day?"

"Autism," she said. "Routine is very important to a lot of people like Alexander. And every morning for the last year, Ryker's sister, Paisley, has been there at Lightman House to greet him when he comes out of his room at seven ten. Then she goes off to work, or back home if it's Sunday. And on Saturdays, she takes him out for a drive-through breakfast treat at Tim Hortons. It means everything for Paisley to let him know she's still there—that he hasn't been forgotten. It's important to Alexander too."

"But she couldn't get there that particular morning?"

"Correct. She was in Fredericton having gallbladder surgery and…"

"Uncle Ryker was going to see Alexander in her stead and was frantic to get there on time."

"Exactly. I'm so glad I stopped."

"I guess, but…" He just couldn't get past the danger aspect.

There was a knock on the passenger window. They both jumped. Between being engrossed in the conversation and the pounding of the rain, neither had noticed anyone approaching the vehicle.

Speak of the devil. Jace rolled down the window.

"Officer Douglas." Jace slid a glance at Ember. Though her lips still looked well kissed, she wasn't blushing like she'd been the last time Harry Douglas had rapped on their window. "Fancy meeting you here. Again."

Douglas didn't appear to be in the mood for reminiscing. "We're asking everyone to get off the roads," he said.

Ember leaned forward to speak around Jace. "Bad storm, huh?"

The old cop nodded. "Power's out in half the area, and there's been an accident up the road."

"An accident? How far from here?" Ember's tone was sharp.

"A mile or so up the highway. The ambulance has been called but there's also been an accident in Upper Crandler."

She keyed the ignition and the car roared to life. "North or South?"

"North," Douglas said, "but the road's closed. We're not letting traffic through. If you need a place to wait it out, the volunteer fire hall—"

"I'm a doctor," she said. "If the ambulance is going to be held up, they're going to need my help."

"A doctor?" Officer Douglas reached for the mic on his coat. "I'll radio ahead and get them to let you through the roadblock."

"Thank you."

"No, *thank you*. And travel safe, now. There's a lot of water on the road. We've already had two cars hydroplane."

"We'll be careful," she said.

Officer Douglas removed his hand from the window so Jace could roll it up again.

As she turned the car and pulled away, his heart beat faster. Apparently he was going to get to see her in action.

– fifteen –

ONE MILE had never seemed so long. Ember badly wanted to push the car harder, but Officer Douglas was right. She couldn't help anyone if she put her rental in the ditch racing to the scene.

The roadblock consisted of a lone Prince Regional Police patrol car with its bar lights flashing, and one officer, dressed in a long yellow rain slicker with reflective stripes. She rolled down her window and identified herself and he waved her on.

She'd barely rounded the bend when she saw the flashing lights of two more patrol cars on the road. With dusk approaching, she almost missed seeing the victim's tan-colored car in the ditch on its roof. From the degree of crumpling and the distance from the road, it looked as though it might have rolled more than once.

"That looks bad," Jace said.

"Yeah." As often as she'd dealt with motor vehicle accident victims, it still made her heart pound. And that was in a fully-staffed, fully-stocked trauma room, not at the accident scene. She had nothing with her, not even a stethoscope. Her medical kit was back at the farm. "Let's hope they were wearing seatbelts."

"Anything I can do to help?" he asked, as she pulled over onto the shoulder.

She glanced at her backpack in the back seat. "The victims will need to be kept warm, which could be a challenge in this rain. You could search my bag, the trunk, and bring anything that's dry or waterproof."

"Got it."

They were expecting her, of course. The senior officer identified himself as Corporal Garrett Ames and his younger colleague as Constable Riley Mason.

"What have we got?" she asked.

"Middle-aged woman and her twenty-two year old daughter," Ames said.

"Names?"

"Mom's name is Margot Hunter. Daughter's name, Kayla. They're both from Crandler." He ushered her around his car.

The two women lay on a tarp on the semi-soft shoulder of the road, each beneath their own Mylar first-aid blanket. The cops had obviously decided to use the squad car as a windbreak, and had rigged another tarp as a roof of sorts to keep the worst of the wind-driven rain off the women.

"Did you move the victims, or did they make their way up to the road themselves?"

"The passenger—Kayla—crawled out under her own steam. She then somehow got her unconscious mother out of her seatbelt and pulled her out through the smashed driver's window. She had already dragged her up here when we arrived." He shook his head. "Musta taken some adrenaline. Mother's probably got sixty pounds on the daughter. She thought the car would catch fire, of course, like they do in the movies."

"Looks like Mrs. Hunter's conscious now."

"She just came around about five minutes before you rolled up."

She looked up at the officer. "Can you bring me whatever first aid supplies you have between these two patrol cars? I don't have my medical bag with me."

"I used a lot of the sterile pads on Mrs. Hunter's head, but I'll fetch what's left."

As the officer rounded the car, Ember knelt beside the two woman. "Hi, Margot. Hi, Kayla. I'm Dr. Ember Standish. Ambulances are on the way, but I'd like to have a look at you."

"Please check my mom first." Kayla tried to sit up.

Ember urged her back down. "I will, sweetie," she assured the girl. "Losing consciousness gets her to the front of the line. But I need you to lie quietly too, okay?"

Kayla subsided and Ember started asking Margot a few questions, her name, where she lived, where they'd been going. Since her daughter didn't contradict any of the answers, Ember figured Margot's mental state was pretty good. When asked about pain, Margot said her head hurt. She tried to lift her left hand to touch the rough bandage job the officer had done, but cried out.

"My elbow!" she gasped, pulling her arm in close to her chest.

Judging from the tears in the older woman's eyes, she was in considerable pain. That elbow was probably broken, but it would have to wait.

"You must have got banged up pretty good," Ember said. "I'll take a look at it in a bit. Right now, I need to know if anyone's bleeding."

The mother looked to her daughter.

"Nothing serious. Not anymore, anyway. That bump on Mom's head bled quite a bit until the officer bandaged it up. But other than that, just some scrapes."

"No breathing issues? Chest pains?"

Both responded in the negative.

"Good." She pulled out her iPhone and took the Tardis cover off it and called up the BP app. "I need to check your blood pressures, but I don't have my stuff with me. We're going to have to improvise and I'll need your help. Can you do that?"

Both women nodded.

"Is your right arm okay, Margot?"

"Yes." She drew it out from under the space blanket to demonstrate.

"I'll need you to hold the phone like so, with your finger over the camera eye." When Margot obliged, Ember guided the base of the naked phone to Margot's chest and held it there until the screen yielded readings. Her BP was elevated, but nothing more than could be expected given the circumstances and the pain she was in.

"Your turn, Kayla."

Having just seen it done on her mother, Kayla took the phone from Ember, covered the camera eye and placed it over her heart as her mother had done. When it beeped, Ember took it back. She was expecting to see another elevated pressure, but what she saw made her heart jump and pound.

Maybe it was a mistake.

"Shoot. Can you do that for me again, Kayla?" Ember said. "I hit a button and lost it before I got the reading."

"Sure."

Ember checked the positioning of the phone and Kayla's finger, which were perfect. She put her own finger to the edge of the phone, pressing down to make sure there was firm enough contact with the girl's chest. As they waited for the result, both Officer Ames and Jace rounded the cruiser, the former carrying two first aid kits and the latter sheltering the dry clothes he'd rounded up under his coat.

The phone beeped and Ember took it from Kayla again. And again, those terrifying numbers.

Her systolic blood pressure was under 80. Shifting her entire focus to the younger patient, she took a pulse. Shit, shit, shit. She squeezed one of Kayla's fingernails. The capillary refill was slow. Way too slow. She must have internal bleeding, which would have been exacerbated by her exertions, dragging her mother out of the wreck. The girl needed EMTs now. They could give her IV fluids and transport her to a hospital qualified to treat trauma.

Ember got to her feet. "I need some help here, right now," she barked at the men. "We have to elevate this patient's legs."

"What's wrong?" Margot asked, alarm in her voice.

"Mom?" Kayla made a move as though to sit up, but couldn't get more than her head off the ground.

"Lie back, Kayla. It's okay," Ember said, even as she directed Corporal Ames to lift and hold the girl's feet about a foot off the ground. She wrapped the space blanket as snugly as she could around Kayla's legs and got Ames to adjust his grip to hold the crinkly material in place.

"What's going on?" Margot asked.

"Your daughter's blood pressure is dipping. I'm just trying to get it up a little bit." She adjusted the top part of the blanket, wrapped it snuggly around the girl. "Jace, I need those dry clothes."

He moved around Ames. When he got into the shelter of the improvised tarp tent, he pulled the clothing out. Ember started piling them around her patient.

"Wouldn't they be better under the waterproof blanket?" Jace asked.

She shook her head. "The Mylar reflects her own body heat back to her. We don't want to get in the way of that, but I'm hoping the extra layers will enhance that effect."

She turned to Ames. He sat on the ground now, the better to support the weight of Kayla's legs. Rain slid down his yellow slicker to soak his uniform pants, but he didn't seem to notice.

"What's the ETA on those ambulances?" she asked.

"I just radioed. One's six minutes out. If they don't run into anymore downed trees."

Downed trees! Dammit, they couldn't afford any more delays. What a nightmare.

"Here," Jace said.

She turned to see he'd taken off his coat and was offering it to her.

"Good thinking." She took it from him and snugged it around Kayla's torso, on top of the Mylar blanket. She quickly removed her own jacket and tucked it up under the back of the prone girl's thighs. "How you doing, Kayla?"

"I'm kinda sleepy."

"I know," Ember said. "But I need you to stay awake for me, okay?"

"Okay." The small voice sounded like it came from very far away.

"Kayla?" her mother struggled to sit up.

Ember looked up at Jace, intending to signal him to tend to the mother, but he'd already moved around to Margot's side. She saw him kneel—that had to hurt his ankle—then heard him quietly reassuring the anxious woman. Ember returned her full focus to Kayla.

She pulled the girl's wrist out from under the blanket to check her pulse. It was weak and rapid, and the skin on the back of her hand was a mottled blue. Her respirations were growing shallower and faster too.

Where was that freakin' ambulance? The patient was in shock. She needed oxygen and IV liquids.

Kayla shivered. "I'm cold."

"The ambulance is just a minute away. They're going to have warm blankets. It'll be just like you're floating on a warm cloud."

"Mmm, that sounds nice."

Ember looked over at Jace, who looked back at her with such faith in his eyes. Did he have any idea how close this girl was to death? All the blankets in the world wouldn't help her if her perfusion to key organs fell below—

"Listen!' Constable Mason came skidding around the back of the car. "Hear that?"

He was right! She could hear the ululating wail of an ambulance's siren in the distance, drawing nearer.

Weak with relief, she sank to the ground beside Kayla. Cold water saturated her already damp jeans, and the rain pelted her back. A hard shiver rattled her, but she didn't care. The ambulance was coming.

Thank God.

— sixteen —

JACE COULDN'T remember the last time he felt so emotionally wiped, and his ankle was starting to throb painfully. Then again, it had probably been throbbing for awhile and he was just now feeling it. Like a hard blow in the boxing ring, you didn't necessarily feel the pain until the bell had rung. It had been a hell of a day.

It was half past six by the time the Gnome Sweet Home came into view. By some miracle, there was still power in the area. For now at least. The storm had abated for a while around midday, but only to catch its breath. The wind had renewed its ferocity as the second ambulance had been loading its passenger. He hoped for both the Hunter ladies' sakes that they had safe journeys.

When they'd finally rolled into the motel, Mrs. Dufour was standing at the window. She waved to them as they drove past the small office/kitchen. She then turned off the single light over the door as though she'd been waiting for them to get back safely before she abandoned that post. As if she'd been worried about her only and unofficial, pay-in-cash guests.

But as long as the day had been for Jace, it had been longer still for Ember.

He'd never seen her like that. She'd taken charge of the scene, assessing the patients calmly, comforting them, directing the police officers. Dr. Ember Standish had been in total command of the situation. Or so it seemed. He'd had no idea how dire young Kayla's situation was until the EMTs arrived and Ember briefed them. They'd had the young woman on a gurney in no time, neck stabilized with a hard collar and what looked like sandbags, oxygen mask strapped to her pale face. A moment later, they'd transferred her to the shelter of the ambulance, heaping more warm blankets onto her. While one EMT checked her vitals, another started an IV.

The first EMT had taken his stethoscope off and declared that Ember had almost certainly saved the young woman's life by elevating her feet.

She'd shrugged off the praise, saying the cops' actions in making them lie down and covering them with the first aid blankets was just as critical. But Jace had no doubt the EMT was right.

He'd half expected Ember to stay with the patient for the ambulance ride, but as they prepared to go, she closed the doors and gave the side of the vehicle a rap with her knuckles. The ambulance pulled away, lights flashing and sirens wailing.

She must have seen the question in his eyes. "I'm a GP, Jace. A family physician. I did do a rotation in the ER during my residency, but those paramedics have undoubtedly seen a lot more trauma than I have."

"You seem to have done all right here."

"I hope so."

With that, she'd turned her attention back to the mother. When the second ambulance arrived, Jace watched her brief them. Margot Hunter's evacuation was efficient, but not as urgent as her daughter's. One of the EMTs took the time to quiz the police about the accident, how the victims got from the wreck to the shoulder of the road, etc. Finally, they'd switched on their sirens and driven off.

Now, Ember opened room thirteen's door and hit the light

switch. A dim lamp in the corner and another beside the bed leapt to sixty-watt life.

"At last." Jace moved over to the bed, propped his crutches against the wall, dropped his plastic convenience store bag on the coverlet, and sat down.

Ember approached the bed too, dropping her knapsack on the floor beside it, along with her own convenience store bag.

They'd stopped at a gas station on their way back for drinks and snacks to get them through the evening. Amongst the touristy merchandise, Jace had spied some men's T-shirts and shorts—the former made of soft white cotton emblazoned with the New Brunswick flag and the latter made from a flannel printed with the provincial tartan. He'd picked up one of each for Ember. While he had dry, reasonably clean clothes at the motel, all of her stuff was damp from being pressed into service as blankets.

"You need to get into dry clothes, then get your ankle elevated," Ember said. She fetched his knapsack from the chair in the corner and dropped it by his feet. "Unless you want to grab a shower first?"

"You go first. But take this with you." He snagged his convenience store bag, pulled out the T-shirt and shorts, and held them out to her. "You'll need something to put on while your other stuff dries."

"What? You mean to say there's no fluffy terrycloth bathrobe hanging on the back of the bathroom door?"

"Bathrobe? Angel, there's hardly any *paint* hanging on the back of that door."

Grinning, she took the clothes from him, but as she looked down at them, she sobered. "Thanks for this. I hadn't even thought that far ahead."

"You had plenty on your mind, including getting us back here in one piece." That latter part killed him. He'd have done anything to be able to take over the task of driving and let her rest, but if a guy was going to try using the wrong foot on the pedals for the first time, it probably shouldn't be in an unfamiliar car during a torrential downpour. "Next time, I'll try to sprain my left ankle. Now get yourself into that shower before you freeze."

"Next time?"

He paused. "It's just an expression, Ember."

When she disappeared into the bathroom, he limped over to check the thermostat. He'd cranked it earlier, and the room was much warmer than it had been when they set out to have their supper at Cupid's Point, but he nudged it up a few more degrees. Best to warm it up real well in case they lost power in the night.

When he turned back to the bed, he noticed the coverlet showed wet outlines from his ass and legs. Time to do something about that. His ankle shrieked in protest, but he managed to trade his sodden clothes for dry ones—gray sweat pants and a black Picaroons T-shirt. If he was going to be sleeping in his clothes, he was going to be comfortable. He dug some ibuprofen out of his bag, located a bottle of water from the convenience store purchases, and tossed the pills back. Then he sat down in the dry chair in the corner.

The pain was enough to make him grimace. As little as he'd contributed out there at the accident scene, he knew he'd overdone it. He also knew the throbbing would settle down when the painkillers kicked in, and when he elevated his foot. No point doing that, though, until he'd had his shower.

He leaned back in the chair and let his eyelids drift shut. Not to sleep. Just to rest his eyes. And to clear his mind. He needed to not think about anything for a while. Not Bridget Northrup. Not the transaction with the Standish farm. And not Ember herself.

He definitely should not be thinking about how badly he wanted to just hold her, kiss her.

Or how much she was going to hate him.

"So what do you think?"

He startled at her voice, and opened his eyes. He hadn't heard the shower shut off, or the bathroom door. He must have nodded off.

Shaking the fog of sleep away, he stared up at her. She stood there barefoot on the worn carpet, her red hair tumbling in a damp mess around her shoulders. The crew-necked T-shirt no longer sported a crew neck. She'd somehow managed to cut it off, turning it into a scoop-necked proposition that showed her delicate collar bones. The bottom hem of the T-shirt cut across her thighs, revealing just a few inches of the tartan shorts.

New Brunswick's colors had never looked so good.

"I don't think that T-shirt looked like that when it went in there," he drawled.

"Oh, right." Her hand went to her chest, splaying to cover the bared skin, rosy from the shower. "I can't stand a tight crew neck. It makes me feel like I'm choking. So I took my manicure scissors to it."

He blinked. He knew that about her. Or he used to. She'd done that to the T-shirt he'd bought for her at that Tragically Hip concert they'd attended in Moncton during senior year. How had he forgotten that?

"Jace, I didn't do it to try to sex it up. I just—"

"I know," he said. "And I promise to be the perfect gentleman. I'll even sleep here in this chair." He resettled himself, showing her how easy it would be to get comfy in the thing. The chair groaned in protest.

"That chair?" she said, eyebrows soaring.

"Sure. Why not?"

"Because you need to elevate your ankle."

He shrugged. "I'll prop it up on the other chair."

She shook her head. "Not happening. You take the bed. I'll take the chair."

There was no way in hell Jace was going to let her do that.

"Also not happening. Ember, you just had a long, stressful drive, not to mention the stressful life-saving bit, and—"

The lights flickered warningly, interrupting the debate.

"Damn. I'd better hurry if I want that shower, huh?"

"Agreed." Ember reached for his crutches and handed them to him as he stood.

As he crutched his way to the bathroom, she dug out her iPhone, plugged in some headphones, and lay down on the bed— on top of the covers. Clearly, sleeping arrangements weren't settled yet.

In the bathroom, he peeled off his dry clothing. He sat on the edge of the tub while he unwrapped his ankle. Turning it sideways, he examined it. The bruising seemed to be a little deeper in color, but the swelling wasn't too awful, especially considering the last few hours' activity. It could be worse.

Reaching for his jeans, he dug out his cell phone. With Ember wearing headphones, now was as good a time as any to try to raise his brother. He hit the auto-dial button and waited.

Terry picked up on the fourth ring. Or rather a giggling female picked up for him and handed the phone over.

"Yeah?"

"It's Jace."

"'Lo, little bro." Terry's words were a little slurred. "Just enjoying Thanksgiving weekend here in tropical paradise." As though to punctuate that statement, Jace heard the pop of a champagne cork, much to the obvious delight of Terry's laughing companion.

"So I hear."

"What's up?" Terry asked. "Thought you were heading out to the old camp for another solo holiday pilgrimage sort of...thing."

"I'm actually off to see a friend of yours tomorrow."

"Oh? Who's that?"

"Bridget Northrup."

Silence.

"Remember her?" Jace prompted.

"Norhtrup," Terry said, as though trying the name on his tongue for familiarity. "Bridgit Northrup…"

Jace clenched his jaw as Terry pretended to search his memory. "Yeah. I'm quite sure you two were an item back when I was in high school."

"That far back?" Terry snorted. "Christ, man, no wonder I'm having trouble dredging her up. That's ancient history."

"Depends on how you're measuring that time," Jace said.

"Wait a sec—I think I *do* remember her. Skinny little thing. Loved to dance. She liked frogs or bats or something?"

"Spiders. She had a tattoo of one on her shoulder."

"Right." Jace heard the *tink-tink* of ice in a glass. From champagne to hard stuff. Terry only used ice when he poured himself a scotch. "What did you want to see her about?"

"I'm going to ask her what happened that night."

"What night? You'll need to be a little more specific. If it's the Bridget I'm thinking of, then she and I had a few memorable nights. I remember this one time we drove down to Fredericton to party with some friends of hers. She was so—"

"You know damn well which night I'm talking about. My nineteenth birthday. The night I got so mysteriously hammered. The night my older brother—"

"Stepbrother," Terry said, his voice acquiring a hard edge. "If we're digging up ancient history, let's at least be historically accurate."

It was meant as a slap. One that Jace had first felt when they were kids, after his mother had married Wayne Picard. Even before Jace had officially taken on the Picard name, Wayne had treated him like a son. Equal to Terry—in expectations, discipline, privileges. And at least by all observations—affection. Terry had resented him for it, especially when they were younger. As hard as Wayne had tried to treat Jace like an integral part of the family, Terry strove always to make him feel like an intruder. Even though they were both adults now, Terry still played the bastard card when he wanted to be a real prick.

"Okay, then, let's talk about the night my older *stepbrother* took me out for a couple drinks for my nineteenth birthday."

"Oh, yeah, I remember that night, all right." Terry laughed heartily. "You got hammered. Absolutely shit-faced. I tried to tell you to slow down—"

"Bullshit."

"—but you just wouldn't listen."

"I could never remember that night."

"Well, that's what happens when a pussy who can't handle his liquor drinks too much." There was that nasty edge again.

"Why couldn't I ever remember that night, Terry?"

"Simple. You got blackout-drunk."

"That was the night I lost Ember."

"Is that what this is about? Man, you never *had* her. Not if it was that easy for me to get into her pants."

Every fiber in Jace's body tightened. If he could crawl through his cell phone, he'd throw his brother through the wall of whatever fancy resort he was currently occupying. Make him pay for that remark.

And for a few other things.

"Look, Jace, she wasn't even that good. Too smart for her own good, for anybody's good. Really, nothing special in the sack. She wasn't worth it back then, and you better not be thinking she's worth it now. Not now, of all times. Don't be an idiot."

The land.

Jace could almost see the light bulb going off above Terry's head as he connected the dots, Bridget-to-Ember. That's what he was worried over. Just that fucking Standish land closing on Tuesday.

Jace's hand tightened on the phone. "You are a complete bastard, you know that?"

"Hey, I'm not the bastard here," Terry said. "I'm the real

deal. The real *Picard*. Talk to Bridget all you want; lament over that nothing-special piece of ass. It changes nothing. As of Tuesday, WRP Holdings will own the Standish land. With the Brooks property on one side and the Dickinson lot on the other, we'll finally have that nice stretch of land we need. The political wheels have been greased. They'll do their little environmental impact study, and we'll get the green light."

"Doesn't it bother you, what you're planning?"

"You're the one who brokered the deal, bro."

"You put me in charge of acquisitions, *bro*."

"Hey, don't pretend you've grown a conscience, Jace. You jumped all over it when Titus Standish put out that feeler. You know as well as I do what this'll mean for WRP's bottom line."

"No matter that it wasn't what the old man wanted for the company?"

"Hey, *I'm* the old man now."

Unbelievable. He said it like he was declaring himself the freakin' godfather. "Got it all figured out, do you, Terry."

"Damn right I do. And you should be thanking me for letting you handle the deal. A gift on a silver platter, if I ever saw one. You get to dish out some payback to that red-haired witch you had such a hard on for. Soon Harkness will be rid of those Standishs. Scattered to the winds, and you'll never have to see that little whore again."

It took every ounce of his self-control not to crush his phone in his hand. To stop himself from grabbing the keys to the rental, driving to the closest airport and going after that piece of shit brother of his in his tropical hideaway. But for now, all he could do was deliver a message. "If you ever call her that again, I'll knock those pretty white teeth of yours down your throat."

Silence.

Seconds later, Terry chuckled, darkly. "I'd be careful who I threatened, if I were you."

"Yeah, well, if I were you, I'd be careful of a whole lot of things."

"What's that supposed to—"

Jace hung up on him, his heart hammering in his chest. He wasn't a violent man. He worked his aggression out in the gym. Saved it for the punching bag. But he'd gladly have kicked Terry's ass if he were here.

He muted the ringer on his cell and watched as two calls, one right after the other, came in from Terry's number. Jace turned the phone right off, taking satisfaction from the act.

Seriously, Terry as *Old Man Picard*? The day anyone in Harkness—hell, anyone in the Greater Prince Region— willingly attached that moniker to Terry Picard would be the day hell froze over.

Pushing thoughts of his brother away, he stepped carefully into the shower. Surprisingly, there was still plenty of hot water, but he didn't linger under the hot spray. He dressed again in the loose clothing, then paused to eye himself in the steamed-up mirror.

He'd shaved earlier in the day when Ember had been off with Groves, so his scruff was gone. Maybe that was why he felt so naked.

Right. It had nothing to do with the flood of emotions seeing Ember had induced. Nothing to do with feeling useless with that damned gimped-up ankle, while Ember carried the load for both of them.

Yeah, let's go with that.

Steeling those emotions away, he picked up the stretchy bandage, grabbed his crutches and left the bathroom.

As he clumped his way across the motel room, Ember opened her eyes, pulled out the earbuds, and sat up. Her brow knit as she looked at him. "What's wrong?"

So much for steeling his emotions away. She always could read him, just as he'd been able to read her. But he had no intention of sharing right now, particularly not about the call with his stepbrother. Everything would be on the table soon enough, but at the moment, she looked beat. He'd had a power nap earlier; she hadn't. She'd also been running on adrenaline since that accident. And now—adrenaline crash.

"Sleep," he said. "We can talk later." He smiled, hopefully reassuringly. "Trust me, okay?"

"All right. Later, then. But at least let me see to that ankle. It needs to be rewrapped."

Jace looked around the room, scanning the sparsely furnished space for another option than that bed, or the spine-contorting chairs. There wasn't one.

"The bed," she instructed. "Doctor's orders. You need to keep that ankle up."

"I could call Mrs. Dufour and see if there's a cot kicking around," he offered.

She lifted a mocking eyebrow. "And have the old girl think there's trouble in paradise? We're supposed to be newly married, remember?"

"I got you a ring."

As soon as the words were out, he wanted to call them back. What was he thinking, telling her that? The fight with Terry—what that prick had said about Ember—must have shaken him more than he knew. Or maybe he was more tired than he'd thought.

Or maybe he'd blurted those words out because he wanted her to know.

Because he wanted *her*.

A thrill of something not entirely pleasant rocked through him. *Terror.* Yeah, he was pretty sure it was terror.

"For my eighteenth birthday?"

He swallowed. "Yeah."

"I thought so," Ember said. "I *hoped* so. I actually thought you were going to give it to me at the camp that night." She turned away with a nervous laugh. "Sorry, this is…weird."

He had to tell. Now. He had to tell her about the deal he'd

made for the land. *Their* land. Standish grounds. "Ember, there's something you need to know."

"No, Jace." She turned quickly. "Not...not now. We agreed, sleep now; talk later."

She thinks I want to talk about that ring. That break up. That damnable night.

He sighed. "Okay."

She went over to "his" side of the bed and threw the covers back. "Now, get in bed. I'll rewrap your ankle and give you some meds."

"I already took some ibuprofen," he said, but he handed her the balled up bandage and foam pieces and lay down on the bed.

She worked with swift, competent, yet gentle motions to wrap the foot and ankle.

"Better?"

"Better," he acknowledged.

She drew the covers up so he could reach them, then crossed the room to the lone dresser. For long moments, she finger-combed her towel-dried hair in front of the mirror. Finally satisfied, she turned. Her gaze flickered over him. Then she walked back to the bed and crawled in on her side. Way over to one side, facing away from him.

"I didn't mean to upset you," he said softly.

She rolled onto her back. "You didn't. It's just been...an intense day, you know?"

"Yeah."

The bedside lamps flickered and the power went out, plunging the room into darkness. The fan Jace had left running in the bathroom died too, leaving a sudden silence.

"Well, I guess that was bound to happen," she said.

"Glad it waited for me to get out of the shower."

They fell silent again. The warm room was a perfect buffer from the wind that blew outside. But it changed the quality of the silence that filled the room now. Made it more complete. Made the space between them…emptier somehow.

He stared up at the ceiling. Those damnable tiles.

He was in bed with her. Fully clad, not touching. Not kissing. Not making love, or making plans. But no mistake, he knew, he was half-way in love with her again.

After a few minutes, she spoke. She'd been so silent and still beside him he was beginning to wonder if she'd fallen asleep.

"Jace?"

"Yeah?"

"Tonight on the highway, when I was helping that girl, Kayla, and her mom…"

Her words trailed off.

"Yeah?" he prompted.

"That's why I went to medical school. To help people. To stop the pain. I…I just want to make people better. But I'd never attended an accident until today. Never been in that situation. I don't mind saying I was scared, not having my medical bag with me, no tools. I was so afraid for that girl. But I proved something to myself today."

"What's that?"

"I made the right choice. All the sacrifice, all the hard work…it paid off."

"It did," he said without hesitation. "You heard that paramedic—you saved that young woman. You're a hell of a woman, Ember Standish. A hell of a doctor. I was proud watching you today. Proud of what you've become."

"What would our lives have looked like if things had been different?" Her voice was sleepy now, and she let the question roll to an end on a big, jaw-cracking yawn.

Jace was still thinking about how to respond to that when he heard her breathing change, followed moments later by soft snoring.

He remained wide awake, staring at the ceiling.

— seventeen —

EMBER'S EBOOK ended on a satisfying note, with espionage agents Dax and Belinda finding their happy ever after, even though she was the honeypot set out to trap him, and he'd been planning to ruthlessly sacrifice her. That's why she loved romantic fiction. People always worked it out, no matter how grim the situation looked, or how wide the chasm between them. In real life, people couldn't seem to get past even the pettiest slights

With a tug, she pulled the headphones from her ears and placed them quietly on top of her iPhone on the nightstand.

The power was still off and the room was in near total darkness. No red digits flashed perpetually from the clock radio or the old VHS player. From the sounds of it, the storm had subsided, so maybe the power crews would get the juice turned back on soon. It had been off now for...well, hours. Since after supper, and it was now what? Probably around ten o'clock.

Duh. Check your phone.

She reached for it. Ten nineteen.

She'd zonked out almost immediately, but after a couple of hours, she'd woken. Jace had been fast asleep. She'd rolled over and chased sleep again, but she'd been too conscious of him beside her, feeling the rise and fall of his breathing. So she'd grabbed her phone and finished the audiobook she'd been listening to.

Even as she'd listened, though, she hadn't been able to cancel out her awareness of him. Every so often, the mattress would shift when he unconsciously adjusted his injured ankle. But it wasn't his movements that disturbed her. It was his scent. It was a short mental trip from savoring that clean, masculine smell to remembering the lingering taste of his kisses.

Somewhere inside, I'm still the same Jace and you're still the same Ember.

His words came back to her, along with the memory of his face when he'd said it. His eyes so hot, expression fiercely intent.

Could it be true? Could it be that easy? Despite everything, at his core, was he still the same boy she'd fallen in love with?

At Chloe's this morning, she'd instinctively leapt to his defence, so she clearly still believed generally in his good character, his decency.

She'd also confided her worries about her dad. Yes, he'd nudged it out of her, but it hadn't taken much work on his part. She wasn't like that. As friendly and outgoing as she was socially, she was extremely private about her personal life. She didn't open up easily to others. Not about stuff that mattered, like family. The fact that she'd shared her concerns meant that she still trusted him on some deeper level, even after all these years. Even after what happened.

Why hadn't she trusted him before? The question sank its talons into her psyche. *When those pictures had surfaced, why hadn't she given him a chance to explain?*

Why hadn't he come after her? The familiar question ran through her brain, along with the equally well-worn answer: *If she'd really mattered to him, he would have come to Ottawa and found her.*

That mantra had been one hundred percent effective at

allaying any stirrings of guilt she might have felt over the way she'd handled things.

Until now.

Now, it was doing nothing to assuage her doubts and regrets.

In retrospect, those romantic notions of him riding after her on a white horse—or at least his father's Lexus—seemed...incredibly childish. Had she really expected that of him? And to what end? To prove...what? She wasn't sure anymore.

But she *was* sure of something else. If this was the start of something new from the ashes, the rekindling of a long-smoldering fire, she'd never make that mistake again. She'd—

Wait a minute—*rekindling a fire?* Panic flash-dried the inside of her mouth as she realized the direction of her thoughts. A few kisses did not mean he was back in her life. Or she in his. Harkness, New Brunswick was a damned long way from Long Beach, California, which was looking more and more like it made the most sense.

But you're here right now, a voice whispered. *And Jace is right beside you in this bed, like he should have been ten years ago, on your eighteenth birthday.*

So much had happened since then. To both of them.

Her thoughts went to Mick, then Harrison. She'd told Jace they'd been too demanding, asked too much of her. That had been part of it, certainly, but it wasn't the whole tale. Those romances had been doomed from the start, if she were honest with herself.

Sighing, she got out of bed, picked up her phone and went to the bathroom where she sent a quick text to Scott, telling him she was still with the patient, not to worry. Even as she typed that last part, she knew he'd worry. Big time. But she couldn't think about that.

Then she'd called the regional hospital where Kayla Hunter had been transported. When she identified herself and explained she'd treated Kayla at the accident site, they put her through to the intensivist on duty, who gave her a report. The young lady was found to have blunt force trauma to both the liver and spleen, with intraperitoneal hemorrhage. The paramedics had done appropriate volume resuscitation, so she'd been fairly stable on arrival, hemodynamically speaking. The trauma team used angiographic embolization to control the bleeding and so far, she was showing no signs of sepsis. He was optimistic she would recover completely, hopefully without the need for surgery. Kayla's mother had a concussion, bruising and lacerations, and was being held overnight in the ER for observation, but seemed to have escaped more serious injury. She thanked the doctor and ended the call.

Thank God.

With a lighter heart, she crept back to bed, using the light from her phone's screen. Putting the phone down quietly, she eased in under the blankets. Beside her, Jace shifted from his side to lie flat on his back. She held her breath and waited to see if he was awake, some traitorous part of her hoping he was.

With the minimal lighting from her still lit phone, she peered at him. His eyes were closed, and his shallow breathing was consistent with sleep, so she took the opportunity to look her fill. His left arm lay at his side, while the right arm was draped across his chest. He was as handsome as ever, but it was a different handsome now, his features more rugged and time-carved.

A lot of girls had swooned over Jace Picard back in the day. Still more had swooned over his family's net worth. But he'd only had eyes for Ember. She knew it. And he had absolutely captured her tender, young heart.

They'd missed out on so much.

Oh, not on life. Life had clearly gone on for both of them, and gone on well.

Her dad had kept her up to date on all the Harkness news that came his way, including Jace's accomplishments. She knew, for instance, that he'd done well in university, though he'd wound up choosing Toronto over Ottawa for his bachelor's degree. Eventually, with a shiny MBA under his belt, he'd come back to the province. He'd been active with the boxing club at university, and on his return, he'd coached school-aged kids locally in his spare time. When his picture had appeared in the *Harkness Times* standing proudly with his boys, Arden had mailed her the clipping.

But Jace had never been engaged. He'd also never showed up at a Standish Christmas Party. She'd never run into him at Drummond's Meat and Produce, The Duchess Diner, or any place else. And yes, she'd searched the crowds.

In ten years, she'd never, ever seen him in person. How weird was that? Granted, she wasn't home all that often, and not for long stretches. Yes, she was aware that he spent time in Fredericton as well as Harkness, which would also cut down the odds. But wasn't it strange that she'd never seen him even once in all that time? Surely he'd come home for holidays too.

Except this was a holiday weekend, and he'd been out at the camp in the middle of the woods. Had he gone out there *because* she was in town? And if so, why? After all this time, why would he feel it necessary to avoid her? Was he that ashamed? Did he resent her that much?

Or...

Did he suspect all along that seeing each other again might rekindle the fire? Within her? Or within himself? The thought made her breath catch.

I might have run, but were you hiding, Jace Picard? Hiding from me all these years?

He turned back onto his side again, facing away from her. In all the rolling around, he'd managed to push the blankets down to his waist, exposing his T-shirt clad shoulder, his strong back. The room had cooled a lot since the power had gone out earlier, and he'd surely waken if he stayed uncovered like that. Reaching for the blankets, she pulled them back up over him.

She let her fingertips linger there on his shoulder a moment. Just as she was going to withdraw them, his hand clamped down on hers. Her heart leapt into her throat.

He rolled onto his back again and stared at her, frowning. "Power back on?"

She shook her head. "No, that's my phone. I was using it as a flashlight to get to the bathroom. It'll shut itself off soon."

Her words came out sounding breathy, but she couldn't help it. He still held her hand, and his roughened fingertips were playing over her palm now. The desire she'd been trying to suppress pooled in her belly.

Could they take this moment out of time? Claim the intimacy that circumstance denied them ten years ago?

"I'd offer you a penny for your thoughts, but I haven't a cent on me," he said.

"Then this one's on the house." She drew her hand from his grip and splayed it on his chest, feeling the hard pounding of his heart that belied his calm, controlled demeanor. "I was wondering how crazy it would be if we made love."

His heart rate took another jump under her palm. "Right now?"

She smiled, letting her hand drift downward. "Yeah. Right now."

He trapped her hand against his abdomen. "Ember, we don't have a condom."

Was he looking for a reason not to do this? Had she read him that wrong? She pulled her hand back. "It's okay. Let's just forget I said that. It was a stupid—"

He leaned in, put a hand behind her head to draw her close, and kissed her. It was a hot, open-mouthed kiss that left no doubt as to what he wanted. When he lifted his head, they were both breathing faster.

"It's not a stupid idea. It's the best one I've heard in years. But without a condom…" His palm cupped her face. "Ember, you're the doctor. We need to be smart."

"Who says we don't have a condom?"

Heat leapt in his eyes. "Seriously?"

"I guess I was thinking further ahead than I admitted, because while you were buying those dry clothes for me to change into, I was buying condoms from the dispenser in the washroom." She met his gaze with clear eyes. "I wasn't thinking about seducing you or anything like that. But it just seemed…advisable, given our history."

"Ember Standish, you are freakin' *brilliant*. But—"

"But what?" Still with the reservations? If he kept this up, she might back away from this madness. She probably should. It was crazy to think—

"My ankle," he said, gesturing to it beneath the blankets. "As much as I want to make love with you, I'm not completely up to par here."

That was what was holding him back? Just like a man to worry about performance issues. But it also melted her heart a little bit more.

"I see what you mean," she said seriously. "You're not exactly able-bodied at the moment, are you?"

A muscle ticked in his jaw and she almost ruined it by laughing.

"No."

"Good thing I am."

With that, she threw the blankets back, and straddled him in one swift, smooth movement.

— eighteen —

JACE HALF suspected he was dreaming. In what world would Ember voluntarily come to him like this? But her weight on top of him was real. So was her warmth. Even through the night clothes they wore, the insides of her thighs practically branded him.

"Kiss me," he grated. As things progressed, he was going to have to rely on her more than his ego was comfortable with, but right now, he could kiss the hell out of her.

Smiling as though she knew what he was thinking, she drew her fiery hair to one side. Bracing herself on his chest, she bent to oblige, her lips teasing his with their feather-light brush.

He cupped her face in his hands and kissed her back the way she used to like, teasing the corners of her mouth, the bow of her upper lip. Sliding his tongue over her lush lower lip before seeking entrance. Then sweeping inside to taste her, to tangle with her tongue. Pulling back to shape and trace her lips again with his in another leisurely buildup to the mating of tongues.

Sweet Jesus, they hadn't lost a beat.

Except the way her lower body moved against his erection bore little resemblance to the innocent way she used to writhe against him. Not that he'd expected it to be the same. She'd had lovers and so had he. And just at this moment, he was supremely grateful for her experience. For the confident way she'd moved astride him and the lead she would have to take.

She reared back and peeled her New Bunswick T-shirt off, baring her breasts. And merciful God, they were beautiful. Fuller than before, but just as milky white as he remembered, their nipples small and the palest, most delicate pink imaginable. She leaned forward, bracing her arms on either side of his head and letting her breasts sway temptingly close to his face. He didn't need a more explicit invitation.

Palming both breasts, he had the satisfaction of hearing her suck in her breath. He guided one exquisite nipple to his mouth and suckled it. She made small sounds of pleasure as he shaped and tasted and nipped.

Tasting her like this, hearing her gasps and sighs—he was beyond ready, his cock hard and aching. He must have communicated that to her somehow, because she drew back.

"I have to get the condom." She rolled away and got off the bed, going in search of her inspired purchase.

He took the opportunity to curl up so he could pull his T-shirt off. He started to shuck his sweats too, but realized it was going to be a problem getting them off over his bandaged ankle.

"Let me help with that." She was there, easing the track pants gently off. Once they cleared his injured ankle, she tossed them. Smiling, she shimmied out of the plaid man-shorts he'd bought her and stood naked beside the bed.

"God, you are so beautiful, Ember." His chest tightened. "Still the most beautiful woman I've ever seen."

"You're not so bad yourself." She handed him the condom. "Would I be hurrying things unduly if I asked you to put this on? Because I want nothing more than to climb on top of that gorgeous erection." The erection in question jerked and she laughed. "Was that a yes?"

"That was a hell, yes!" He had the condom in place in record time.

She climbed onto the bed beside him. Despite her words of mere seconds ago, she didn't move to straddle him immediately. Instead, she looked at him, her gaze traveling down then back up the length of his body. When her eyes met his, they held as much hunger as his probably did. But there was something else there too.

"I'm kind of nervous," she confessed. "Is that crazy?"

"If it is, then I'm crazy too."

"You're nervous?"

"Of course. I mean, not like I would have been back then. The blind leading the blind, worrying about hurting you."

She grinned. "Or finishing before you got started?"

"God, yes. *That*."

Her smile faded. "Then why are you nervous? Why am *I* nervous?"

Because maybe you're feeling as vulnerable as I am? Maybe what we're about to do is going to matter more than you think? More than you want it to?

But he didn't say any of that. He knew Ember. That kind of talk would have her reaching for that oversized T-shirt again. So instead, he shrugged. "I suppose anything a person waits this long for is going to be charged with some...expectations."

That seemed to satisfy her. Either that or she didn't want to dwell on the real reasons in case it got in the way of the sex her body craved.

"I *do* have expectations." The smile curving her lips was purely carnal. "No, I have *plans*. Ones that involve an orgasm in the very near future."

Taking his cue from her, he gave her his wickedest smile. "I am one hundred percent on board with that plan. Now come here so I can kiss you again."

She moved astride him, trapping his sheathed erection between them, and bent to kiss him hotly. When they were both breathing hard, she pulled back, lifted off him to position his cock at her entrance, then sank down on him.

The hot, tight clasp of her sex enveloping him was exquisite. He closed his eyes a moment to absorb the shock and delight of it. But then she was moving on him, rocking. He opened his eyes, feasting on the sight of her. Slim, strong, beautiful. Her breasts swaying as she rocked on top of him at a pace designed to throw them over the edge. He lifted his gaze to her face.

Her eyes were closed, her face a mask of concentration as she sought her release.

As she fucked him.

Suddenly that wasn't good enough.

"Ember, open your eyes," he commanded hoarsely. "Look at me."

Her eyes opened, her gaze locking with his.

"Slower," he said, cupping one of her breasts.

"Your ankle." She stilled. "Am I hurting you?"

"God, no." His hands went to her hips, urging her to movement again. "I just don't want it to be over too fast. I want to look into your eyes while I'm inside you. I want to feel every touch."

"Jace," she said warningly, even as her body had started up a slower, sweeter rhythm.

Yes, *Jace*. Not some memory to be exorcised. Not a convenient bed partner with whom she had good chemistry, here tonight and forgotten tomorrow.

He saw the moment she dropped her mask, felt it in the brush of her hands on his chest, the languid way she lifted off him and sank slowly, slowly back down, taking him more deeply inside.

Her phone chose that moment to wink out. Though they no longer had eye contact, the sudden darkness seemed to intensify their connection, heighten the sounds of their breathing. It was impossibly, intoxicatingly sweet, but ultimately unsustainable. Her motions gradually gathered speed again, and this time, Jace was right with her, hands clamped to her hips, rising beneath her to meet every thrust. He could feel his own release drawing nearer, tighter.

He moved a hand to the juncture of her thighs, parting the lips of her sex to find her clitoris. She quickly came apart, her inner muscles gripping him as she came. He held her hips as she bucked against him, and his own climax took him.

She collapsed on him, and he held her there. Neither of them spoke as their heart rates slowed. He wished he could stay like that forever, but he needed to take care of business.

"I guess you'd better deal with that condom, huh?"

"Yeah."

She moved off him and rolled to her side. By the time he'd cleaned up and hobbled back to bed, she was curled up on her side of the bed, facing the wall. His heart ached as he looked down at her.

Had he been wrong to make her open her eyes and acknowledge it was him, Jace, the man she used to love, who was inside her? Did she regret initiating sex now?

Well, if she doesn't regret it now, she sure as hell will when she hears about the land.

Yeah, the land he'd bought out from under her family. He'd finally remembered. Though even if he'd thought about it earlier, he wasn't sure he'd have been strong enough to refuse her.

He eased into bed, wishing he had the right to put his arms around her and pull her close.

One thing he knew. He loved her. Loved her still, but loved her anew too. The girl and the woman. He loved the single-mindedness with which she'd pursued her dream. Loved the physician she'd become, who'd driven through torrential rain to attend to strangers on the roadside. Loved the woman who'd nursed his sprain so carefully despite her justifiable hostility. The woman who'd agreed to come on this quest with him. Who'd made love with him moments ago.

And he would earn her love back somehow. The kernel of it was still there. She couldn't have made love to him like that if it weren't.

He'd win her back, and this time, he wouldn't lose her.

— nineteen —

EMBER SLID out of the bed. The room was still in darkness, but from the pale light leaking around the curtains, she knew it was morning. With a minimum of fumbling, she located her phone on the night table and turned it on. Almost seven.

And yes, a missed call and a couple of texts from Scott. She really had to call him before he blew a gasket or something. The man worried enough for all of them.

She glanced at Jace. Eyes adjusted to the low light level now, she could see he was lying on his back. The pillow had been shoved out of the way, and he held one arm crooked over his head as he slept. It was all she could do not to crawl back under the covers and snuggle up to him. That raised arm would come down around her and—

And that was enough of that. Firming her lips, she headed for the bathroom. After taking care of nature's call, she ran the tap a moment to see if there was any warm water left in the tank. Tepid was the best she could get. Wetting a facecloth, she did a quick clean up in the dark and brushed her teeth. Then she picked up her phone and called Scott.

He answered on the first ring. "I'm up."

"Well I should hope you are," she said. "It's almost seven o'clock."

"I've been up for hours," he said. "In fact, I've been sitting here working on my *second* pumpkin pie latte waiting for your call. And yes, I did get whipped cream."

She rolled her eyes. As if a Standish man would be caught dead sipping something so frivolous as a latte. "I'm just checking in, per Titus's protocol."

"Still with your patient?"

"Yes, I am. Okay then, I'll—"

"Have you seen the river?"

The river? Not since she and Jace had parked at Cupid's Point at supper time last night. "Why?"

"It's pretty rough. With all that rain, the runoff could make it breach its banks. Your lame patient might want to stay put until it blows over rather than trudging back along that shoreline."

Yikes. She didn't like to lie to Scott, but if he knew they were already out of the woods, he wouldn't leave it alone until he knew where she was, and more importantly, who she was with. She wasn't ready for that just yet. "Yeah, um, good idea. I'll suggest that."

"Great. Just give me a call when you set out and I'll meet you halfway."

"No!"

"No?"

"I'm not coming out yet. The patient still needs attention. But I'll check in. Thanks, Scott."

"Wait," he said before she could hang up. "Is everything okay out there, kid?"

"What? Yeah. Everything's fine. And don't call me kid."

"At least tell me the name of the guy with the ankle."

"Sorry. Doctor-patient confidentiality."

There was a pause, then he sighed. "All right. Call back within six hours."

"Sure. But I'll probably text you instead of calling." Before he could protest that, she changed the subject. "What's up with Titus's situation?"

"He's called a couple times. Last night he sent up a white flare from the cabin."

"Really? His phone must be dead or something."

"Nah, phone's fine. I'd just talked to him within a half hour of the flare."

She snorted. "Does that sound like a Standish man or what? Send up a flare rather than pick up the phone twice in an hour. You are men of few words."

"Hey, he's been more talkative than you, Miss Texter. And who knows? Maybe he was showing off for Ocean."

"One could only hope." She gave an exasperated huff. "If that brother of ours had half a brain, he'd see what a sweetheart Ocean is."

"Maybe she isn't anymore. People change."

Not Ocean. But to keep the conversation short, she said, "Maybe. But you know as well as I do that she had a ginormous crush on Titus when we were in high school."

"I plead the fifth."

"We're Canadian, Scott. We don't plead the fifth, we—oh, never mind."

The line went silent again. For a moment, she was tempted to tell Scott everything, to spill it all out. She hated keeping secrets from her brothers. But if Scott knew—

"Ember? You still there?"

She pulled a deep breath. "So, when you do see Titus, will you tell him something for me?"

"Sure, what's that?"

"Tell him not to freak out."

"Wait...*what?*"

Outside the bathroom door, she heard Jace stir, then call her name.

She lowered her voice. "Scott, I've got to go."

"Why are you whispering? Ember!"

"Just trust me. I'm fine."

"A penny for your thoughts."

Ah, there it was. The test to make sure things really were all right in case she needed help but couldn't say so outright. They'd been using that code since she was in junior high.

"Make it ten bucks and we have a deal," she said, giving the correct answer. Then, for good measure, she added, "I'm okay. Don't worry. But, Scott…"

"What?"

"Don't you freak out either."

She hung up, then turned her ringer off.

Jace wakened to a persistent *tink-tink* sound. He opened his eyes to a blast of light from the bedside lamp and glanced over at Ember's side of the bed to find it empty. The digital clock radio on the night stand blinked incessantly. The lamp in the corner was on too, but Ember was nowhere to be seen. No sliver of light showed from under the bathroom door.

"Ember?"

Where would she have gone?

He threw off the blankets and sat up. He'd pulled on his T-shirt and was reaching for his track pants when she stepped out of the bathroom.

"Oh, power's back," she said, glancing around at the lights.

Ah, it must have still been off when she'd slipped into the bathroom. "Yup. And the heater kicked in too," he said, finally recognizing that *tink-tink* sound as the ancient radiator.

"Good thing. It's freezing in here."

She wore the shorts and T-shirt he'd bought her, which were nowhere warm enough.

He patted the bed. "Come get under the quilts."

"Just a sec." She crossed to the door and snapped the light switch off. All but his bedside lamp went out. Then she darted to the bed and dove under the covers.

He dropped the track pants and crawled back under the still-warm blankets.

"Brr." She gave an exaggerated shiver. "I think I saw my breath in the bathroom. Or would have if I'd turned the light on."

He grinned, relieved to hear how normal she sounded. "Yeah, it's cold, all right. Which is why I'm staying put under these blankets until the place warms up a little."

"Oh, yeah? You think a bigger bladder is going to save you from freezing?" She put her bare feet—her cold-as-freakin'-ice bare feet—on his right leg.

"Hey!" He scooched away. "No fair. Isn't there some medical oath prohibiting that kind of conduct?"

"On the contrary. It's actually highly therapeutic."

He snorted. "Yeah, for *you*."

She grinned. "Exactly."

She was still smiling when he leaned over and kissed her. Her mouth was warm and welcoming. And minty fresh. He pulled back. "Guess I'll get up after all. I refuse to be the only one in this bed with morning breath."

The water was barely lukewarm, so his ablutions were quick. He brushed his teeth, splashed his face, and slicked back his hair. He glanced at the result in the mirror. That would have to do. He needed to get back to Ember before she decided last night was a huge mistake.

Last night.

He rubbed the back of his neck. Much as he wanted to talk to her about it, he knew she wasn't ready. From her demeanor this morning, it was obvious she needed to keep it light, and that's what he'd do. For now. And who knew? Maybe that was the right approach. Maybe they needed to create a new space between them where they could be easy with each other before tackling the past. The hard stuff.

And maybe you're looking for another reason to delay telling her about the farm.

Not that he needed another reason. He already had an excellent one. If he confessed now, she would peel out of this motel and leave him stranded. No way would she hang around to hear what Bridget had to say. And he needed her to hear it. Needed them to hear it together.

She was fully dressed in her own clothes when he emerged. "Are those dry?" He went over to squeeze his own pants, which were hanging on the back of a chair. They were still a little damp.

"Dry as they're going to get in here, unless we're planning on lolling around half the day. Which I'm guessing is not on the agenda if we're going to drive all the way to Edmundston."

He went to the night table and retrieved his watch. Dammit. Almost seven-thirty already, much later than he'd thought. Edmundston was better than two hours' drive. "You're right. I told Bridget we'd be at her place before noon, so I guess we should get moving. If we get on the road now, we can stop for a nice, leisurely breakfast along the way."

"Just give me a minute to do something with my hair," she said. "It really needs shampooing, but I'm not getting in a frigid shower."

She disappeared into the bathroom and he turned his thoughts to getting ready. He limped over to the chair and grabbed his jeans. Their dampness had him thinking seriously about sticking with his sweats, but he quickly discarded the idea. He never wore sweat pants outside of his house or the gym, and he wasn't about to start now. He dressed in the jeans and a dry flannel shirt from his backpack. It would be good to get into the car and get some serious heat going.

He bent to retrieve his briefcase, plunking it on the bed beside his backpack. Only then did he realize he'd been moving around the room without crutches. Limping, of course, and not putting much weight on the injured ankle. But just the fact that it wasn't screaming at him to sit the hell down was a huge improvement. It must be starting to heal.

His eyes fell on the slender briefcase again.

He thumbed in the three digit combination and opened the case. The contract for the purchase of the Standish lands lay on top of the other files. Terry had assigned Jace to handle all acquisitions, but he'd been especially keen for his little brother—stepbrother—to handle this one. He thought—correctly—that the Standishs would trust Jace more than they would trust him. It had also suited Terry's twisted sense of humor to hand Jace the power to hurt Ember.

Now Jace held the contract he'd negotiated in his hands.

He would show her this and all the other documents. He would explain everything. Just not until they got back from seeing Bridget Northrup. And when he told Ember *everything*, she'd understand.

God, he hoped.

Ember emerged from the bathroom. He clicked the briefcase shut and turned toward her.

Wow. In a matter of a few minutes, she'd done something amazing to her hair. It looked liked she'd twisted it all up, then tucked it together somehow into a wide knot at the back of her neck. Not high up on top of her head, which he thought could look harsh, but low on her nape. She looked fantastic.

"That was quick."

"Practice." She shrugged. "When I was a med student, I learned lots of ways to make dirty hair look passable."

"Passable?" he said. "It's beautiful. How'd you do that?"

"Thank you." She touched the the back of her head. "It's actually three fat braids, each made into its own bun, then all pinned together to look like one piece."

"And it's all yours?"

Her brows shot up. "Who else's would it be?"

"You'd be surprised. Nothing like trying to take a woman's up-do down and pulling out clip-in hair extensions."

She laughed. "You've done that."

"Once. I'm a quick learner."

"Now you can spot the extensions?"

"Hell, no. I'm still clueless about that stuff. I just let the lady take it down herself."

"Smart." Still smiling, she went over to the nightstand, picked up a convenience store bag he'd presumed was empty and pulled out a bright pink scarf. Crossing to the mirror mounted on the dresser, she tied the thin fabric around her neck. Apparently satisfied with her reflection, she crossed to him, went up and tiptoe and kissed him.

Jace fingered the scarf. "You were missing it, weren't you?"

"You know, me and scarves."

"We'll go back for that red one as soon as—" It was quick and tight, but Jace caught it—the flash of conflict in her eyes

"Right." She pushed the awkwardness back with a smile. "So, are we ready?"

"We're ready." He kissed her quickly on top of the head and released her.

Five minutes later, their stuff packed in the car, they stopped to check out of The Gnome Sweet Home for the second time in twenty-four hours.

Mrs. Dufour was sorry to see them go. "Be sure to tell your friends about my little place," she said to Jace. "Well, your *discreet* friends. I keep a few rooms fresh and ready." She gave him a conspiratorial wink. "You don't even have to be newlyweds stranded in a storm."

He laughed out loud at that.

Back in the car, Ember drove. She'd tried to get him to take the back seat so he could elevate his ankle, but he refused to be chauffeured so utterly. When she saw how far back the bucket seat would go, she agreed it would be okay for him to ride in front...so long as he was prepared to recline the seat and put his foot up on the dashboard for fifteen minutes of elevation every hour. He'd readily agreed.

They stopped at Tim Hortons and grabbed breakfast sandwiches and coffee. Well, coffee for him, tea for her. Then they hit the road.

He watched the countryside passing by. Yesterday's wind and rain had ripped a lot of leaves from the trees, but some still clung stubbornly. Mostly yellow ones. With the browned grass, grey maple trunks, and white birch stands, it made for a subtle, understated palette. Beautiful. How could anyone want to leave here?

How could Ember?

"Where will you go?" The words were out before he'd thought about them.

"I thought you had the address?"

"No, not in Edmundston. I mean, after this weekend. Where will you set up your medical practice?"

Her lips pressed thin; her hands tightened on the steering wheel. "I've been thinking about California."

"California?" He felt like he'd just been throat punched. "Wow."

"Nothing written in stone yet. But...yeah. I'm leaning toward Long Beach."

"Why California?"

She told him about Joanne and Hannibal's offer, right down to the attractive buy-in terms and the ready-made roster of patients. "Not that establishing a practice, finding patients, would be difficult anywhere," she added.

"It's a great offer," he conceded. "Though you'll be working with a guy named Hannibal."

"No jokes," she said sternly. "He's vegan."

Jace snorted.

"Seriously, they're good people. And I'd be working in a state-of-the-art facility."

"Would you enjoy it?"

She flicked him another glance. "Why wouldn't I? I'd be doing what I studied all my life for—helping people."

"Like on the highway yesterday."

She nodded. "Hopefully not quite like that, on the side of the road. But yeah, helping. Speaking of which, Kayla is going to be all right. When I was up in the night, I phoned the Regional and talked to the intensivist who was caring for her."

"That's good news. What about her mom?"

"Concussion. They were keeping her overnight for observation."

Silence fell. A few kilometers rolled past.

"So, you never told me," Ember said.

His muscles tightened. "Never told you what?"

"About your past romances. Well, other than the thing about pulling out that woman's hair extension."

He grinned. "That *was* pretty funny, though it was pretty mortifying at the time."

After another brief silence, she prompted him again. "Well, come on, Jace. Aren't you going to dish? I told you about mine."

Yeah, but she hadn't exactly been...comprehensive, had she? She'd left out Terry. Of course, what woman wouldn't want to leave him off their résumé? He was such a pig when it came to women. A misogynistic jerk.

"So you did," he said, "but if you'll remember, you *volunteered* the information."

She sent him a surprised look before returning her attention to the highway. "Sorry. I didn't mean to pry into anything you're not comfortable talking about. Obviously, you don't have to—"

"Just messing with you. I don't mind talking about it." Well, he kind of did, but only because he wasn't terribly proud of some of it. "Let's just say I've had my fair share of lovers over the years."

"How many is a fair share?"

"I don't know. I wasn't keeping a tally."

"More than you could count on the fingers of one hand?"

He pinched the bridge of his nose. "Yes. More than the fingers of *both* hands, probably. But less than fingers and toes combined. Is that good enough?"

"So ten-ish. That's like…one girlfriend a year."

"Ember, they weren't all girlfriends. Some of them were hookups, women I met at parties. Mostly when I was off at university. I was young, away from home, and I couldn't have the woman I loved."

Silence stretched so long, he thought the subject had been dropped. Then she spoke again.

"Anyone I know?"

He shook his head. "Probably not."

"Any that were serious?"

He sighed. "Some had the potential, but none ever made it that far."

"What happened?"

"I happened."

She glanced at him. "Care to elaborate?"

No, he did not care to elaborate. Not at this moment, anyway. Fortunately for him, her timing was perfect. He didn't have to. "Take the next exit."

"Here?" She took her foot off the gas but didn't signal. "That's not the exit to Edmundston."

"Trust me," he said. "There's something I want to show you, and we have the time."

After the briefest of pauses, she hit the turn signal and slowed for the exit.

— twenty —

SHAMROCK FALLS? What could Jace have to show her here?

Ember hadn't been in Shamrock Falls since she was twelve years old, when her mother had brought her here on an outing one summer day. Titus and Scott had been home helping their dad in the fields. For once, Ember got an exemption from chores to go on a mother-daughter jaunt to the neighboring town where Margaret Standish—nee McGill—had grown up. Even now, she smiled at the memory.

They'd set off early, Ember chattering away happily, her mother listening to every word. They'd walked around the town, investigating the places her mother had haunted as a child. When the sun was high in the sky, they'd had lunch in what Ember considered a *real restaurant.* That is, one where you didn't look up at a sign above the counter to place your order, or unwrap the food when it came. It was, in fact, an old Victorian-style house with several large, elegant dining rooms. An enterprising local had converted it to a fine dining establishment. Ember had ordered the fanciest thing on the menu she could pronounce. *Vichyssoise.* It had sounded so fancy. So exotic. So Julia Child! Except it turned out to be cold potato and leek soup, the same stuff her mother made from time to time. Though truthfully, the restaurant version had been so much better. Her mother, of course, had wisely ordered a full-sized entre and shared it with her daughter.

Afterward, they'd gone to see the house where her mother had grown up, a large, red-brick house on Honey Street. Ember got to see the wide front steps where Margaret McGill—long presumed to be destined for spinsterhood at twenty-eight—had been kissed goodnight for the first time by the slightly older Arden Standish.

They hadn't knocked on the door of that house on Honey Street to bother the new owners. They hadn't even stood outside and taken pictures. Nevertheless, it had been a perfect mother-daughter time, and Ember hadn't needed photos to preserve those treasured memories.

But now, as they cruised slowly along the main drag of the quiet downtown, Ember noted there were very few people out and about. And it looked like every other storefront had a *For Sale* sign in front of it. Even stores she thought would have been thriving—a thrift store, a hunting shop—were closed and shuttered.

It was the economy, she knew. Even Harkness hadn't escaped the downturn and the out-migration of young workers.

Not so in California.

"Turn here, on the right," Jace said.

She obliged, and found herself driving through the old town in a westerly direction. If she'd thought Main Street had changed a lot since her mother-daughter adventure, the changes were even more profound in the residential areas.

Many of the houses along the roadsides sported for sale signs, just as the commercial properties had, but it wasn't just that. While some of the quaint houses were neat and well-kept, many more showed signs of chronic neglect—overgrown lawns, dilapidated fences, weathered siding in need of a coat of paint, curling asphalt roof tiles...

It made Ember's heart ache to see the once-thriving place so deserted. So many of the residents gone west to seek better opportunities.

"Wow, the recession has really taken a bite out of this place," she said.

"A very big bite," Jace agreed.

"Is the whole town like this?"

"Pretty much." He gestured to the intersection again. "Turn right up there, onto Sunbury Street."

Ember complied, and he pointed a little ways up the street. "That's where we're going, that big building on the left."

"The ugly grey monstrosity?"

"Yeah."

Ember turned into the yard and pulled up to the front of the building. What had once been Fredrica's Fine Furniture, according to the sign, was clearly vacant. But unlike the other shuttered commercial properties, this one had a *Sold!* sticker plastered across the Realtor's sign.

She stopped the car and killed the engine. "What's this?"

"Come see."

Jace got out of the car and headed toward the building. As Ember levered her own door open, she realized he'd left the crutches in the back seat and was walking with a minimal limp. The treatment was obviously working, but if he wanted it to continue to improve, he had to be careful about putting weight on it. She opened the back door and grabbed his crutches.

She caught up to him in time to see him digging a set of keys out of his jeans pocket. He stopped at the front door, flipping through them.

"Let me guess," she said. "Company building. I'd heard you guys were buying properties up here."

He turned the key in the lock and held the heavy glass door open for her. "Not this one."

The place was cold, barren. A grey concrete floor stretched across the emptiness. The wide but short windows near the ceiling barely let in any sunlight. She looked up. There were big fluorescent lights embedded in the high, industrial ceiling above.

"Where's the light switch?" she asked.

"Power's not connected yet."

"So if this isn't a WRP property, is it yours?" She handed him the crutches.

"Yep. All mine." Fitting the crutches under his arms, he moved into the center of the expansive room. Ember walked with him. "You're currently standing in what is soon to become Shamrock Falls' first and only boxing club. I'm thinking about calling it *O'Bryan's Boxing Club*. That or *Spar for the Course*."

"Ha! *Spar for the Course*! That's cute. You should reserve the name, before someone else grabs it."

"Already have. Locked up the URL too. But I kind of like the simplicity of *O'Bryan's*. I grabbed that one too."

"As in Coach Lee O'Bryan, your old boxing coach?"

He nodded.

"Didn't he just retire from high school coaching last year?"

"That's right. Worked right up till he was sixty-five. He'd have stayed longer if it weren't for the school board's mandatory retirement rules. Especially with Mrs. O'Bryan dying just the year before."

Ember wasn't surprised to learn that he'd stayed in touch with his old coach. Jace had been one hell of a boxer, and had been exceedingly dedicated to the sport. Lee O'Bryan had coached him through to winning the provincial championship for his weight class in his senior year.

"So, will Coach O'Bryan be involved with the club?"

"He's going to run the place. We'll have a training area over there." He gestured to the far end of the room. "And the ring right here. It's going to be fantastic."

"Do you think there'll be enough business in Shamrock Falls?"

As soon as the words were out of her mouth, she wished she could retract them. Unless Arden had gotten slack about updating her, this was Jace's first solo business venture. The last thing she wanted to do was knock that smile off his face. But with the hard economic times in the region, was a gym the kind of place where people would spend their money?

She needn't have worried. His smile didn't falter. "We'll see. But I'm not looking to do anything more than break even. I've gone over the business plan—I should be there in a couple years. Four tops." His eyes danced as he looked around the place. "It'll be good for the area, Ember. Give the young guys a place to hang out. Take up a sport. Work toward goals. Get ripped. Learn sportsmanship. All of it."

She slanted him a look. "Just the guys?"

"Ah, somebody's seen *Million Dollar Baby.*"

Well, yes she had. Eastwood's best movie, in her opinion. But that was beside the point.

"Step into the twenty-first century, Picard!" She took up a boxing stance and one-two punched him playfully in the shoulder. "Combat sports aren't just for men anymore."

"Way ahead of you," he said. "It's going to be a co-ed gym. I don't know how much interest we'll get from Shamrock Falls's kinder, gentler sex, but there'll be a place for them here."

She smiled. "That's good. But I'd recommend you not use *kinder, gentler sex* in your advertising."

"Okay, good point. But these doors are going to be open to everyone, regardless of gender or age."

No age limits? Her physician antennae quivered. "Surely you must have minimum age restrictions? I mean, you can't have little kids boxing."

"Okay, I take that back. There will be a minimum age requirement, which I've left to Coach to work out, but it's probably younger than you're thinking. Like maybe six or seven."

"But—"

"Relax, Ember. We're not planning kiddie cage matches. The young ones wouldn't be allowed to spar at all, not until they're much older, like thirteen or fourteen. Obviously, no heavy bag work, which could injure young bones. But they could be taught the fundamentals—stance, guard, footwork, one-two. And without getting into anything heavy that could stunt their growth, they could safely jump rope, shadowbox, maybe even do some mitt work. Bring them along slowly."

"I guess that's reasonable," she allowed. "If you have buy-in from the community."

"I've already talked to one of the local youth organizations. There's good interest in getting a program going for some of the disadvantaged kids in the community. Might be a big help to them, and Coach O'Bryan is excellent with kids."

"He's a good man." He'd certainly been good for Jace. He'd been like a second father figure, and Jace had been devoted to him. Apparently, he still was. "So are you looking to the local service clubs to fund the programs for the kids who can't afford a membership?"

"No, that won't be a problem."

That was all he said, but Ember knew. The kids who couldn't afford to pay would attend for free.

She watched him crutch his way over to a row of lockers to the left, obviously just installed. A pang of longing pierced her. With that mixture of pride and hope for the youth of the region written on his face, he'd never looked more attractive to her.

Damn him. He was breaking her down.

He'd done it last night too. Slowed the sex down, drew it out. Changed it.

Part of her had wanted to know what they'd missed all those years ago. Another part of her had wanted to do it— okay, do *him*, to put it crassly—then move on. Get him out of her system. But he'd reached another part of her with his tenderness. A part she hadn't planned on ever letting off the chain again. That scared the crap out of her.

So far, she'd managed to keep panic at bay by keeping it light. So far, he'd played along.

She'd slipped up, though, in the car, asking him that stuff about his former lovers.

Asking him? She'd practically grilled him. And even as she pressed for answers, she hadn't known what she wanted to hear. Legions of women, none of whom meant anything? Serial monogamy involving a couple of really serious, adult relationships?

She should have known the answer would be somewhere in between.

And what had he said when she asked him what happened to those relationships that did have lasting potential? *I happened.*

So what did that mean? Had he done something to cause the breakup? If so, and despite what happened ten years ago with Bridget, Ember was pretty sure it wasn't infidelity. Jace was a good guy. She was beginning to appreciate that all over again.

Witness this project. It would have been all Jace's doing, of course. The concept, the business plan, recruiting Coach O'Bryan, getting the community and service clubs behind it, buying and renovating the building. She was pretty sure, too, that this was just a start, one prong in his efforts to rejuvenate the region.

How different Jace was from his brother. Terry had always been the playboy, looking out for no one but himself. Always with the angle. Always with the agenda. And never, ever to be trusted.

"They'd be proud of you," she said.

He frowned. "Who?"

"Your mom. Wayne." She shrugged. "I'm proud of you too, Jace. This…this is awesome. What you're doing for the community, the region. For Coach O'Bryan."

"I'm a businessman."

"Yes. But you're also a good man."

He looked at her, his expression an odd mixture of sadness and tantalizing possibility. "Ever wonder, Ember?"

She swallowed to ease her suddenly painful throat. She should lie, but she couldn't. "Yes," she breathed. "So many times."

The ring of Jace's cell interrupted them. Cursing, he dug the phone out of his pocket and looked at the call display. "It's Bridget Northrup," he said for Ember's benefit, then answered the call.

Ember watched his brow furrow as he held the phone to his ear. "I'm sorry to hear that," he said. "I gather it was quite a serious accident."

"What is it?" she mouthed.

He held up his hand in a *just a minute* gesture.

"Of course. I understand." He paused to listen again, then said, "Okay. That works. See you at five o'clock instead."

"Postponed until five o'clock?" she said as he pocketed his phone.

"Yeah. She's no happier about it than we are, but it couldn't be helped. That accident on the highway yesterday? Apparently, Kayla Hunter's older sister Shelley is a friend of Bridget's and is living in Edmundston. Bridget agreed to look after Shelly's twin girls so she could go visit her sister in hospital and help her mother cope. But the girls' dad will be home to take over about four-thirty, leaving Bridget time to get home and grab a bite before we descend on her."

Well, it could be worse. She'd half expected Bridget was calling to beg off. "Looks like we'll have lots of time to explore Shamrock Falls."

"Maybe we can find out where the cool kids hang out."

His grin was so wickedly sexy, her heart turned over.

God help her.

— twenty-one —

"THANKS, JACE. That was the best sandwich I've had in...forever. Seriously."

"It's the homemade sourdough bread and the gourmet mayonnaise."

Jace looked up in time to see the approaching waitress's expression change. She must have heard Ember say his name. The older woman pasted a smile back on her face, but she was obviously nervous.

"Mr. Picard. I'm sorry I didn't recognize you earlier, when I took your order."

"No reason why you should...Sarah," he said, reading her name from the tag on her tasteful black shirt. "And please, call me Jace."

"Thank you, Mr...Jace. Can I offer you dessert?"

He looked at Ember and raised his eyebrow.

She shook her head. "Not for me, thanks. Not after demolishing that huge sandwich."

"Coffee or tea?"

"Can we get one of each, to go?" Jace asked. "I'd like to show my friend around the hotel a bit."

"Of course. How would you like your coffee and tea?"

"Coffee black and tea with...?"

"Milk," Ember supplied.

"Coming right up. In fact, if you want to head out to the lobby, Hank at the front desk can assist you with the tour, and I'll bring your drinks to you."

Jace smiled gratefully. "That would be perfect."

For a small town hotel, The Shamrock Arms lobby was surprisingly comfortable. Large, sink-into-me chairs, a fireplace decorated with fall foliage, small pumpkins, gourds, and thick unlit candles in shiny hurricane lamps. He was glad to see those touches, since the old hotel was now part of the WRP Holdings portfolio, as of two weeks after Wayne Picard's death. The transaction was the first of Terry's acquisitions since assuming the CEO role, and so far, one of the few Jace hadn't objected to.

The front desk was temporarily unmanned, but that was no cause for alarm. Jace knew the place operated on a skeleton staff, and the receptionist/reservation clerk probably also served as bellhop when needed, or kept the public washrooms' paper towel supply topped up. Just as the waitress served as hostess and cashier, as well as waiting tables.

Sarah bustled into the lobby with their hot drinks in paper cups. Her bright smile dimmed when she saw no one was behind the reservation desk.

"Oh, dear." She put the beverages down on the antique marble-topped table between them. "Let me page Hank for you."

Sarah crossed to the desk and picked up the phone. "Front desk, Hank," she said. Then turning her back to Jace, she urged "And hurry. Seriously, this time."

Jace and Ember shared a grin at that.

When Sarah turned back to them, Jace noted the worry on her face. Ember must have too, because she jumped in to engage the older woman.

"So, Sarah, have you been here long?"

Sarah smiled, but it was a nervous smile. "This is my thirtieth year."

"Wow," Ember said.

Jace was equally impressed too. "You worked for the previous owners then."

"I did," she said. "I worked in the main office—nine to five, five days a week, until recently."

"What happened recently?" Ember asked.

Jace had a sickening feeling he knew.

"Oh, just changes." Sarah forced a laugh. "The Old Man reorganized things."

"The Old Man?" Jace said. "You mean Terry?"

Sarah looked alarmed at his reaction. "I'm sorry, sir. No disrespect intended. It's just that Mr. Picard—Terry—was adamant we call him that."

Jace and Ember exchanged glances. Terry really took the cake. He might have taken over their father's company, but the idea of him taking over Wayne's legacy? Freaking laughable.

"I hope I haven't offended—"

"Not at all," he hastened to assure her. "Can't disregard the boss's orders, right?"

"Right," she said, almost wilting with relief.

A scrawny older man—familiar looking in a can't-quite-place-him way—rushed into the lobby. He gave his crisp, short black jacket a final shrug as he sidled up to the desk.

"Hank, I have to get back to the dining room, but Mr. *Picard* and his guest would like to look around the facility," Sarah said. "I told them you could help."

"Picard?" Hank straightened. His eyes narrowed as he looked at Jace. "Are you related to Old Man Picard?"

"Terry, you mean?" Jace grated.

"I was going to say Wayne, but I guess if you're related to Wayne, you're related to Terry too." Hank swatted the air dismissively at his mention of Terry. "Your father and I used to fish together. You might not remember, but one time he took you up to Bright River with us to fish trout. You were bound and determined—"

"To use hot dogs for bait." Jace laughed at the memory. It was just after he and his mother had moved into Casa Picard. He'd never fished before in his life. A tragedy, according to his new stepdad. As soon as he learned of Jace's deficiency, he'd set out to rectify it immediately.

"Why hot dogs?" Ember asked.

"Hot dogs were my favorite food at the time. I figured they had to be equally irresistible to the fish."

"They didn't work half-bad," Hank said. "You should have seen the size of the trout he caught!"

"You have a good memory," Jace said.

"Faces, yes. Names, not so much."

Jace stuck out his hand. "I'm Jace Picard." The older man's grip was firm, but Jace could see his fingers were bent, knuckles enlarged. Probably arthritic. He kept the handshake short.

"And who would this young lady be?"

"Ember Standish," she supplied.

"Amber, like the gemstone?"

"No, Ember," she said. "Like the fire."

"Oh, sorry."

"Happens all the time." She reached for Hank's hand and shook it. Gently, Jace noticed.

"Good to meet you folks. You're sure different than your brother," he said to Jace. "That fellow's a bit of an—"

"Hank!" Sarah warned.

He glanced at her, and finished anyway. "Arse."

Sarah moaned. "Hank, you're already on probation. We both are."

Jace turned to Sarah. "Probation? For what?"

"Well, I'm on probation because it's company policy," Sarah said. "Mr. Picard…The Old Man now puts all employees on probation for the first six months they take up a new position. No matter how long they've been with the company. And this is my second position since your brother re-organized."

"Front office, right?"

She ducked her head. "Housekeeping. The front office job was before the motel changed hands."

Ember frowned. "When you say you're on probation, that means what, exactly?"

It was Hank who answered. "It means if we screw up, our ass is grass."

Dammit. What the hell had his brother been doing, jerking these good people around? "Tell me more about Terry's changes."

Sarah and Hank exchanged glances—hers a cautious one, his definitely not.

"Got time for a coffee?" Hank said.

As a matter of fact, he did...

Half an hour later, Jace sat on a bed in one of the standard rooms, ice from the dining room packed around his ankle. Ember's orders. She'd noticed his limp getting a little worse and insisted if they were going to do any more touring of the town, he had to agree to twenty minutes of rest, elevation, ice and ibuprofen.

Sarah had suggested they take the executive suite—Terry always insisted it be made available for him whenever he stayed—but Jace insisted on a regular room. He felt bad enough that someone would have to come and re-clean the tiny room for the sake of his short occupation. No way would he make them clean a big suite.

"Terry really is an ass, you know that? What he's doing to those people is a tragedy."

His skin crawled just to hear Terry's name on her lips, and he knew it showed on his face. No doubt she thought it was because of what an eager Hank and a more reluctant Sarah had shared with them about life at the Arms.

Great. Let's go with that.

He pretty much had to, didn't he? Unless he raised the subject himself, it didn't look as though Ember was going to come clean. And he sure wasn't going to raise it before they'd talked to Bridget. If he pushed her into a corner, made her admit to an action she no doubt regretted and clearly wanted to forget about, how likely was she to hang around for the trip to Edmundston?

"Earth to Jace." She waved a hand in front of his face.

He blinked. What had she said? Oh, yeah. Terry = asshole. "*Terry*? Don't you mean, *Old Man Picard*? Right about now, I'd say he's more than an ass. He's in contention for Asshole of the Year. Dad would roll over in his grave if he knew what Terry was putting those people through."

She laughed. "I can't believe you gave them your lawyer's name."

He shifted his foot. "Terry deserves to get hit with a lawsuit. At best, that's constructive dismissal. He must have someone in mind for some of those jobs—probably some chick or other whose pants he wants to get into or some guy whose family connections he can use—and he's employing these tactics to try to clear the positions."

She grimaced. "It must be hard to have to claim him as your brother sometimes."

"Stepbrother, as he's quick to remind me."

She moved to the edge of the bed, leaned down and kissed him. "You are so much better than he is, Jace Picard."

Better in bed too?

Chrissakes, what was wrong with him? Ember had no affection for Terry. And she'd been a virgin, for God's sake. Screwing his brother might have satisfied her immediate thirst for revenge, but it was a pretty safe bet it wouldn't have been pleasant. No matter what had happened all those years ago, it meant nothing. *Nothing.* He needed to just get over it already.

He lifted a hand to her hair. "Hey, we should have showers while we have this room."

She took a step back. "Are you telling me I smell?"

"Not a bit. But I know I wouldn't mind cleaning up, and figured you might want to too."

"I do. And since you have to finish the ice therapy, I guess that means I get to go first."

He smiled. "Guess so."

She disappeared into the bathroom and his smile faded.

Forty minutes later, on Sarah's recommendation, they hit the local farmers' market. It was good to finally see something thriving. For Jace's benefit, Ember drove as close to the large, open-air structure as she could, parking behind a kiosk with two barbecues going full out. A tattooed man in an apron with Kiss the Kook emblazoned across it was turning foot longs on the grill.

It was a short walk to the building itself, but by the time Jace got there, he ditched the crutches, took a seat at one of the picnic benches, and ordered a coffee. That was good enough for him.

Not so much Ember. "I haven't been to a market in eons!"

"Eons?"

"Okay, years," she said. "I've got to look around. You?"

"Think I'll sit this out."

"Oh right, the ankle."

In fact, the ankle felt pretty good after the rest and ice, not to mention the ibuprofen. But they had a long trip ahead of them in the car, and he wanted to keep it under control. He was coming to appreciate that when the pain got ahead of him, his mood got pissy. It was too easy to dwell on the negative when he let that happen.

She hauled over a plastic chair and ordered him to put his foot up on it.

"Okay," she said when he'd complied. "You've got coffee, got your foot up—"

Her smile faded as her phone buzzed in her pocket. She pulled it out, read the text, then pocketed the phone again.

"Scott?" Jace asked.

"Titus."

Her expression hadn't changed, so that must mean Titus hadn't told her about the sale yet. "Not going to respond?"

"It'll wait. I have some shopping to do."

He waved her on. "Go. Knock yourself out."

She evidently didn't need to be told twice.

Her first stop was a table marked *Blushing Moon Scarves.* He watched as she sifted through the assortment of colorfully painted scarves. She settled on a blue and gold one and paid for it. Then she took off the cheap convenience store scarf, shoved it in her backpack, and tied the new scarf around her neck. Sensing his regard, she looked over at him and struck a corny fashion model pose. Then he lost sight of her as she disappeared into the crowd.

The market was teeming with shoppers this Thanksgiving Sunday. All the usual things one would expect to see— vendors selling their holiday and country harvest goodies— pumpkin pies, homemade preserves, farm fresh eggs. There was also more modern fare. Samosas, and soy wax candles. There was a petite lady in a bright green shawl applying a henna tattoo on a young girl's hand. From the back of one particular booth hung home knit sweaters—bright and colorful, each one unique.

He recognized quite a few of the people—nodded hello to couple of them as he sat there sipping his coffee. Despite the hardships of the region, the people were the same as they'd always been—friendly and laughing, talking to their neighbors about that crazy storm they'd had yesterday.

Jace would have enjoyed it a hell of a lot more had his thoughts not kept drifting back to The Shamrock Arms. What the hell was Terry doing to those people? Probation for someone like Sarah who'd been with the Arms for thirty years? He hoped she would take his advice and call his lawyer, Chris McGrath. Hank too. His brother had no qualms about running people into the ground if it suited his purposes. At this point, probably no one could rescue the situation for the current workers. Not with Terry in charge. But McGrath could at least make sure that WRP Holdings paid for Terry's arrogance with some fat constructive dismissal settlements. Maybe Terry would even learn a lesson.

"Mister, I think you need a walking stick!"

Jace turned his head to see a young boy who'd suddenly popped up beside him. He looked to be about eight, and smiled at Jace, displaying a gap left by a missing front tooth.

"You think so?" Actually, it wasn't a bad idea at all. He didn't really need crutches, but neither did it feel great to put full weight on the ankle.

"My grampy makes the best darn walking sticks around." The boy held his gaze with dark brown, intelligent eyes. "He's got a little booth at the back here, Calhoun's Carving. And that's not even the best part."

"What's the best part?" Jace strove to keep a serious expression in the face of the kid's sales pitch.

"I get what's called a 'commission' for everyone I bring to the booth who buys something. Do you know what a commission is?"

"I've heard the term before."

"A commission is another word for a dollar."

Jace nodded, thoughtfully. "How's business?"

That missing-tooth made an appearance again. "About to get better, hopefully!"

Ten minutes later, Jace found himself deep in the market and the proud owner of a polished beech walking stick, hand-carved by Grampy Calhoun himself. It took him a little while to get it right, mainly because he tried using it on his weak side. But as the senior Calhoun explained, it should be carried on the strong side and moved with the weak leg. Once he got the rhythm figured out, he decided it was possibly the best fifty bucks he'd ever spent. The commission earner was already off again scouring the market for his next mark. Jace caught a glimpse of him escorting an older woman by the arm towards his grampy's shop.

Jace made his way back to where he had parted company with Ember, intending to wait for her there. He didn't have her zeal for market shopping. He was more of a get in, get out kind of guy. When he did have to shop for something, he knew what he was after, made a bee-line for it. And that's exactly what he did when he spotted the Callaghan's booth.

He could take or leave booze, but he really enjoyed Callaghan's products, which included a number of organic fruit wines. He selected a blackberry-gooseberry-plum blend, and another honey mead/rhubarb concoction. Hopefully he and Ember would get a chance to drink one of them. Except this time, he'd be damned sure not to wash down any painkillers with it.

He thanked the merchant and turned around to see Ember standing there smiling approvingly at his purchase. Not only did she wear the new bright scarf around her neck, new earrings dangled from her ears. Small silver hoops. She carried a shoulder tote made of simple burlap, but finely crafted. It bulged with her purchases. But what really struck him was how beautiful she was. He couldn't take his eyes off her.

"Penny for your thoughts."

"Just a penny?" Jace grinned. "You should work on commission. Pays better."

"Pardon?"

"Long story." He moved to stand by her.

"Well, look at you. I see you got yourself a walking stick."

"Hand carved by Odbur Calhoun."

"Does he have other wood crafts, or just the walking sticks?"

Jace started to tell her that he was all about the sticks and canes when she leaned around him.

"Are you kidding me?"

He turned to see what she was gazing at with such awe. "What?"

She brushed past him, crossing quickly to a booth directly behind them full of what he'd taken to be yard sale quality odds and sods. She went straight to a colorful dish and picked it up.

"Oh my God. Just...*oh my God!*"

"You've got good taste, young lady," a woman said from behind the counter.

Jace peered closer to see what Ember held "A gravy boat?" He looked at the tiny price tag. A hundred bucks? "A pretty expensive one, isn't it?"

Ember slid him a dagger look. "I'd pay ten times that."

Whoa, way *not* to negotiate. But as Ember turned the dish gently in her hands, he noticed it had a Christmas pattern on it. And then it clicked.

"This is it—the exact match to the gravy boat I broke when I was nine." She lifted shining eyes to him. "Remember, Jace?"

He did remember. She'd told him about it years ago. She'd been *helping* her mother with Christmas dinner. Not very effectively, but Margaret Standish hadn't said a word. Not until she turned around from cutting the pies on the counter to see Ember attempting to drain the gravy into the gravy boat she held in her hand. Her mother had cried, "No, Ember!" and rushed to stop her, knowing she was bound to burn herself badly with the hot gravy if she tried to do it that way. Ember had managed to put the gravy pan down with the only casualty being the stovetop, which got heavily splattered. But she'd bobbled the gravy boat and dropped it. Not a big deal. That's what her mother had told her. *My fault, sweetie. I should have got you to cut the pie while I dealt with the hot gravy.* But on their first Christmas as a couple, Ember had confided to him how much she'd regretted breaking that gravy boat. She loved those Christmas dishes. Her family's Christmas dishes.

A hundred bucks no longer seemed like that big of a deal.

Ember already had her wallet open. "This is crazy," she said to the smiling clerk. "I've scoured the Internet, looking to find this dish. You wouldn't also have a sugar bowl?"

Jace suppressed a grin. There must have been another mishap Jace hadn't heard about.

The woman shook her head. "I've only that one piece from that pattern."

"I guess that would be too much to ask."

Ember watched with satisfaction as the other woman wrapped the china dish in tissue and then bagged it in a pretty hand-stenciled paper bag.

"That'll be one hundred dollars."

Ember handed over two fifties. The merchant tucked it away inside a cash box, then passed her the bag. Ember tucked it carefully into the pretty burlap shopping bag.

Back at the car, Jace shoved his crutches into the back seat but kept the walking stick with him as he climbed into the passenger seat. Ember slid behind the wheel, putting her purchases on the seat between them. Jace waited for her to turn the key.

"Maybe it's a sign," she said.

"A sign?" It took him a moment to figure out what she was talking about. "Finding that dish, you mean?"

She nodded slowly. "I know you'll think this is crazy. But Jace, I've looked for those pieces—the gravy bowl and sugar dish—for years. I've looked everywhere. *Everywhere.* Then here it is in Shamrock Falls, so close to home. And here we are too."

"Yes, here we are," he said softly.

Her green eyes were luminous, brimming with emotion. He couldn't have stopped himself if he wanted to, and he didn't want to. He leaned toward her, captured her head with a hand and pulled her close for a breath-stealing kiss. Only the laughter of nearby children kept him from losing his head.

With a groan, he pulled back. "Not the best place to suck face, as those kids might say."

"There are kids?"

He laughed. "Yeah. Coming right up on our six."

She checked her side view mirror, then turned horrified eyes on him. "Thank God you heard them. They'd have walked right past the car while we were making out."

Even as she spoke, they filed past, each bearing cones piled high with ice cream.

"I doubt they'd have passed us by."

She blushed. "No more kissing in cars."

"I don't know. That seems pretty radical. How about no more kissing in cars in broad daylight, in busy parking lots?"

"Deal." Her gaze dropped to the burlap bag between them. "God, I can't believe I found that piece. As soon as I get home, I'm going to put it in the cupboard with the rest of the dishes. I cannot wait for Christmas dinner now. The gravy never tasted quite right in a different gravy bowl." Her eyes widened. "Or wait, maybe I could serve up a late Thanksgiving dinner... No, no, I'll save it for Christmas."

Except home wasn't going to be home much longer. He'd have to tell her soon, before Titus did. But not until they'd spoken to Bridget. He wished he could advance the clock and get that conversation over with. But at the same time, he wished he could stretch these hours out. They might be the last ones they spent together, no matter what Bridget had to say.

He swallowed, stared straight ahead out the windshield. "So, we still have two hours before we need to be on the road. Are there any other sights you'd like to see?"

"Could we get that room back at the Arms?"

That brought his head around. Her eyes held an invitation he was unable to deny, even though she might damn him for it later.

"We absolutely could."

— twenty-two —

"AND *THIS* was only twelve dollars." Ember held up the last of her purchases—a colorful, beadwork barrette done up in a simple but beautiful red and gold four-petal flower design.

"Very nice."

She appreciated his focus. A lesser man's eyes would have glazed over long ago. As it was, Jace was just on that glassy edge. She put the barrette back in her bag.

When they'd landed back at The Shamrock Arms. Sarah and Hank were still on duty and were glad to put them back in the same room. Both employees seemed more at ease now, especially Sarah. She still had that little bit of worry behind her smile, but that huge ball of tension Ember had sensed in her seemed to have dissipated somewhat. Jace had done that, given them reason to hope their situations could improve.

They were sitting now on what was just about the most comfortable queen bed Ember had ever experienced. The room had more of a country inn feel than a hotel vibe. Ember loved it—right down to how the windows were angled to give the most spectacular view.

She reclined on her side, propping herself up on an elbow. "So let's see what you bought?"

"My walking stick? You saw it. And it was cheaper than the gravy boat, I might add."

"Ah but not nearly so awesome. But I was talking about the wine. What did you get?"

He explained that they were organic fruit wines, made from blends of things like blackberries, blueberries, gooseberries, plums, apricots, and so on. Most blends, he explained, contained up to five different fruits to give it complexity and layers.

She sat up. "Can we open one?"

"Sure. We could each have a glass, then leave the half bottle for the maid."

Ember jumped off the bed and fetched the two thin-stemmed wine glasses and a corkscrew from the rustic sideboard that served as an entertainment unit. She handed the glasses over to Jace, while she herself uncorked the wine.

Jace held the glasses as she poured.

"You look like you've had practice with that."

"Jealous?" she teased, then immediately regretted it. "Sorry, Jace, I—"

"Yes."

She could feel the rise of heat in her cheeks as she set the wine on the night table beside them. "I shouldn't have said that. I was trying to be...I don't know...playful, I guess. I shouldn't have. I'm not..."

"Not what?"

She bit her lip. "Not unaware that the weekend won't last forever." She looked away, up into the chandelier that hung down over the bed. Anywhere but into Jace's eyes.

"Well for as long as it lasts, it's a weekend for truths, isn't it?"

His soft words surprised her. Yes, there had been truth between them, but he was also holding something back. And there would be more truth to come, hopefully, from Bridget.

"Yes," she agreed. "It's certainly shaping up that way."

"Then let's make a rule." He placed the glasses of wine on the night table on his side of the bed. "Nothing's off the table."

This time she didn't even try to hide her surprise. "Really?"

"Really."

Her heart pounded, but she kept her voice steady, normal. "You said you never really had a serious relationship."

He nodded.

"You sort of intimated that *you* were the reason why those relationships didn't progress. What did you mean?"

"Oh, I was the problem, all right." A distant look came to his eyes. "No matter how beautiful or amazing or kind those women were, they weren't you."

Though she hadn't had so much as a sip of wine, her head whirled. Was that why her own attempts at relationships had failed?

At first, she'd been quite wildly attracted to Mick's long hair, slightly androgenous face, and metrosexual vibe. He was so...cool. But as the relationship progressed, the things she'd told herself she liked about him turned out to be the very things that drove her crazy. He spent more time on his hair than she did, and probably had better facial care products. And then there was the way he fussed about his clothes. She'd had to break it off when she started fantasizing about cutting his ponytail off with the kitchen shears.

With Harrison, she thought she'd chosen more wisely. Short cropped hair that would never see a man-bun, more masculine features, conservative attire. But she'd found other things to nit-pick. Like the faint clicking sound his jaw made when he chewed, or his excessive neatness. Eventually, her irritation level had made it easier to be alone.

Could it have been that their only real failing was that they weren't Jace?

Yes. Absolutely yes.

While she might tell the world those relationships had failed because they'd gotten in the way of her doctor dreams, the truth was the issues could have been worked out. The push-pull over her time could have been managed. They were good men, both of them. The negatives she'd focused on were foibles, superficial. But somewhere in the back of her mind, she'd pulled back because...dammit, there was only one man she'd ever imagined linking her life to.

To think that Jace might have been handicapped the same way made her heart squeeze. Had he ever sunk his hands into a woman's hair and inhaled, only to find it didn't smell right? Or find himself struggling to make conversation with someone he was beginning to think he didn't even like, for the lamest reasons?

God, if only things had been different...

"Jace, that night..." Her heart thudded so hard, she felt dizzy with it. "These last few days..." She paused again, drew a deep breath. "I wanted you to be my first. My only. I know it wouldn't have been great sex, but it would have been you and me. It would have been everything."

"Oh, Ember."

There was so much emotion in his voice. It throbbed with the same regret that resonated in her own chest.

She didn't know who reached for whom, but she found herself on the bed, on top of him, limbs tangled.They kissed hotly. Desperately. Hands streaked over her clothes, arousing a fire everywhere they touched. Then he flipped her over, pressing her into the mattress with his weight.

She caught the hem of his T-shirt and dragged it up so she could lay hands on his bare, heated skin. "Can we get these clothes off?"

"God, yes."

He moved off her long enough to shed his clothes. She wasted no time stripping her own off, but before she tossed her flannel shirt, she retrieved the condom she'd put in its pocket.

He came back down on top of her, his weight pinning her, his chest crushing her breasts, his hands framing her face, fingers burrowed into her hair. And then his mouth was on hers again, fiercely this time, taking everything she could give.

She dropped the condom beside her so she could use both hands on him. She glided them over his back, thrilling to the hard muscle beneath warm skin.

He'd parted her legs and was poised at her entrance before she remembered protection.

"Wait!" she panted. "The condom." Casting blindly around with her hand, she found it where she'd dropped it in the sheets.

After the briefest of pauses, he sheathed himself and moved between her legs again. As fast and furious as the buildup had been, now that he was poised to enter her, he held himself still.

"Please," she arched up against him. "Don't hold back, Jace." She bit him lightly on the point of his shoulder and he shuddered. "Let's set this bed alight," she murmured against his throat. "We tore the Band-Aids off last time with that slow love-making. This time, let's cleanse those wounds with fire."

"Ember..."

Her name on his lips sounded like a plea for reason, for caution, but she was beyond heeding it. Evidently, so was he.

Bracing himself above her, he pushed into her, sinking himself to the hilt. She cried out with shock and delight. When he withdrew again, she rose to meet the next thrust and the next. Together they built an inexorable rhythm, drawing them closer and closer to the precipice. When she felt her orgasm coming, she fought with tooth and nail to hold it back, wanting to draw out the agonizing pleasure. But it took her with a ferocity that ripped the top right off her world.

His thrusts grew faster, wilder, until his own orgasm claimed him a moment later, leaving him shuddering in her arms.

Tonight, she decided, as she held him tight, glorying in the weight of him. No matter what came of the visit with Bridget Northrup, she would tell him later tonight. She'd fallen in love all over again.

— twenty-three —

AT JACE'S direction, Ember took Exit 105. Fifteen minutes later, they were cruising through a quaint little neighbourhood.

She felt her cell phone vibrating in her sleeve pocket.

And there it was again.

Titus. Or Scott. An earlier text from Titus had revealed they knew she was with Jace, and they were just as pissed as she'd known they'd be. *Well too bad.*

Except she couldn't shake the feeling there was more to Titus's anger than the usual big brother bullshit. Though why she should think that, she didn't really know. His message had been terse, not giving her many words to read between. Yet she knew there was something more behind those words than could be accounted for. It had to have something to do with whatever he'd called them home for. She kept coming back around to their father. Could something be wrong with him?

"This is it—Two Goldenrod Lane."

Ember felt a little flip in her stomach as she braked. Of all the things she'd thought she'd feel if she ever ran into this woman, nervousness wasn't one of them.

She pulled into the narrow gravel driveway and killed the engine. The screen door creaked open immediately, and a trim, friendly looking woman held it ajar. Smiling nervously, she waved at them.

Jace raised a finger in a *just give us a second* way, and Bridget Northrup, looking a little bit more apprehensive, disappeared back inside.

He turned to Ember. "I don't have any idea what she's going to say in there. But whatever she says—"

"It won't change what we did last night, and again today. We made love." Her words came out on a rush. She drew a deep breath, and continued, more slowly. "Let's keep that, Jace. Let's own it. Let's just...see."

He leaned across the console and kissed her, tenderly and oh-so-sweetly.

When they broke apart, she put a hand on his chest. "We don't have to do this," she said, surprising herself with her urgency. "The past is gone. We can back right out of this driveway, head back to Harkness and face the music."

"The *music* being the combined wrath of your brothers for leading their kid sister astray."

"Leading me astray?" She marked him with a *get serious* look. "First of all, I seduced you."

"And second of all?"

"Don't call me kid."

She kissed him, hard, and let her left hand smooth over his chest. But he grabbed her hand and pinned it in place over his heart.

"As tempting as that offer is, sweetheart, we have to go in there. We've come this far, and I need to know what happened that night."

"Okay." She drew a deep breath, nodded. "I get it. I really do. I want to know too. But I just wanted you to know that whatever she says in there, it doesn't matter now. The past is the past."

"Let's go talk to Bridget, and then..." He rubbed his temple. "Well, let's just get through this."

Ember nodded, but her mind was racing to finish the

sentence he'd left dangling. And *then...what*? She was practically in Long Beach, California already.

They both climbed out of the car and started toward the small house. Before they were half way up the walk, the door opened again.

"Please come in," Bridget said. She held the door for them as they stepped into the cozy home.

Up close, Bridget looked more and more familiar as the seconds ticked by. Seconds counted out by the spider clock above the small stove. The arachnid motif was repeated on the teatowel hung to dry on the oven door handle.

Still *Bridget with the spider*.

"Hope you didn't have any trouble finding the place," she said.

"Not at all," Jace said.

She glanced at Ember. "Nice car."

"It's a rental."

The two woman exchanged an awkward look as they traded forced pleasantries. And if Ember wasn't mistaken, there was a hint of apologetic discomfort in Bridget's eyes.

Bridget led them into a tidy but tiny livingroom. A love seat faced the world's smallest picture window. With an unspoken agreement, Jace and Ember sat there. Bridget settled into a glide rocker, but sat perfectly still.

"How's your friend's sister?" Ember asked.

"She's going to be okay, but get this—her mother said if that doctor hadn't come along and taken charge at the accident scene while they waited for the ambulance, she might not have made it. Internal bleeding, I guess. Was that lucky or what?"

Ember met Jace's gaze, saw the pride there. "Very lucky," she murmured.

"That's her—Kayla—with her sister, my bestie." She pointed to a picture on the tiny mantle. "It was taken last year, at the Hunters' cottage."

"Beautiful girl," Ember said. Her gaze fell on another

picture. Bridget with her arms around an equally happy looking middle-aged man. They were on a tropical beach, the sun setting behind them, umbrella drinks in hand, posed in a lovers' embrace.

"That must be your fiance," Ember said. "Jace told me you were engaged. Congratulations."

"Thanks. He's a great guy. It'll be a second marriage for both of us." Bridget put a hand to her chest, clutching the chunky necklace she wore, and looked from Ember to Jace. "But I'm guessing you two didn't drive up here to talk about my wedding plans."

"Right," Jace said. Ember felt the brush of his knee on her own as he sat forward on the sofa. "We didn't. As I said on the phone—"

"You want to know what happened that night you joined Terry and the rest of us."

He grimaced. "Not sure I want to, but I need to hear it."

Ember reached for his hand. Jace squeezed back.

"Fair enough." She took a deep breath. "Terry called me that afternoon. He said he'd twisted your arm into going out for your first legal drink." Her words came out fast and precise. Practiced.

"Correct," Jace said. "It was my nineteenth birthday."

Ember knew it wasn't just his first legal drink, it was very nearly his first drink, period. Coach O'Bryan didn't approve of his athletes drinking. More importantly, Margaret and Arden Standish didn't approve of anyone who was dating their teenage daughter drinking either.

"Well, you didn't exactly take to alcohol," Bridget said. "It took you forever to down your first beer. So, Terry bought you a shot to go with that second. You drank it. Against your better judgment, I think, but he goaded you into it. We all did. It hit you like a ton of bricks. You could hardly stand on your own two feet."

"So, we've established that he was inebriated," Ember said.

Jace could feel her tension. Her anger. "Not just over the legal limit for driving, but really, really intoxicated."

"He was completely wasted," Bridget confirmed, looking Ember square in the eye. "But I didn't get him there."

"Leaving that aside for the moment, would you say he was in no shape to make critical decisions? To be responsible for his actions?"

Bridget's face stiffened. "That's basically the definition of wasted, isn't it?"

Before Ember could lash out, Jace jumped in. "What happened next?" he asked.

"Right." Bridget clasped her hands tightly in her lap. "So after a couple near misses on the dance floor, Terry poured you into the car. We drove home. I sat in the back with you, you rested your head on my shoulder. You were so—"

"Wasted. Yeah, I got that."

"That too. But I was going to say you were so *sweet*. Okay, not exactly Mr. Charming, but you couldn't stop talking about your girlfriend. Wanted to call her then and there. You couldn't find your cell phone so you kept pestering me for mine. But I was thinking your girlfriend's dad might not appreciate the late night call. Not even, as you put it, to tell her she was the love of your life."

Ember's heart pounded painfully in her chest.

Beside her Jace sat without moving. "I don't remember any of this."

"It happened. I have no reason to lie."

"Of course not. I'm not suggesting you would." He dug his fingers into the edge of the sofa. "Go on. Please."

"So we went back to your house. There were five of us. You and me, my friend, Kendri, and some guy she was seeing—I don't remember his name, but it's not important. And then there was Terry."

"What about Terry?" Jace demanded.

"He...uh...thought you should have a souvenir of the

night." Bridget flicked a nervous look at Ember, then returned her attention to Jace. "It was supposed to be a lark. Terry said you'd get a kick out of it."

The knot of anger in the pit of Ember's stomach flared, burning blindingly hot. What the hell had they done to him? His own brother had fed him alcohol until he damned near passed out. Hell, he'd probably spiked that shot with GHB or something. She felt sick for Jace.

She couldn't help herself—she glared at Bridget.

"Get a kick out of what?" Jace asked.

Bridget shrugged. "Going to a college bar, getting a hickey from a college girl. He said you'd be thrilled. You know, the stories you'd have the next day at high school, that sort of thing. Bullshit guy stuff."

Ember's eyes narrowed. "You wanted guys to spread stories about you?"

"Stupid, I know." Bridget looked away. "But I was…"

"Young," Jace said. "You were young, intoxicated, and you did something at Terry's behest that I'm guessing you otherwise wouldn't have done. Is that about right?"

Ember looked at Jace. He had every right to be angry, but there was nothing in his expression but compassion.

"Exactly." Bridget looked like the weight of the world had been lifted from her slim shoulders. "I was young, drunk and completely crazy about your brother."

"Were the two of you dating seriously?" Jace asked.

"Yes. Or at least I thought so. We were going steady, as they used to say."

"I don't suppose it lasted long?"

"He broke up with me not a week after." She grimaced. "I guess I should have known what I was getting into. I mean, I'd seen him burn through a lot of girls, but you know how it is when you're that age. You think you'll be the one to tame the bad boy." She laughed, but it was a nervous, hollow sound.

"Anyway, like I was saying, after the bar closed, Terry

drove us all back to your place—the Picard house. Your father was away, of course. Terry dumped you on the bed, but the rest of us kept drinking." She looked down at her hands clasped in her lap. "I remember I had to help my dad at the market in Harkness the next day. He had a little specialty sweets shop. I told that to Terry, whose answer was to hand out little white pills."

"What kind of pills?" Ember asked sharply.

"I don't know," Bridget said. "They made me feel pretty euphoric, but who knows? They could have been Tic Tacs, for all I knew. But Terry said they'd make me feel great and they did."

"What next?" Jace said.

"We got hungry, so he ordered pizza. When we ran out of our own booze, he kept us going with the old man's scotch. I hate scotch, but drank it and smiled because Terry gave it to me. He was the leader of our little gang. So when he got the idea for the souvenir…it sounded like a harmless prank at the time. And like I said, I was crazy over Terry. I'm ashamed to say I'd have done pretty much whatever he asked. Then. as I said, less than a week later, he dumped me. Said I wasn't his type after all. I felt like such a fool." If the blush rising in her cheeks was any indication, she still did. She touched a hand to her forehead quickly, as if she'd subconsciously been about to hide her face then caught herself. "Oh, God, I'm so, so sorry, you guys."

Ember felt her anger abating in the face of Bridget's story. "We all do stupid things when we're young," she said.

"Really?" Bridget's eyes sparkled with unshed tears. "I have a hard time believing you ever did anything that stupid."

Ember felt a chill go through her. More and more, with every passing moment, she was beginning to think she'd done something much, much stupider than anything Bridget had done. She'd let Jace go. No, she'd run like hell from him without giving him a chance to explain. "Oh, I did," she said. "Believe me."

"But the souvenir wasn't just a hickey, was it?" Jace's words broke across Ember's. "There were those pictures..."

"I know." Bridget actively blinked back tears now. "Jace, I cannot tell you how sorry I am. Nothing happened. I mean, not sex. I kissed you and posed with you, but that's all." She rubbed her hands together. "If this were reversed...if I'd passed out and you'd—"

"Kissed you? Taken pictures in sexually suggestive poses?" Ember said. "I'm pretty sure you'd have gone to the cops."

"You're right." Bridget's tears broke. "I'm so sorry. The worst of it is I know I broke you two up—"

"No," Jace said, his voice so hoarse Ember barely recognized it. "*Terry* broke us up, and I'll never forgive him for it."

"Nor will I," Bridget said. "For using me, and using me to hurt you."

Ember knew she should say something comforting to the other woman. Forgiving, Or at the very least, understanding. She'd seen many of her friends over the years—male and female—who'd been that hopelessly smitten over the wrong person.

Did it absolve Bridget? *No.*

Was her apology sincere? *Absolutely.*

"It was Terry who took the pictures, wasn't it?" Jace said. "Terry who decided I needed a souvenir. Terry who used your affection for him to manipulate you into those suggestive poses."

She cringed. "Yes, but I—"

"But nothing. Listen to me, Bridget. It took a lot of guts, speaking with Ember and me," Jace stood. "Terry's the one to blame."

Ember got to her feet, as did Bridget.

"I'm really sorry," Bridget said, wiping her blotchy face. "I know."

"That was hard on her," Jace said.

"It was. And it was good of you to forgive her."

There was silence in the vehicle for a few moments before he spoke again. "Terry has some things to answer for."

As she drove on, Ember's throat ached. *Oh damn, she would not cry!* Jace hadn't betrayed her. At all.

She'd betrayed him by not believing in him. By running. By not giving him the chance to explain the void in his memory.

But it wasn't just Jace she'd betrayed. She'd betrayed *them*; their life plans.

And she'd tell him this. Own up to it. But it was not a conversation to be had with one of them behind the wheel.

She flicked another quick glance his way. He was looking out the window, staring into the dense trees along the road.

"Can you help keep watch for wildlife?" she asked. "Two sets of eyes are better than one."

"Of course." He sat up straighter, scanning side to side.

Several hours—and four deer, two raccoons, one coyote, and one porcupine—later, they hit the outskirts of Shamrock Falls. Minutes after that, she pulled into the motel parking lot and killed the engine. In the ensuing silence, neither of them made a move to get out.

"Jace, there's something I have to confess about that night I ran away. Something I have to tell you."

The seconds ticked by until she began to wonder if he was going to respond.

"All right," he said at last. "Let's talk inside."

— twenty-four —

JACE STEPPED aside to let Ember enter first. He closed the door behind them.

She had a confession about that night.

He'd waited so long for her to admit that she had slept with his stepbrother. For so long, he'd tortured himself with images of the two of them.

And how many times over the years had he fantasized about her making this confession? Of course, in those fantasies, he'd pictured her broken apology, his righteous indignation. Always he would tell her how grievously her actions had hurt him. How they'd gutted him. And with those words, he would hurt her back.

But as he looked at her, the absolute last thing he wanted to do was to cause her pain. To hurt her. Ever again.

She crossed the room and dumped her backpack on the bed beside his briefcase. Then she peeled off her jacket and tossed it on the bed too. When she finally turned to face him, there were tears in her eyes. He wanted nothing more than to wipe them away, now and always.

He didn't give a damn if she'd had sex with Terry that night. It didn't matter.

Yes, he'd let those damned crazy-making mind pictures intrude these last few days, despite his determination to forgive and forget. They'd kept showing up, stealing some of his happiness even as he and Ember reconnected. But no more. All he'd needed was for her to confess. In stepping up to the plate and owning her actions, the images would be exorcised.

None of that crap mattered anymore.

What mattered—*all* that mattered—was that they were here together.

"It's all my fault," she blurted out, her eyes sheening with tears. "My fault that we broke up."

She was standing by the bed where she'd dropped her stuff, looking forlorn. He wanted desperately to comfort her, but he had to dump his walking stick and backpack first. He crossed to the bed and deposited his burdens with the other stuff. Hands free at last, he turned to her and grasped her shoulders.

"Don't do this to yourself," he said, massaging her upper arms. "The past is past. Let's leave it there."

Tears broke and slid down her cheeks. "But—"

He lifted both hands to cup her precious face. Tear-streaked and blotchy as it was, it was beautiful to him. Perfect. "These past days, we managed to love each other like there was no yesterday. Only today." He bent to press his lips to hers gently, tasting the salt of her tears. When he lifted his head, more tears brimmed and spilled. He wiped them away with his thumbs.

"Don't cry, Angel. We'll put all of this in the past where it belongs, so we can finallly reclaim the future."

"But it's my fault," she said again, her voice high and strained. "All those lost years. Years we could have had together."

"We still have lots of years. It doesn't matter."

She looked up at him, her face a picture of cautious hope. "Do you mean that?"

"That we can make a future together now?"

She nodded.

"Damned right I do, with every bit of me. Every last corner of my heart."

"Thank God!" She slid her arms around him and hugged him tightly, burying her face in his shirt.

He eased her away a few inches so he could tip her chin up and kiss those beautiful trembling lips. She lifted her arms around his neck and clung as he kissed her again. Their kisses grew more fevered and he waltzed her over to the bed. Pushing their backpacks and his briefcase to one side, he urged her down on the bed and came down beside her. He gathered her into his arms and hugged her tight. She hugged him back just as fiercely.

He lifted a hand to brush a strand of red hair off her face. "God, I wanted so badly to come after you. You have no idea."

"I wanted you to." She stroked a hand over his chest. "So many nights, I used to look out my dorm window, hoping to spot you making your way along the paths below. And I'd search for you in crowds. On campus, off campus... I had this whole fantasy."

"I'm so sorry. I should have—"

"No." She put a finger to his lips to stop him. "It's still my fault. If I hadn't bolted, there'd have been no reason for you to chase after me. Well, no further than the farm."

He leaned in and kissed her, tenderly. "No more blame. Terry and Bridget made it look bad. Damning. It's in the past. All of it." He brushed his knuckles over her still-damp cheek. "None of that matters now: not that you bolted. Not that you slept with Terry."

Ember went stiff in his arms.

Then she pulled back, eyes intent on his face. "What did you say?"

His body went still too as he heard the echo of his own words in his head: *you slept with Terry.* They felt alien now. Distancing. Wrong.

A fucking lie.

Dammit, why had it never occurred to him before that Terry might be lying?

"I asked you a question, Jace."

He blinked her face back into focus. "Terry told me you and he were together before you left town."

"And you *believed* him?" She looked completely appalled. Furious. "When?" she demanded, sitting up in bed. "When did he say I slept with him?"

"Before you went to Ottawa." He sat up too. "The night before you left."

"The night *we* were supposed spend together?"

"Yeah. "

Her narrowed eyes were like knives to his heart.

"So that's what you think of me? That I would break up with you and immediately sleep with your brother? That I'd save my virginity so long, then throw it away on Terry, of all people?"

"Think about it, Ember," he pleaded. "You'd just seen those supposedly incriminating pictures. You were in a rage. Why wouldn't I believe you wanted to revenge yourself on me?"

"With *Terry*? Are you freaking kidding me?" She practically yelled the words. "Yes, I was hurt. Furious. Betrayed," she said in lower tones. "But since when have I ever gone for that sleep-with-anything-in-panties type?"

"Ember—"

"Oh my God, *that's* why you didn't come after me?" Her eyes widened. "That's why you switched to another university for your undergraduate degree. That's why you've been avoiding me all this while. Because you thought I slept with your disgusting brother."

He reached for her. "Ember, if you'd just—"

"Don't touch me!" She leapt up off the bed, grabbed her jacket, and jerked it on.

Dammit, she was doing it again. She was going to bolt.

"Ember, don't," he said, his voice cracking. "Please don't run away. I'm sorry I let Terry sell me that pack of lies. I was still reeling from what you'd told me about those pictures. Heartsick that you'd left, that I'd blown it so badly and couldn't even remember doing it."

She hesitated. Her hand was on her backpack, but she hadn't yet picked it up.

He got off the bed. The adrenaline coursing through his veins screamed at him to do something, to take control of the situation, to seize her before she could run. But he knew if he did that, it would only escalate her fury and he'd lose his chance. So, heart thudding in his chest, the width of the bed separating them, he used his words instead of his muscle.

"Hear me out, Ember. Please. You have to understand that back then, it made sense when Terry said it. He pointed out I'd just fucked you over, throwing our love away for a piece of tail. Why wouldn't you be thirsting for revenge?"

Her shoulders dropped and she looked down at the carpet. "I was *devastated*, Jace. Humiliated. And yes, furious. But mostly just overwhelmed with pain, betrayal, loss. I had to get away. I couldn't stand for anyone to look at me with pity. Or worse, satisfaction. There were people who'd have taken pleasure in seeing me get my comeuppance. People who thought I was too uppity or too nauseatingly wholesome. I couldn't stick around for that." She lifted her gaze to meet his, her green eyes turbulent. "But I sure as hell didn't make a pit stop on my way out of town to bed your sleazy brother."

"I know." He rubbed both his temples. "As soon as I heard myself say the words out loud just now, I knew."

She made a choking sound. "You should have known *then*, Jace."

"Yes, I should have. I should have trusted what I knew about you. But can't you see how it was for me? I couldn't even trust myself anymore. My own memory. My body. I loved you beyond reason. You were my *soul mate*, Ember. Yet I'd cheated on you, or so I thought. I couldn't trust my own judgment about anything after that, and I let Terry convince me of those vile lies."

She let go of the backpack's strap. "Damn that bastard! I'm not a violent person, but right now, I could cheerfully do violence to that brother of yours."

"Stepbrother." Relief washed over him, making him almost dizzy. "He has a lot to answer for. And believe me, I'll make sure he does." He sank back down on the bed before he fell down. "I guess it's a good thing he's in the Bahamas. Otherwise I might wind up in jail for aggravated assault."

"Promise you won't do that." She crossed to his side of the bed and took his face in her hands. "Terry has already taken enough from you. From *us*. Whatever you do, don't let him goad you into anything."

"I won't." He put his arms around her and pulled her to the edge of the bed, between his knees. "I love you, Ember." He put his arms around her, pressed his face to her belly.

She went still in his arms. Then he felt her hands on his head, in his hair. "I love you too, Jace. I'm not sure if I love you still or love you all over again, but I love you."

He pulled back so he could look up into her eyes. The depth of emotion he saw shining back at him made his heart soar. Then he remembered.

"I have something else to tell you."

Unease flickered in her eyes. "Does it have to do with what happened back then?"

"No."

"Will it ruin this moment?"

"Maybe." He felt a muscle in his jaw tic. "Yes, probably."

Another pause. "Will it destroy us again?"

"No." His answer came quickly. Maybe too quickly.

Dammit, how could he explain?

He'd bought her family farm. Yes, him—not WRP

Holdings. He'd done it to protect it from Terry's development plans, but he'd still be the guy who bought out her heritage. He'd have let Arden stay and work the farm, but with Titus gone, Scott following wherever his wanderlust led him, and Ember busy with a practice, Arden had flat out said he wasn't up to doing it alone. The economics of hiring a foreman and a crew weren't tenable, given the narrow margins in farming. He'd insisted he'd rather vacate the place. All perfectly understandable. But Ember wouldn't see it that way. She'd see it as Jace forcing her father out to pasture. "I mean, it shouldn't. Not if you trust me."

She closed her eyes while she digested that. The seconds ticked by. When she finally opened her eyes, they were clear, beautiful.

"Then I don't want to hear it."

"What?" She could have knocked him over with a feather. "This from the gal who faces everything head on?"

She took his face in her hands again, studying it. "I'm not planning on burying my head in the sand forever. Just for a little while."

"How much longer?"

"A week?" She brushed a strand of hair off his forehead. "I have some time before I have to make a decision about my future, where I'm going to set up practice. I'd like to spend it with you."

"But— "

She put a finger to his lips to silence him. "We've lost so much, Jace. But despite everything, we found our way back to each other. I don't want to risk this happiness being ripped away. Can't we take this time to be together? Shut the world out? I want to see what it could be like, just the two of us. Don't you?"

"Of course I do."

"Then what's to stop us?"

A honeymoon. That's what she was asking for. His heart

felt like it was being squeezed by a giant fist. If Terry's vindictiveness hadn't changed the course of their lives, they'd have had a real honeymoon. What could it hurt to grant her wish?

It might even help. A carefree week together could strengthen these new tendrils of attachment into a more powerful bond, one that stood a better chance of surviving the news when the moratorium on the outside world ended.

The trick would be to get the outside world to leave them alone.

"What about your family?" he asked. "Won't they be anxious about you?"

"I can handle them," she said briskly. "What about your job? Can you take the time?"

"I'll *make* the time. Though with Terry away, I'll have to check for messages, return calls, stay on top of email, that kind of thing. But that's maybe a couple of hours a day. Can you work with that?"

She smiled victoriously. "Just watch me."

— twenty-five —

EMBER FOLLOWED close on Jace's heels as he led the way down the third floor hall of the apartment building on Second Street.

He'd offered to take her anywhere she wanted to go within reasonable flying distance. She smiled at the memory of his expression when she told him where she really wanted to go—his apartment in Harkness.

Laden as they were— him with grocery bags and a backpack and her with a backpack and his briefcase—they'd ridden the elevator to spare Jace's ankle, something he said he hadn't done since he moved his furniture in. At the door to his apartment, he put down the grocery bags he'd been carrying, dug out his keys and unlocked the door. "Remember, it's nothing special. A place to lay my head when I'm in Harkness."

She held up her free hand, palm out. "Understood. No judging."

He held the door for her, then picked up the grocery bags and followed her in, kicking the door shut behind him.

"Just dump your knapsack and the briefcase anywhere. We'll square everything away as soon as we deal with the groceries."

She obliged, putting them down beside a black leather love seat.

He headed straight for the kitchen. With a quick, sideways glance at the sparsely furnished TV room, she followed. The kitchen was actually quite large, but it did contain a small dining table and two chairs, which ate into the usable space. The refrigerator and electric range seemed newish, as did the built-in dishwasher. He deposited the bags on the counter, shrugged out of his backpack, and started unpacking the food.

"Wow, granite countertops?"

"Nope." He rapped his knuckles on it, producing a much hollower sound than granite would have. "Granite-look arborite or laminate of some kind."

"Looks nice just the same," she said, doing a quick visual tour. "So, what can I do to help?"

"How about checking the fridge to see if there's anything in there that might kill us? I haven't been around much."

The fridge was just as sparsely populated as the rest of his place, but he was right about the spoilage. She wound up dumping soured milk down the drain and chasing it with some orange juice that was well past its best before date. She also discarded some dried-out Chinese takeout, some salad dressing and a package of deli meat. Knowing he had new meat to go in the meat tray, she pulled it out and washed it with hot, soapy water before replacing it. Then, for good measure, she did the same with the vegetable crisper trays.

Working together, they put everything away. He dealt with the cupboard staples while she squared away the refrigeration-required stuff. By the time she closed the fridge, it was bulging with fresh fruit and vegetables, meat, poultry, fish, milk, eggs and juice. Oh, and the white wine Jace had bought at the market in Shamrock Falls, as well as a six-pack of local micro-brewery beer they'd picked up at the liquor store.

She surveyed the kitchen with satisfaction. "We are going to eat so well."

"I still think you're crazy." He pulled her into his arms. "I *can* afford to take you out for dinner now and again, you know."

"Are you kidding? I'm dying to cook. I have so little time for it, day to day, so when I do get time off, I like to indulge." She put her arms around his neck. "And don't worry. I'm a pretty good cook."

"I never doubted that, after all those years of helping your mother pull off those big meals."

He bent to kiss her, a surprisingly sweet, chaste kiss, his lips sliding warmly over hers. Then he released her and stepped back.

"Ready for the ten cent tour?"

Ember's phone vibrated in her pocket, but she ignored it. One of her brothers, no doubt. She'd purposely switched the ringer off, intent on checking for messages just once a day.

"I'm ready."

He picked up his knapsack and they backtracked to the TV room, directly off the entry way. It was as sparsely furnished as she'd thought from her initial glance. A big flatscreen TV on the wall, with an entertainment center below it. A small leather love seat and a matching recliner. No coffee table, but an end table sat beside the recliner, its surface covered with newspapers and a pair of remote controls.

"No video games?"

He shook his head. "Not a gamer. If I don't have work that I've brought home with me, I prefer to be outside. I've been thinking about getting a boat."

She frowned. "Didn't your dad have lots of boats? A sailboat and one of those bass fishing boats?"

"He did. A high-powered motorboat too. And now Terry has them. But I need something smaller anyway. Something I can put into the river by myself without a crew or a crane." He looked around. "Seen enough of this room?"

She laughed. There wasn't much to see, considering there

wasn't a piece of art or bookcase or picture frame or knick-knack to be examined. "Yeah, I'm good."

He bent and picked up his briefcase. Before he could scoop up her knapsack, she beat him to it. Though they'd ridden the elevator, his ankle must be feeling it from carting all those groceries.

The next room was probably intended to be a second bedroom, but it was furnished as a workspace. A U-shaped desk with stuff spread out on it and a big chair sprouting several ergonomic adjustment levers on its undercarriage. He dropped his briefcase on the desk.

Unlike the TV room, this room at least had photographic prints on the walls. She wouldn't call it art; it was more like commercial photography. Old buildings and decrepit houses and empty lots sectioned off by weed-covered chain link fences.

"Your office away from the office?"

"More like my other office. I do some WRP Holdings stuff from here, but mostly it's for running my independent projects."

She scanned the photos on the wall again and spotted the big grey building they'd visited yesterday. "Like the boxing gym?"

"Exactly."

"Does your brother know about these projects?"

He shrugged. "I don't know. I don't talk to him about this stuff. But it's a small town. I imagine he'll get wind of it sooner or later."

"Is your activity in conflict with the company?"

Something flickered in his eyes, but was gone before she could decipher it.

"Not this stuff." He waved a hand to indicate the photos on the wall. "These are definitely not WRP Holdings style investments. Way too micro-level."

"I really like this room. It has a lot of positive energy." She looked up at him and smiled. "A great vibe."

She wasn't sure, but it looked like he was blushing.

"Thanks. Shall we move on? Just two more rooms."

"Lead the way."

The bathroom was right down the hall from the office. Because it was so tiny, he gestured for her to go in, then stood in the doorway watching. She wasn't sure what to expect in terms of cleanliness. As well as they'd known each other back then, she'd never been privy to those intimate details. To her relief, the place looked as clean and tidy as her own bathroom. The tub was small, but it had one of those curved shower curtain rails that hotels often used to make it more spacious for showering. She pulled back the curtain to find a sparkling tub surround. His shampoo, body wash and shaving cream sat in a neat caddy suspended from the shower head. Full marks for organization too.

"Nice. Now can we tour the bedroom?"

"It's not much," he warned as he gestured for her to enter the room directly across the hall. "Just a place to crash."

She stepped inside. If the TV room had been spartan, she didn't know what to call this. The queen bed sat against one wall, but had no bedframe, no headboard, no footboard. Just a box spring and mattress. It was made up, though, with a duvet throw and queen-sized pillows. No pillow shams or bed skirting or anything fussy. The window was equipped with simple bamboo blinds. A single night table stood beside the bed.

"No dresser?"

He went to the closet and opened the white bifold doors. Inside, she saw suit jackets, shirts and pants hung neatly. On the shelf above, jeans, T-shirts and sweaters were stacked perfectly. But on the floor sat three cardboard boxes, the kind offices used to archive old files. One box held footware, another socks, and another underwear.

"Brilliant."

"My Fredericton condo is more put together," he said. "It

has a walk-in closet with built-in shelving in the master bedroom and built-in cabinets in the living room. It even has some art on the walls."

She turned to him. "This makes sense, especially if you're still splitting your time between here and Fredericton."

"I've been thinking about selling the condo." he said. "The deeper I get into these Prince Region projects, the more I need to be here."

"What about what you were doing in Fredericton? Are you winding that up?"

"Pretty much. Since Dad got sick, I've taken on more at WRP. Between that and my side projects, I knew I had to scale back the consulting service. I won't leave anyone in the lurch, but I've put all my clients on notice that as specific projects finish, I'm done."

"Good." She stepped close, moving into his arms. "The Prince Region is certainly going to win under that scenario."

"Speaking of winning, I was thinking I might talk you into testing out my bed. It doesn't look like much, but it's got this super-expensive, chiropractic mattress."

He slipped his hands under her sweater and ran them up her back, sending tingles of excitement dancing along her nerve endings.

"That," she said, going up on tiptoe so she could whisper the words against his ear, "sounds like a win-win proposition."

He shuddered at the warm breath in his ear. She laughed, but it turned to a gasp of surprise as he whipped her off her feet and into his arms.

"Your ankle!" she protested.

"It's suddenly feeling better."

He carried her the few feet to the bed and deposited her there before following her down to crush her under his weight. When his hands slipped under her sweater again, she forgot to worry about his ankle. Or pretty much anything else.

— twenty-six —

"ANOTHER CUP of tea?" He held aloft the new china teapot he'd bought yesterday. They'd found it at a yard sale they'd happened upon, along with matching mugs, for ten bucks. It wasn't especially beautiful, but Ember assured him tea demanded china. It just wasn't the same in the stonewear mugs he used to swill coffee. "There's plenty left."

She held out her mug. "Hit me."

It had been four days. Four of the most incredible days of Jace's life. He knew they couldn't go on like this forever, inside this bubble. But dammit, he was going to make it last as long as he could.

He'd been ambivalent going into the arrangement. Accepting her terms meant delaying unburdening his conscience, and he'd feared that weight might overshadow their idyll.

But as it turned out, he needn't have worried. Oh, the guilt and apprehension were still there, but once he committed to the week, he'd successfully pushed those feelings to the back of his mind, living only in the present. If he woke once in a while in a cold sweat of fear, it was a small enough price for this unsullied time together. The longer they loved and laughed, the stronger the bonds of love and trust would grow. He had to believe that.

They'd just finished a late lunch. Late because they'd gone back to bed mid-morning, napping to make up for lost sleep last night. And when they'd woken, they'd made love again, this time on their sides, her sweet ass tucked up against his groin, his hands free to explore her breasts and belly. And to slide down into the thatch of curls to stroke her intimately, catapulting her into orgasm.

Jace had never enjoyed cooking, but he loved doing it with Ember. At her instruction, he'd heated the chicken stock she'd made last night from the bones of the chicken she'd roasted. Meanwhile, she'd cut up sweet potatoes and shallots and carmelized them in a skillet. Then she'd pureed the potatoes and shallots with the hot chicken stock, salt, pepper and cumin. Eaten with crusty rolls they'd picked up at the baker, the meal couldn't have been simpler. But it was as delicious as anything he'd ever eaten.

"What do you think about chicken quesidillas for supper?" she asked.

"Sounds great." He collected the dishes from the table and loaded them into the dishwasher with the skillet and saucepan. "But I don't think we have flour tortillas, do we?"

"We'll need to hit the grocery store," she agreed. "I'll need some Monterey Jack, too, to go with the cheddar. We've got everything I need to make guacamole and we already have salsa and sour cream."

Jace knew when she said "we", she meant she would drive them to the grocery store and he would go in. She didn't want all of Harkness to know they were together. Not yet. And neither did he. The fewer people who knew or suspected, the easier it would be to keep the bubble intact around them.

His phone buzzed and he pulled it out of his pocket. Carly, from work. He looked at Ember. "I have to take this."

She waved at him to answer. "Of course. Go ahead."

It was a quick exchange. Carly had some cheques that needed to be signed. She had signing authority, but because of the dollar figure of several of them, she required a second signature. In Terry's absence, that meant the signature had to be his. He hung up and turned to Ember.

"I have to run into the office to sign a few things. Do you mind? I can stop at the grocery store on my way back."

"Would you like me to drive you?" He'd hired a garage to retrieve his vehicle from the parking lot where he'd left it before his fateful hike out to the cabin. They'd delivered it up to his parking lot last night, but he hadn't yet driven it. He knew she planned to return the rental today and was looking forward to piloting the Escalade.

"No, I can drive myself. The ankle's about eighty percent."

"You did have an excellent doctor," she pointed out.

"So I did."

He showered and dressed quickly. At the door, Ember gave him a quick kiss goodbye, but he growled and grabbed her. The quick kiss turned into a passionate clinch against the door. When he pulled back a moment later, his heart swelled at the look of her. Hair disheveled, lips swollen, eyelids drooping with drugged arousal. It was all he could do not to drag her off to bed again.

Instead, he put a fingertip to her full lower lip. "Hold that thought. I'll be back in half an hour."

Smiling, Ember closed the door behind him and leaned against it.

God, she loved him. Loved being with him like this. Cooking, eating, drinking wine at night, talking, making love, even watching TV. If his ankle wasn't still healing, they could have jogged together like they used to. Rented kayaks and run the river or hiked up Harkness Mountain.

If she stayed here, could they have this life?

Of course you can. What's to stop you?

Her conversation with Stuart Kirkpatrick came to mind. He'd looked so hopeful when he'd asked if she were considering setting up practice in the Prince Region. She'd said something non-committal at the time, but truthfully she'd never planned to come back to Harkness to live and practice. Too many bad memories. But now...

Now you should check your messages. If she got that out of the way for the day, she'd be free to pounce on Jace the moment he came home. Smiling again, she pushed away from the door and headed for Jace's office where she'd left her phone plugged in and charging. But when she got there, she spied his briefcase on his desk.

Would he need it for whatever work he had to do? And had he left yet? She went to the window to see him standing by his car in the parking lot below, talking to a neighbor. If she was quick and used the stairs, she might be able to get it down to him before he left.

Grabbing the case by the handle, she took off with it. Except the case fell open, strewing its contents on the floor. *Whoops.* He'd been into the briefcase yesterday when he'd checked in with the office manager. She'd seen it propped open by his side when she'd brought him a coffee. He must have closed it but not latched it.

She bent to scoop up the papers, but froze when she recognized her father's name on a document on top of the pile. Dropping the other papers, she stood. An agreement for purchase and sale between Arden Standish and WRP Holdings, Inc.? She frowned. What could her father possibly have to sell to WRP?

She read further and the answer became horribly clear. *The farm. Her home.* She read it again to make perfectly sure she wasn't mistaken. She wasn't. Her father was selling the farm, lock, stock and barrel, to the Picards' company.

The paper in her hands began to tremble violently. She

sank down in Jace's chair and dropped the document like it was on fire.

That's why Titus had insisted she and Scott come home for Thanksgiving. What he'd been poised to tell them before the search and rescue calls had come in.

And that's what Jace had been working himself up to tell her when she'd shut him down. When she'd proposed this week away from the world. This fucking escape from reality. God, what a fool she'd been!

But why would WRP want an organic farm? Agriculture, organic or otherwise, wasn't exactly in their wheelhouse. What use had they for orchards and strawberry fields and blueberry bushes? They were developers.

The waste treatment facility.

Her stomach roiled violently as she realized why they wanted the property. She put a hand to her mouth, but it did nothing to quell the nausea.

Hazardous waste. That meant risk to the water supply, to agriculture, food safety. Even very low levels of chemicals in drinking water could cause carcinogenic and mutagenic effects in humans, pets and wildlife. And the river...the beautiful river.

How could Jace do this to her? How could her father? Titus? What the hell was going on?

She had to stop it. She'd just talk to Arden. There had to be a way out, a means to void the agreement.

She snatched up the document, searching for the date of the closing.

What the hell? It had already closed, on Tuesday. *Two days ago.* While she'd been playing house with Jace, the transaction had gone through. Her home—the land that had been in her family for over eighty years—was gone. It belonged to the Picards now.

And Jace's name was on the agreement for purchase and sale. He'd brokered the deal that stole her heritage even as he'd been professing his love for her. Making her love him back.

Their conversation came back to her:

"I have something else to tell you."
"Does it have to do with what happened back then?"
"No."
"Will it ruin this moment?"
"Maybe. Yes, it might."
"Will it destroy us again?"
"No. I mean, it shouldn't. Not if you trust me."

What alternate universe was he living in where he thought she'd be able to swallow a deal that turned their organic farm—*her childhood home*—into a toxic waste treatment facility?

She sat there for a moment, bringing her heart rate and respirations under control. When she felt less like she might shake apart from sheer rage, she picked up the sale agreement. In the kitchen, she calmly sorted through his utensil drawer, drew out a pointed knife, held the document up to a cupboard door and stabbed it, pinning it in place.

She stepped back and surveyed her handiwork. He'd be coming in with groceries—the stuff for the quesadillas she'd asked him to pick up—so he'd go straight to the kitchen. A grim smile twisted her lips at the thought of his reaction.

Screw you, Jace Picard.

— twenty-seven —

"EMBER, I'M back." He let the apartment door close behind him. "Got the stuff you wanted and some fresh pasta too. I know we haven't planned our meals yet, but I couldn't resist."

He dropped his keys on the narrow table in the entryway.

"Ember?"

Still no answer. Had she gone back to bed? His heart rate quickened at the thought of joining her, sliding between the sheets, pulling her slim, warm body close.

Smiling, he headed for the kitchen to put the groceries away. He'd actually stowed most of the stuff in the refrigerator before he saw the knife protruding from an upper cupboard door. The sight almost gave him a heart attack.

"Ember?" Jesus, was she all right?

He raced to the bedroom only to find it empty. The bed was still rumpled. He was dashing back to the kitchen when the mess inside his office caught his eye. He backed up to stand in the doorway. His briefcase lay on the floor, its contents spilled across the carpet.

Shit. He strode back to the kitchen.

The good news? Ember hadn't been abducted.

He pulled the knife out and took down the agreement for purchase and sale.

The bad news? She'd fled again, just like before. Without giving him a chance to defend himself or explain.

Anger leapt to life. How could she do this to them again? Had she learned nothing? Hadn't he asked her to trust him?

He drew out his phone and dialed her number. His call went straight to an excessively cheerful voice mail.

Hi, you've reached Dr. Ember Standish. Please leave a message and I'll get back to you as soon as I can. Unless your last name is Standish or Picard, in which case, don't bother. Have a great day!

Well at least he wasn't the only one on the shit list. Not that the thought was any comfort. He never did subscribe to the misery-loves-company axiom. Arden had to be suffering. Titus too, since his desire to leave had prompted the sale. They didn't deserve that treatment.

And neither did Jace, evidence notwithstanding.

Well, if she wouldn't answer her phone, maybe her host would answer his.

He called directory assistance for a number and dialed it. One hand on the back of his neck, he waited for an answer.

"Groves Construction. We nail it."

"I need to talk to her."

Groves had the good sense not to pretend confusion. "I'm afraid you're S.O.L. right now, 'cuz she's not taking calls."

Jace's hand tightened on the receiver. "I need to explain some things. It's not what she thinks."

"I'm glad to hear that," Ryker said, his voice pleasant. "Because if it *is* what she thinks, I might have to express my displeasure personally. Fist to face, so to speak."

Jace suppressed a sigh. "Could you please have her call me?"

"We're talking about Red here." Jace could hear the shrug

in the other man's voice. "I can't *have* her do anything. She's gotta sort that shit out for herself."

This time, he did sigh. "Got it," he said. "Thanks."

"Hey, Jace?"

He'd been about to close the connection when he heard Groves's unexpected words. He put the phone back to his ear.

"Yeah?"

"Have faith, man. If you really didn't sell her down the river, along with this whole damned region, with this toxic waste crap, she'll come around. Give her some space."

The ache in his throat forced him to swallow before he could reply. "Thanks, Ryker."

The line went dead. He shoved his phone in his pocket and leaned against the kitchen counter.

As much as he hated to admit it, Ryker Groves knew Ember. There was no way he was going to get to talk to her until she was ready to listen. Emails? She'd delete them on delivery. If he was really lucky, maybe she'd just let them rot in her inbox. But until she was good and ready, he couldn't force her to read his messages or take his calls.

There was no way Terry was getting his hands on the Standish farm. He'd seen to that. And when Terry discovered what he'd done, Jace would be getting the boot as a WRP executive. Not that he cared about that. He'd hung in there to try to counter Terry's megalomania, but he wouldn't be sorry to leave. It just meant he'd have to continue the fight from outside the fold.

The fight. His conscience twinged. It was just semantics, but if this truly was a fight, he wasn't acquitting himself very well. His coach would be ashamed.

Yes, he'd taken measures to protect the Standish farm, but was he doing as much as he could to protect the rest of the region? A hazardous waste treatment facility was so *not* the kind of development they needed. Not to mention that if Terry pulled it off, Wayne Picard would be rolling in his grave.

That's it. That's what I have to do.

Rather than sit around twiddling his thumbs while he waited for Ember to come around, he could be doing something, getting in the fight. Whether he won her back or not, he had to act. He had to be the man Wayne Picard had believed him to be. The man the region needed him to be.

Fired with new purpose, he strode to his office for his contact list.

— twenty-eight —

"DAD, YOU sold the farm? To the *Picards*? How could you?"

There were very few things in this world that Arden Standish could not stand. That new car smell that was really the offgassing of toxic chemicals. The taste of warm beer. Reality television. A rat in a barn. But most of all, he couldn't stand to hear pain in his little girl's voice. He was hearing it now as he held the phone to his ear. He pinched the bridge of his nose.

He'd known where she was—known she was safe. But he'd had no idea how heartbroken she was.

Until now.

She'd been out of touch for days, letting all their calls go to some voice mail purgatory. Only through Ryker's good graces did they know she was with him. He'd had the good sense to call Arden on Thursday to tell him not to worry. Ryker also told Arden she'd learned about the sale and was coming to grips with it, but while she did, she'd be staying with him.

Even knowing she was safe, the household was in turmoil. Scott was worried, Titus was angry, and Arden was heavy with guilt.

She'd found out in the worst possible way. And now they were paying the price. He should count himself lucky that she'd finally answered his call this Friday morning.

He sighed. "I should have told you and Scott myself, Ember. Before you heard it from someone else."

"The time to tell me would have been before you sold it!"

"Sweetheart, like I told you in the messages I left you, Titus deserves—"

"His chance to get out and follow his dream. I get that and I'm not denying it. But Dad, there had to have been another way. Any other way than to lose the land. God, what would Grammy Clara and Grampy Edward say?"

It was all on the table now—the sale, the move at the end of the month, Titus's plan to leave on Sunday for RCMP training. Who knew how long Scott would be sticking around? He took a deep breath, exhaled slowly. "I'm sure—"

"So why was I the last one to know?"

"That's not how it was intended," he insisted.

"Yeah, right!"

She sounded so young. Hurt. *Betrayed.* And it was that latter sentiment in her voice that cut him the hardest. She'd had enough of that in her life. Lord above, what had he been thinking when he'd sent her out to see Jace Picard at the cabin? What had he been hoping for?

"When are you coming home?" He knew her friend Ryker would take good care of her, but she needed to come home. The sooner she came back, the sooner fences could be mended. And yes, they would be mended—they were family. The Standish Clan. He just hoped they'd be mended before Titus left Harkness. But he'd already told her Titus's departure date. All he could do now was hope she came around in time to say goodbye.

"I don't know, Dad."

He cleared his throat. "Someone called the house looking for you."

There was a long pause. "Who?"

"A friend of yours from med school—Joanne Pine. Said she was calling from California."

"She's more than a friend," Ember said. "I might be working with her. Setting up practice with her and her husband."

"In California?"

"Yes."

Arden was taken aback. It was the first he'd heard of it. He knew his brilliant daughter had more than a few offers, but California? That was so far away.

But what was to keep her in Harkness now?

"Come home soon, Sweetpea. You can tell me all about this California proposition."

"I...I still need some time. A few more days. Okay?"

Will that be before Sunday? he wanted to ask, but held the words in. If he pushed her, his girl was almost certain to dig in her heels. He rasped the whiskers on his neck with the back of his knuckles. "Okay."

"Dad?"

"Yes?"

"Why didn't you tell me it was Jace stuck out there at Old Man Picard's camp? What were you thinking? What were you trying to do?"

"I thought if you guys..." He felt suddenly weary, like the phone receiver was too heavy to hold. "I don't know what I was thinking. And I'm afraid my meddling has backfired on another front."

"What do you mean?"

"I sorta gave your brother Titus a push toward Ocean Siliker."

"Titus and Ocean? I'd have thought that was a good match myself." Her acknowledgement was grudging, colored, no doubt, by her own experience of his meddling. "But I guess just because a pairing looks good from the outside doesn't mean there'll be a spark there."

"Oh, there's plenty of spark. Enough to burn down the old barn. And they get on well together too. Since they came down off the mountain, they've been inseparable, working side-by-side, putting the farm to rights for winter."

"Readying it for winter?" Her question was sharp. "What's the point of that? The Picards are just going to plow everything under and build a toxic waste storage facility on it."

The words were a knife to his heart. "We don't know that for sure," he said. "And nothing like that was ever mentioned when your brother and I talked with Jace."

"What else would they do with it?" she demanded. "And do you seriously think they'd tell you they were planning to turn our organic farm into a toxic waste dump while they were trying to wheedle it out of you?"

"Now wait a minute. I'm the one who decided to sell. Titus approached the Picards on my behalf. If it turns out they've got dubious plans for the property, that's on me for not asking. I just figured...I don't know...that they'd parcel it up for residential development or something."

Ember sighed. "Sorry, I'm still processing this whole thing. Tell me about Titus and Ocean instead. If they're so perfect for each other, what's the problem?"

From one sore subject to another. "Their paths are headed in different directions. Now that Titus is finally free to join the RCMP, nothing's gonna keep him from it. He'll be bound for the West and cadet training on Sunday. Lord knows when he'll get assigned back to these parts, if ever. Meanwhile, Harkness is where Ocean is determined to stay, according to Faye. She's got it in her head that Faye needs her help."

Ember snorted. "Faye Siliker needing help?"

"Could be she does," he said. "She's not getting any younger and she shouldn't be alone over there in that big old house. But the upshot is, my interference accomplished nothing except heartache for Titus and that sweet girl."

"Don't beat yourself up over it, Dad. If they really love each other, they'll figure it out."

He pinched the bridge of his nose, blinked rapidly. He wasn't so sure anymore. Hadn't that been his line of thinking when he'd sent Ember out to help Jace? And just look at how that worked out.

"I'm sorry, Ember," he said. "About everything."

"Me too. Bye, Dad."

The line went dead.

"Bye, Sweetpea."

Arden replaced the receiver.

— twenty-nine —

"ICE CREAM? Again?" Ember said. "Are you trying to fatten me up?"

They were sitting on top of Ryker's covered boathouse. Accessible from the French doors at the back of the house, the boathouse roof doubled as a patio. Ember had to admit that the up-close view of the Prince River was pretty spectacular. Currently, they sat in stripes of shade from the naked limbs of the tall poplars that flanked the house.

"This evening's specialty," Ryker said. "Chocolate chip cookie dough."

"Why didn't you say so?" She leaned forward in the Adirondack chair to take the bowl Ryker offered. She looked down at the contents. "That's a pretty meager looking serving, isn't it?"

"I can fix that." He reached for the bowl.

"Kidding!" She drew it back out of his reach. "That's enough ice cream for two people, which sounds about right, since we're talking cookie dough."

He picked up his own heaping bowl and took a seat in the matching chair beside her.

She dug into the ice cream, feeling just a little bit guilty. Ryker had opened his home to her without hesitation. For the last three mornings, she'd woken up to an empty house, but one that was divinely scented with fresh brewed coffee and perfectly crisped bacon. All she'd needed to do was scramble some eggs and make toast. And each night, he'd come home by five o'clock. Given that it was still prime construction season, she knew he was leaving the work site hours early to keep her company. He'd even worked Saturday. This morning—Sunday—she'd tried to repay him by making him a full breakfast, but he'd taken charge again at lunch time, making them tomato soup and homemade biscuits. Now with the ice cream...

Maybe that was a good thing, the guilt finally surfacing. It meant she was coming around enough to appreciate how much she'd been imposing on him.

She took another bite of the chocolate chip cookie dough goodness. Obviously, she hadn't come around to the point that she was beyond a little Ben & Jerry's consolation, but who could blame her? Her whole world had been turned upside down.

Betrayed.

She had never felt so betrayed in her entire life. Which was saying a hell of a lot, considering what she'd thought Jace had done to her ten years ago. But this was worse because she felt betrayed on so many fronts at once, by so many people.

Appetite evaporated, she set the bowl on the table without making much of a dent in it. She wasn't really an eat-her-emotions kind of woman, but she appreciated her bestie's thoughtfulness all the same.

"Want to talk about it?" Ryker asked. He could have added *some more*. He'd heard it all, a couple times already.

She smiled. "I'm good."

He nodded, dug into his own ice cream. She smiled as she watched him. Poor guy. He was probably relieved that she'd given him a pass on the offer of a heart-to-heart.

Her smile faded. He'd been awesome during these last few days. She'd driven straight to his house from Jace's apartment, storming in unannounced. Ryker had been going over some construction plans, costing out an upcoming job. He'd put everything aside, and while he hadn't tried to hug her—they were friends, but that would have just been too awkward for both of them—he'd leant her a sympathetic ear. And he'd let her crash in his spare bedroom, a small but surprisingly airy-feeling room. The next morning, he'd followed her to Faulkner's to return the rental, then driven them straight back to his house. Other than that necessary errand, she'd been content to lay low during the day while he worked. And sleep. If she'd accumulated a sleep deficit, it should be well and truly rectified by now. The evenings she'd spent hanging out with Ryker.

Okay, *hiding out* might be a more apt description than hanging out.

She wasn't just hurt. She was furious. Mostly at herself for letting her guard down. But she had lots of anger to go around for everyone—Jace, her father, her brothers. She had no desire to talk to any of them, though she had broken down and answered her father's call on Friday. She knew Ryker had phoned Arden to assure him she was all right. She knew this because he'd told her so. And she was okay with that; she had no desire to be cruel or to cause her father needless worry. She also knew she could trust Ryker to keep her confidences. He wouldn't have told her dad anything more than that she was with him and was safe.

The string of messages from Scott went unanswered. Likewise for Titus. Well, for the most part. She hadn't been able to resist one blistering text for him.

Before she'd discovered Jace's duplicity, she'd responded to one of Titus's incessant texts with yet another *Still with patient* message. Titus has blown up and texted back, *Cut the crap. We know you're with Jace.* Feeling guilty about her lies of omission, she'd let his curt text ride, but after seeing that agreement for purchase and sale… Where did he get off being so freaking...*accusatory*? She'd let him have it with both barrels. Since then, she'd ignored all further messages from her family.

The thought gave her a pang. Titus would have left this morning. He was probably half way across Quebec by this time. She should have gone home to see him off, but she hadn't been able to summon the energy for any kind of confrontation. She'd call him later, when he got to Regina and had a chance to get settled in.

And then there was Joanne and Hannibal. She'd called them on Tuesday, two days before everything had blown up, but instead of giving them her answer on the California partnership, she'd put them off, bought some more time.

Why? Because she'd allowed herself to think things were going to work out with Jace? That she'd be staying here?

Dammit. she still didn't know what she wanted to do. Jetting off to California would be so easy...

Pushing further thought from her mind, she snuggled down into the oatmeal-colored cable knit sweater Ryker had loaned her and gazed out over the river. Midstream, a fish jumped, a quick flash of silver in the dying evening light, and then gone.

"Men are pigs."

She glanced sideways at him. "Nice try. But really, I'm good. All talked out."

"Maybe I'm not."

She raised an eyebrow. "You really want to have a discussion about how men are pigs?"

"Sure. Why not?"

"Because it's not universally true." She fixed him with a gaze. "Not all men are pigs. Case in point, you."

He grinned. "'Preciate the vote of confidence, Red. But you gotta admit that men do pig things. Take Jace, for instance. Cheating on you all those years ago with this spider woman, Bridget What's-Her-Face."

She sat up straighter. "But he didn't cheat on me. If anything, he was the victim."

He shrugged. "Doesn't sound like it to me."

Why was he saying this stuff? "We've been over this, Ryker. He did nothing wrong back then, except maybe not telling me about the blackout, the missing time. And hiding that stupid hickey, of course. He definitely didn't cheat on me. Terry got him drunk—probably spiked his booze to make sure he got completely wrecked—and manipulated Bridget into posing for those pictures. He was innocent. But like a child, I ran without giving him a chance to explain."

He sat forward in his chair. "Why'd you do that?"

She looked down, unable to hold his piercing gaze. "I guess I didn't trust him enough, since I let those pictures persuade me so completely."

"And?"

She glanced up briefly to see he was still studying her intently. She dropped her gaze again and shrugged. "I don't know. Maybe part of me needed to do medical school alone. Devote myself to it." She picked at the cuff of the oversized sweater. "Maybe I just needed to be on my own, to grow up."

When he said nothing, she glanced over to see a smile playing on his lips.

Her eyes narrowed. "Okay, I see what you did right there. What you're trying to do with this whole discussion."

"What's that?" He looked at her with such innocence from beneath those ridiculously thick lashes.

"For one thing, you just got me to acknowledge that there may have been other factors at play when I ran away all those years ago. That no situation is ever as simple as it might appear."

"Hard to argue with that."

"But it's totally different this time." Her fingers tightened on the chair's wide arm rests. "This isn't me running off in a fit of jealousy, or to find out if I could stand on my own. This is about the farm. Standish land. My *home*."

He nodded agreeably. "Like I said, never trust a man. We're all—"

"Ah, yes. *Pigs.* Which brings us to the other thing you did."

He gave her those innocent eyes again.

"You attacked Jace unjustly, forcing me to defend him. You made me acknowledge that he's a good, decent person."

"Is he?" Ryker pinned her with his gaze again.

"Yes," she said slowly. "Yes, he is."

He'd been a good guy back then, and he was a good man now. How many times had he proved that to her? His concern for people, for the region. The boxing club that would turn no member away for inability to pay.

What had he said when she asked him if the thing he wanted to tell her could destroy them?

It shouldn't. Not if you trust me.

But she hadn't trusted him. She hadn't hung around to demand explanations. She'd run.

Again.

It was time to rectify that.

"Thank you, Ryker."

"What for?"

"Everything. Giving me a place to hide out and lick my wounds. Listening to me." She gave him a tremulous smile. "For being such a great friend. A really, really smart friend."

"Careful, Red. You'll make my head swell."

"Ha! Considering you could make a living as a body double for Joe Manganiello. I don't think anything I could possibly say could swell that head of yours."

"Body double, huh?" He laughed and slouched back in his chair. "Maybe I should give that a try. Give up this construction gig and go to Hollywood."

"Nah," she said. "Too much sitting around waiting between

takes. It'd drive you crazy. Plus it would be dangerous, with all those pyrotechnics and crazy stunts. I like you with all your limbs intact."

"Glad someone does."

She slanted him a *get real* look. "Um…I think there are a whole lot of ladies around who appreciate you that way."

He gave her his most wicked grin, the one that made his dimples flash. "Yeah, but the trick is finding the right one."

"Which maybe you could do if you gave up working from sunup to sundown. Well, when I'm not here, guilting you into cutting your day short so you can babysit me."

"No guilt involved. Seriously, Ember. I'm happy to spend the time with you."

Well, he wouldn't have to do that much longer. "Mind if I go make a call?"

"Mind if I eat your ice cream?"

She laughed. "No."

"Then be my guest." He swiped her dish of melting ice cream and dug in.

She took her cell phone out of her pocket, crossed the deck and entered the house through the French doors.

Jace answered on the second ring.

"Ember?" He sounded surprised to hear from her. And was that a hopeful note beneath the surprise?

"I shouldn't have run away," she said without preamble. "I should have given you a chance to explain." He said nothing for a second, so she added, "In case you missed it, this is me, giving you that chance."

"Ember, I just took a seat on a plane. A middle seat. Quarters are a little tight."

A plane? Well, that hadn't taken long. Where was he? Las-freakin'-Vegas? The Mayan Riviera?

As though he could hear her thoughts, he said, "I'm in Ottawa, for meetings. I'm bound for Fredericton now,where I'll pick up my car and drive home."

"I see. So, not the best timing for a conversation like this."

"No. And I'm going to have to turn my phone off in a second anyway." She heard the tinny sound of a recorded pre-flight safety message running in the background. "Can I call you when I get back?"

She inhaled a deep breath, released it. "I'd prefer face-to-face."

"Okay. I'll come see you at Ryker's early tomorrow morning. By the time we land and I make the drive back from Fredericton, it'll be really late. We should both probably be fresher for—"

"Tomorrow's fine, but I'll be home. At the farm, I mean. If that's all right with you? I know the deal has already closed, but Dad said they have until the end of the month to get out."

"Jesus, Ember. Of course it's all right."

For a moment, neither of them spoke.

"I gotta go," he said, breaking the silence at last. "They're telling me I have to turn off my phone."

"Tomorrow, then." She slipped her phone back into her pocket. When her heart rate dropped into a more normal zone, she went back out onto the deck.

Ryker stood, empty bowls in hand.

"Mind driving me home?" she asked.

He didn't.

— thirty —

TITUS'S TRUCK was still in the yard. What was the deal with that? She'd had the impression from her father that he was planning to drive to Regina. Had she gotten the wrong handle on that?

"Want me to hang around?"

Ember glanced over at Ryker and shook her head. "No, I'm good. Thanks, Seven Ten. For everything."

"You're welcome, Red."

She hopped out of his car, shouldering her rucksack. With a wave, he turned the Infiniti around and headed back out the long driveway, dust billowing behind him.

She looked at the old farmhouse where she and her brothers had grown up. Where she'd learned to cook, done her homework, had sleepovers with her girlfriends, mastered the art of mascara application. God, she was going to miss it. And not just the house. The land. The activity cycles around the different crops as one season segued into the next. Even the chores she'd grumbled about. She pivoted to survey the Far South Barn. That might be the thing she would miss the most, the celebrations. The times the community came together and all seemed right in the world.

She heard the front door slam and whirled. Her first thought was Titus. Her father had said that he and Ocean had gotten close, but that the affair seemed doomed. She wished she'd known that when she'd blasted Titus with that one text she'd answered. No wonder he was like a bear with a sore head.

She prepared herself for his anger. Not because she feared it but because she'd promised herself she'd give him a free shot or two before she came back at him. An opportunity to vent some of the simmering anger. But since restraint didn't come naturally, especially when dealing with with her siblings, she had to be mindful.

Except when the figure emerged from the shade of the porch, she realized it was Scott.

"Hey, kid. You're back!" He sprang lightly down the wide steps and crossed to enfold her in a hug. She could practically feel his relief. Always the worrier.

"Hey, Scott." She hugged him back. "Good to see you."

He released her and gestured toward the porch. "Helluva homecoming, huh?"

For the first time, she noticed there were professional packing boxes stacked in the shadows, a long row of them running against the house, piled two boxes high. She pulled in a shakey breath. Of course there'd be boxes. They were preparing to vacate by month's end.

"Yeah. Not exactly what I had in mind when I said I'd come home for Thanksgiving." She sniffed back tears that she refused to let fall. "I wish I'd known. All that time I was nursing Jace's ankle and sorting out the past, I wasn't paying any attention to what was going on right under my nose. I knew he was holding something back. I should have pressed him."

"Well, he told you about it eventually. That must have taken some cojones."

Her laugh was harsh. "He didn't tell me, actually. I found the agreement for purchase and sale. Unfortunately, not until after the deal was closed."

Scott whistled. "I'm impressed you're still here and not as

far away from Harkness as you could get. You're making progress, kid."

She punched his arm, hard.

"Ow!" He rubbed his bicep.

"The first *kid* was free, but you'll pay for the privilege if you keep that up."

He grinned. "That's the Ember we know and love."

"Yeah, I'm the same Ember, all right." She pushed her loose hair back from her face. "When I saw that document, I still ran. Just not as far away as last time."

"How is Ryker?"

"As hard-working as ever."

"Did Jace track you down there?"

She shook her head. "He knew I was there, but I made it clear I wasn't going to talk to him."

"We're familiar with your voice mail recording."

The words came not from Scott, but from Titus, who had emerged from the house with a worried-looking Ocean at his side. "*Messages will be erased unheard, texts deleted unread. Wasn't that the gist of it?*"

She shrugged. "Sorry. I was a little upset."

Leaving Ocean on the porch, Titus descended the steps and crossed to her. "No, *I'm* sorry," he said. "I shouldn't have gotten pissy when I realized it was Jace you were tending. You're a big girl. All grown up. A doctor."

His gaze slid to Ocean, who looked on with an approving expression that left Ember in no doubt as to who had influenced that sentiment. If Ocean had convinced even one of her brothers that she was old enough to take care of herself, then this family needed more Ocean.

"I'm sorry too about not telling you about the sale. I should have told you when I first talked to Jace about the possibility. Certainly before the deal was signed."

Her father, who she hadn't even seen come down the steps, came to stand beside Titus.

"That's easy to say now, Son, but the truth is you needed to get away, and I needed to make it happen. Which is why we agreed we wouldn't break the news until after the fact."

"I appreciate that, Dad, but I'm the one who pressured you into selling." His voice was gruff. "I'd been wanting to get away from Harkness for so long. Wanting to join the RCMP and start living the life I'd dreamed of since I was a kid."

Oh, Titus.

"I feel so selfish, so *oblivious*," she said. "We left you behind to deal with everything. I'm so sorry."

"Nobody left me behind," he said. "I volunteered to stay."

"Yes, you did. And we were so grateful when you stepped up to the plate. But after a while, we—okay, I shouldn't speak for Scott—but I know I'm guilty of taking you for granted. After a few years passed, I just assumed you'd always be here, carrying on. And I know you didn't know what WRP Holdings had planned for the property." She glanced at Arden. "Dad already told me that."

Scott cleared his throat. "This is one instance where you could have spoken for me, since I've also been equally guilty of taking the status quo for granted. Sorry, Titus."

"None of you are sorrier than I am." Arden's voice was thick with emotion. "I left so much to you, Son. When your mother was sick, and later, when I was missing her so bad."

Ember had to clear her own throat. Time to get this conversation on more positive ground before they all started crying. "Well, you're free to go now, bro. That's the main thing, right?" She grinned. "I can't wait to see you in the Red Serge. I hope they tailor those babies, though." She punched his upper arm. "I can't see those guns fitting into a standard issue uniform."

Titus looked to Arden, then down at Ocean by his side. Scott stuck his hands in his pockets and looked everywhere but at Ember.

"What?" She frowned. "What'd I say?"

Titus shifted. "Well, it's like this. I'm not going to join the RCMP after all. I'm staying here."

"*What?*" She searched his face, unable to remember the last time she'd seen her older brother look so abashed. Elementary school, maybe. She half expected him to kick at a rock like he might have done back then. What could possibly keep him from his dream now? It was right there, within his grasp. Unless... "Did they uninvite you to cadet training?"

"No, nothing like that. Nothing on their end," he rushed to assure. "In fact, I was all set to go this morning. Had the truck packed. Made it to the end of the driveway. Then I looked in the rearview mirror and saw Ocean standing here in the yard, waving goodbye."

Titus looked down at Ocean, and the look on his face stunned Ember. He was in love with her! Totally and completely in love.

Titus lifted his head to meet Ember's gaze, not even trying to hide the emotion blazing from his eyes. "I know I'm a little thick when it comes to this stuff, but as I sat there with my signal light clicking, it hit me like a thunderbolt out of the clear, blue sky. I couldn't leave. Everything I need is right here."

This time, Ember couldn't stem the spurt of tears. "Oh, Titus. I'm so happy for you."

"Thank you," he said, but the clouds had crept back into his eyes. "Unfortunately, there was a price for my thick-headedness. That thunderbolt came too late to save the farm."

Ember blinked. "But not too late to avoid making an even worse mistake—driving away from the woman you love."

His arm tightened around Ocean. "Exactly."

Ember frowned. "If you're staying here, and with the farm sold, what will you do?"

"I thought I'd ramp up the classic motorcycle restoration business. I'd been doing it more or less as a hobby, but now..." He shrugged. "Now I guess I'll find out if I can make a living from it."

"Won't be a problem," Scott put in. "I've already told Titus that I could have sent him dozens of referrals over the years, if he'd been interested. And this just from folks who admired my Ducati outside truckstops or pool halls. If he actually beats the bushes for business, he'll be swamped."

"Let's hope," Titus said.

"Sounds like a good plan." She smiled at Titus. "Now let the girl go. I want to give her a hug."

Titus obliged, and Ember hugged Ocean tightly. "Congratulations, Osch. I'm so happy for you. I always thought you guys would be good together."

Ocean hugged her back, hard, then pulled away. Her face was radiant, but just as tear-damp as Ember's. "Thanks, Ember. I'm so glad you're happy for us. In the circumstances, with the rumors of a waste storage and treatment facility—"

"Let's hold off on the gloom and doom for a little while," Ember found herself saying.

"Thanks, but I'd rather face reality," Titus said. "We may have let the farm go, but that doesn't mean we—or this community—will stand still while the Picards turn the place into a toxic waste dump."

"But the reality might not be as grim as you think it is." God, was this her saying this? Trusting Jace?

Apparently so.

"What do you mean?" Her father's eyes sharpened. "What do you know that we don't, Ember?"

She wet her lips. "No one's been harder on Jace than I have. And I was so pissed at him—"

"And us," Titus put in.

"Yes, I was furious with you guys too, for keeping me in the dark. But the point is, I blew up at him and ran away. But he said something…"

"Go on," Arden prompted. "What'd he say?"

Her heart started to pound. "That I should trust him."

— thirty-one —

THE NEXT morning Arden made his way stiffly down the stairs. At the bottom, he noted the time on the clock on the entryway wall. It was Margaret's clock. She'd bought it on a visit to Calgary with her sister twenty years ago. It had been her only souvenir from the trip.

So much of Margaret was in every nook and cranny of this place. Though much of the house's contents had been packed away, evidence of her touch still abounded. He saw it in the books that still lined the bookcase—her beloved mysteries and detective stories. He smiled. For such a gentle woman, she sure loved to read some bloodcurdling stuff. He saw it in the kids' graduation pictures, each in a matching black frame. He suspected that when every last photo and trinket and dish had been packed up, some part of her spirit would still linger.

But most of all, he saw Margaret's influence in his children. Not just Ember, but his sons too. The way they looked out for each other, cared for each other. Family had meant the world to Margaret.

Scott and Titus glanced up at him as he walked into the kitchen, then stared back down into their coffee.

"Any left?" Arden asked.

"Half a cup, maybe," Scott said.

"I'll make another pot," Arden volunteered. "It's going to be a long day."

"I can fix up a sandwich if you're hungry, Dad," Titus offered.

"Not hungry, Son."

Arden grabbed a cup and poured the dregs from the coffee pot into it. That would do till the second pot was ready.

Titus and Scott must have gotten up at the crack of dawn. Or maybe they'd just stayed up all night; Arden wasn't sure.

He looked down at Axl's bowl, which was empty. "Dog fed?"

"Yup," Titus said. "He's ouside, on squirrel patrol."

Arden snorted. Axl hadn't chased a squirrel in a year or more, thanks to his stiffness, but he did like to pad slowly around the front yard in the mornings, sniffing everything and annointing his favorite places before settling down in front of the porch for a nap.

The boys were quiet as he measured the coffee, poured the water and hit the brew button. Likewise when he took a seat at the table to sip his coffee. Clearly, they were all talked out.

When the coffee finished, he grabbed the carafe. "Top you up?"

Titus pushed his mug closer, as did Scott. Arden refilled them, then topped up his own coffee. Plunking himself down again with about as much grace as Axl, Arden toyed with his old, chipped mug. He turned it until the wording showed: *World's Greatest Husband*. It had been a gift from Margaret. She'd made it years ago in ceramics class at the Harkness Community Center.

Dammit, he didn't feel much like world's greatest anything. Certainly not world's greatest father.

God, the look on Ember's face when she'd come home yesterday… Saying goodbye to this place was going to tear a piece of her heart clean out. No matter how much she said she understood, it would hurt her badly.

She'd calmed down a lot, though, since he'd talked to her on a phone a few days ago. She'd obviously done a lot of thinking since then. He'd been relieved to see how strongly she empathized with Titus's situation. She didn't blame him for wanting to get away, follow his own path. Miraculously, she didn't appear to blame anyone. Well, except for shutting her out of the decision-making and then dragging their heels telling her about it.

Arden glanced at Scott, who appeared to be searching for answers in the depths of his coffee cup. Scott's reaction had been much the same as Ember's. Unlike Ember, he wasn't one to talk about his feelings, but that didn't mean he didn't have them. He'd been just as hurt to be left out of the decision to sell the farm. If anything, he'd probably been hurt a little deeper. Scott always thought he was on the outside of things. He'd never said as much, but Arden knew.

His gaze slid to Titus, who seemed to be studying the landscape beyond the kitchen window. Except Arden doubted he saw the rows of straw covering the neatly mowed strawberry plants in the distance. He almost felt worse for Titus than the other two. It was in his nature to be responsible. To protect and serve. To take care of others. It had taken a lot for him to finally put his needs first. Then Ocean happened.

His son had found his match in that young lady, and Arden knew the two of them would be happy. But in deciding to stay and make a life here with Ocean, Arden knew his eldest son's guilt about selling was deeper than ever.

Then there was the issue of how his boys felt when he'd confessed to sending Ember out to help Jace. They had been beside themselves. And the questions they'd lobbed at him had been ones he'd already asked himself. *What were you thinking? That Ember and Jace would get back together? Or that somehow, she could use her influence with Jace to fix this?*

What had Ember said yesterday? Jace had asked her to

trust him. But trust him to do what? Prevent the property from being turned into a toxic waste depot? Maybe he'd just meant she should trust him to know best.

All Arden knew was that if Jace Picard built up his daughter's hopes just to disappoint her again, he was going to have three Standish men to contend with.

"Ember still sleeping?" Titus asked. He directed the question to his brother across the table.

Scott shrugged. "I'm not sure. She's quiet up there."

"She's awake." Ember walked into the kitchen.

Arden turned in his chair. Though she seemed a little paler than usual, she also looked as strong and determined as he'd expect from a Standish woman.

"Morning, Sweetpea."

"Morning, Dad."

"Coffee?" Scott offered.

"There's cake," Titus said.

"Thanks, I'm good."

She walked over to the box of half-packed Christmas dishes. She looked at it, then looked to the china cabinet, then back to the box again. She took one of the dainty holly-trimmed teacups from a hook inside the cabinet and turned it over in her hand, examining it.

A knock sounded, drawing everyone's attention to the kitchen door. *Way to go with the advance notice, Axl.*

Ember put the teacup back. "Did I mention Jace was coming by this morning?"

— thirty-two —

IT COULD have been anyone on the other side of that kitchen door. It might have been Ocean to see Titus. Mrs. Budaker delivering yet more gingersnaps to him. It could be any one of their neighbors who'd gotten wind of the news and came to see if it were true—that the Standishs had sold the homestead.

But Ember knew in her heart who it was. She held her breath as her father opened the door.

Jace stood there, holding the screen door open, a tail-wagging Axl at his side. Despite herself, her heart fluttered.

Gone were the jeans, T-shirts and hoodies she'd seen during their days together. Today, he'd dressed in tan khakis, a black cashmere crew neck sweater and a tweed sport jacket. On his feet, he wore desert boots. She suspected the footwear choice had more to do with ankle support than fashion, but they looked great with the business casual look he was rocking. His dark hair was neatly combed and his face clean-shaven.

Axl trotted into the kitchen. Jace waited for an invitation.

"Good morning, Arden."

Her father acknowledged him with a nod and moved aside to let him in. "Jace."

Jace stepped inside, letting the screen door close behind him. His eyes locked with Ember's. "Ember."

Before she could respond, Titus thumped his coffee cup down on the table. "What are you doing here, Jace?"

"I've come to speak with your sister," Jace said, evenly.

"Well, my sister might not want to speak with *you*." Scott stood, his chair scraping back. He stared at Jace, matched him toe to toe. "I know the warning I gave you was years ago, but it still stands. I told you not to hurt her, man."

Jace drew a breath, seeming to grow taller, bigger. "I believe I told you I never would."

Hello? Right here and able to speak for myself. "Scott, for the love of—"

"WRP got the land," Titus said, "but you'll never get that hazardous waste project off the ground. Not as long as there's a Standish left in Harkness. Not as long as there's breath in—"

Ember's mother's clock began to chime, cutting across Titus's words. Everyone stilled. It was as if their even-tempered mother were interjecting herself in the conversation, telling them all to calm down. Telling the men to lower their voices.

But she was also telling her daughter to speak up.

"Jace." She held a hand up toward her brothers as she faced Jace. "You said this wasn't what I thought, the sale. That there was something you needed to explain."

"And I can," he said. "I can explain it all, Ember."

"You also asked for my trust. I lost you all those years ago because I chose not to trust you." She could hear the way her voice vibrated, but couldn't seem to help it. "I know I ran initially, hid out at Ryker's. But I'm not running anymore. I won't make that mistake ever again. I *do* trust you. I've seen how much you love this region, the people. And I know you share Wayne's ethos about the environment. And because I know all of that—because I know *you*—I know there's a good explanation."

"That's exactly what I'd like—a fucking explanation."

At the voice from outside, all heads swiveled to the screen door. Terry Picard stood on the porch.

Axl, who'd gone to lay under the kitchen table, leapt to his feet, barking his deep, scary alarm bark. Titus took him in hand. "Easy, boy."

Terry opened the door and stepped into the kitchen. "What the hell is going on here, Jace?"

A muscle-bound man—presumably Terry's henchman—let himself into the house behind Terry. Ember's eyes widened as she recognized the man as Dundas Bloom. Definitely muscle. He didn't have the smarts to occupy a higher level position in a company like WRP. This was the jerk who'd spread stories about her in high school. She wanted to claw his eyes out still.

Axl growled low in his throat at Dundas. Titus kept a good grip on his collar, but made no attempt to quiet him.

"You shouldn't be here, Terry," Jace said.

"You know damn well why I am here, little brother."

Scott stepped forward to stand beside Jace. "Judging by what you just dragged in,"—he glanced sideways at his archenemy, Dundas—"I'd say it looks like you're spoiling for a fight."

The testosterone-fueled tension in the kitchen was thick enough to cut with a knife.

"Everybody just simmer down!" Arden said. "The first man to throw a punch in this house is going to feel my boot up their—"

Arden was interrupted by the sharp crack of Ember's palm across Terry's face.

That shut everyone up. And despite her stinging hand, it felt pretty damned good.

Terry put a hand to his face. "You little—"

He didn't get a chance to finish whatever nasty epithet he'd planned to say. With a roar, Jace bulldozed him out the screen door, across the porch and down the steps. Terry landed on his feet, but stumbled against the side of his own vehicle, a big yellow Hummer he'd parked too close to the door. Jace launched himself down the steps after his brother.

"Hey!" A slow-to-react Dundas lumbered after him.

The rest of them spilled out of the kitchen and onto the porch.

Before Dundas could come to his boss's aid, Scott shot down the steps and barred his path. "Don't even think about it, Bloom."

Titus, still holding back a snarling Axl, joined Scott, reinforcing the message.

Dundas stepped back, holding his hands up, palms out. "Whoa. Take it easy."

"You *asshole!*" Jace spat the words at his brother, drawing everyone's attention back to the Picard brothers.

Ember bit her lip. She wanted to call out to Jace, remind him that he'd promised not to let Terry goad him. But after that slap, she didn't have much of a leg to stand on.

Jace grabbed Terry by the shirt front and shook him. "You told me that Ember *slept* with you."

Ember's glance flashed to Scott, whose head had jerked around at Jace's words. His body held a whole new tension, muscles bunching for action. She rushed down the steps and grabbed his arm. He looked down at her, his eyes hazed with fury. She dug her fingers harder into his arm and shook her head. Thankfully, that seemed to reach him. Some of the tension flowing out of his muscles.

"I was all set to go after her and you told me not to bother," Jace said. "That she didn't give a shit about me anymore. You lying son of a bitch! You cost me everything."

"Oh, so what!" Terry shoved Jace's hands away. "That's ancient history." He touched a hand to his grazed forehead. She could already see the lump forming from where he must have clunked it against the vehicle.

Good.

"*So what?* You broke us up with that stunt with Bridget Northrup, and you made damned sure we stayed broken up with those vicious lies."

"Grow up, man." Terry drew himself to his full height. "I did you a fucking favor. She had you wrapped around her little finger. No sex, no drinking, no fun. I saved you from a future as a pussy-whipped loser. At least I *thought* I had…"

Jace punched his brother. Not a fancy jab or an uppercut; just a furious roundhouse that would have left him wide open if Terry'd had an ounce of boxing skill.

Terry went down, but he didn't stay down. Spitting blood, he got to his feet and glared at his henchman, but it was clear Dundas wasn't getting past those Standish men until they were ready to let him through.

Terry turned back to Jace, his face flushed and bloodied. "That make you feel better?" he said. "Go ahead, take another shot." He thrust out his chin and pointed to it. "You were a provincial champ, weren't you? Let's see what else you got."

Jace dropped his hands to his sides, unclenching his fists.

"No?" Terry jeered. "Well, here's some truth for you, *brother*. You can get your panties in a knot all you want, but if your pathetic puppy love couldn't survive a few lumps and bumps, it wasn't much of a love, was it? It deserved to die."

Jace's fingers balled into fists again, but his voice remained calm, controlled. "I'm not going to hit you again, no matter how hard you try to make me. You know why?"

"Yeah." Terry spat more blood and wiped his mouth with the back of his hand. "Because you're still a pussy."

"Because you're done pulling my strings. And I'm done at WRP too. I quit."

"You're right about being done, but you don't get to quit. Your ass has already been fired. I wrote up a press release on the way over here."

Jace shrugged. "Okay with me, long as I'm done."

Terry got in his face. "We'll see how okay you are with it after I drag you through the courts. You were paid to negotiate a deal for WRP, but you had the deed drawn up in your own name. You stole it right out from under the company."

What? Ember shot a look at her brothers and her father. They all looked as stunned as she did. Jace had bought the Standish farms, not WRP Holdings?

"So you finally noticed." Jace stood toe-to-toe with Terry and smiled. "I was beginning to wonder if you'd ever quit swanning around long enough to see what was happening in your own company. I mean, making employees call you *Old Man Picard?*"

Terry's face flushed an even deeper red. "I wasn't looking over your shoulder because I trusted you to do your job! Until last night, when I got wind of you agitating politicians in Ottawa and interest groups in the region against a waste treatment facility. When I heard that, when I saw you were working against the company, I checked with the lawyer's office and found out what you'd done."

"I didn't have a choice, Terry. Believe it or not, I *have* been operating in the best interests of WRP. At least, the WRP I worked for under Dad's watch."

"Bullshit! WRP Holdings was going nowhere. Dad was satisfied with the status quo. He didn't pay enough attention to growing the company, and if you're not growing, you're dying."

"Talk about bullshit." Jace snorted. "That's the philosophy that's killing this planet and it's unsustainable. Wayne knew that."

"Well, I hope your organic farm investment pays off for you, Jace, because you're going to need something to fall back on. When I'm through with you, you'll never work again. Not as a CFO, not as a consultant, not as a fucking *bank teller*. I will crucify you for corporate wrong-doing. And the judgment I get against you? The sheriff just might have to seize this big, old parcel of dirt to satisfy it, in which case I'll get it for a song."

"You might want to re-think that lawsuit, *brother*." Jace's smile turned menacing. "I've been working at WRP long enough to see how you operate. The bribes, the kickbacks, the payments to so-called contractors whose only work was done in the back seat of the company car. And you'd better believe I kept proof."

Terry's complexion was approaching an unflattering plum color. "You bastard!"

"Yeah, so you kept reminding me when we were growing up, Terry. But I'm the one following in Dad's footsteps. Or at least trying to," Jace said. "But you're kinda right. I can't say I'm proud of the methods I've had to stoop to in order to protect this land. But you know what they say about fighting fire with fire…"

"You're going to regret this!" Terry uttered the promise so vehemently that blood-flecked spittle flew out with the words.

Jace sighed. "You're nothing if not predictable, Terry. Which is why I've taken measures to ensure that if anything remotely untoward should happen to me, the evidence of your shady deals will be made public. That goes double for Ember or any of the Standishs. You do anything to hurt any one of them, there will be consequences. For you and for everyone whose palms you've greased."

"Fuck you." Terry dug his keys out of his pocket. "Fuck you all."

"Back atcha," Jace said.

Terry jumped into the Hummer and fired it up.

"Hey, wait for me!" Dundas edged around Scott to get to the truck, but Terry put it in gear and peeled out before he could reach the passenger side. Dundas ran down the drive after him. "Hey, wait up! C'mon, Terry."

Terry turned onto the highway and nailed the accelerator, leaving a patch of rubber on the road. Dundas stopped running a few yards short of the mouth of the driveway. He looked back at the group outside the house, then down the highway after the disappearing Hummer. Correctly gauging the likelihood of Standish help, he spat on the ground and started trudging toward town.

— thirty-three —

AS HE watched his brother's Hummer race off, Jace expelled the breath he'd been holding too long.

Ember came to stand beside him, her eyes luminous as emeralds. "*You* bought the farm?"

"Yes."

"But the agreement I saw—it was between Dad and WRP Holdings."

"You're right." He lifted his gaze from Ember's face to meet her father's confused eyes. "I got Arden to sign two agreements. I led him to believe they were duplicates of the same contract, but one listed WRP as the buyer and the other listed me. The first one—the one Ember saw—was for Terry's benefit. Terry watched me like a hawk until that agreement was in hand, signed, sealed and delivered. Then he jetted off to Nassau for his vacation, leaving me free to present the other agreement to the lawyer and have the documents drawn up accordingly."

"Pretty slick, Son," Arden said. "I sure didn't notice anything amiss, even when I signed the deed. But why go to all that trouble? I'd have been much happier to sell the place to you personally than to the company."

Jace grimaced. "Terry might have been out of the country, but he has spies aplenty in the community. I needed you all to behave as though the sale was to WRP, at least until the transaction closed. You had to be seen packing the house up, talking to people about it, that kind of thing." He shrugged apologetically. "I figured the best way to pull that off was if you really believed it."

"I don't get it." Ember said. "Whether they sold to you or WRP, Dad and Titus would still have been packing the place up, right? They could easily have pretended the sale was to WRP."

"Actually, whether or not Arden moves is completely up to him. I own the property now, but Arden, if you'd like to stay on in the house, you're more than welcome to rent it." Jace glanced at Titus. "I know Titus is RCMP-bound, so I'm not sure what your wishes are about the farm."

Titus shifted. "Actually, I'm not."

Jace blinked. "Come again?"

"Something has since…uh…happened." Titus cleared his throat. "My situation has changed."

"*Something happened*?" Ember laughed. "More like some*one* happened. Ocean Siliker, to be specific. It seems Ocean is putting down roots in Harkness again, to help take care of her mom, so…"

"So I'm available to work the farm again," Titus said. "We could lease the land back from you. Put me back in the traces, and we won't miss a beat."

"Wouldn't you rather have the farm back in Standish hands?" Jace looked from Titus to Arden.

"Really?" The old man's eyes filmed with tears. "Wouldn't that cost a lot to change the title again? Transfer taxes and such?"

"The deed hasn't been registered yet. The land is still in your name, Arden."

"So if we were to return the money…"

"I'd tear up the deed. But only if you want to. If you'd rather keep the cash and lease it back, that's cool too. I won't be hurting. Either way, the property will be safe from Terry."

"If it's just the same with you, I'd like to have it back in the Standish name." Arden's voice was gruff. "I was thinking just this morning how much of Margaret's spirit is here. Some of it we could take with us, like that clock on the wall or the dishes in the cabinet. But so much more is worn into the bones of this house, or rooted in the soil like that Bramley tree out front."

"Then let's do it that way," Jace said.

"I'll go to the bank today," Arden said. "But if we're going to do this, I'm going to have to insist on one change."

Jace felt Ember tense beside him.

"Dad, I don't really think you're in a position to dictate terms," she said, her consternation evident. "Jace just saved the homestead for you and he's offering to hand it back."

Arden held up a hand. "Sorry, I didn't mean that comment for you, Jace. This is an issue for us Standishs to resolve. What I was going to say is that we can't go back to business as usual. Titus has been carrying too much of the weight. He was planning to devote himself fulltime to the motorcycle restoration business, build it up. Was looking forward to the challenge, I'm pretty sure. So I think he should still do that."

"But Dad—"

"Hear me out, Titus. I'm not saying you shouldn't come back to the farm. It needs you. *I* need you, if this is going to work. But we need to make sure you have enough time to pursue other things. I can step it up and do more than I have been doing, but I'm not getting any younger. Come spring, we need to find a reliable foreman. Someone to shoulder some of the burden."

"I can help," Scott said.

All heads turned to him.

"What?" Scott looked at their stunned faces, then turned to look behind him. "Did a bomb go off and I didn't notice?"

"Son, that's a kind offer, but—"

"But nothing. And just to be clear, I'm not saying I'll stay forever. I'm just talking about giving Titus a vacation."

"That's not necessary," Titus said.

"It is," Scott said. "When's the last time you got away from this place?"

Titus didn't have to think long about it. "Other than a trip to buy machinery or see a specialist for dental work? I guess that would be college."

"Exactly. You need a break. You can hit the road or hang around, whatever you want. I'll be here with Uncle Arden. Well, after a quick trip to Montreal to finish up some odds and ends from that last job. But that's a few days' work, at most. I'll come directly back. I can stay for a month, or two."

"You sure?" Titus said.

"I'm sure. Why wouldn't I hang around?"

"Thanks, man," Titus said. "Ocean will appreciate this almost as much as I do."

"No trouble." Scott glanced at Arden. "I intend to make myself useful while I'm here, Uncle Arden. I notice the chimney liner in the fireplace needs to be replaced, and the plaster is cracked in the living room, in the corner up near the ceiling. I have to hand it to you and Titus—you've taken great care of the place. But it's gotta be better than ninety years old. If I really looked around, I'm sure I could find a few more things to keep me busy."

The tears that had gleamed in Arden's eyes earlier fell now. He dashed them away. "That would be appreciated, Son."

"I'll help too."

This time, all the astonished gazes turned on Ember.

Titus was the first the break the silence. "Um…you're a *doctor*."

"So? I can still be a doctor and drive a tractor in the evening, can't I? Well, maybe not this year; it looks like you have things pretty much set for winter already. But I can help next spring. And at harvest time."

"What about California?" Arden said. "Your friends who called...I thought..."

She glanced at Jace, then back to her family.

"I was tempted," she admitted. "Really tempted. But what's a state-of-the-art facility and a lucrative practice got on a resource-challenged area with a doctor shortage and a capped income?"

Her father and brothers surrounded her, laughing and congratulating her. After much hugging and back-patting, she emerged from the knot of Standish men and turned to Jace.

He was waiting for her. When their eyes met, electricity arced between them.

Behind her, her family scrambled.

Titus suddenly had to go see Ocean. Scott and Arden, overcome with hunger, disappeared inside to make a "proper breakfast".

Then Jace and Ember were alone.

— thirty-four —

EMBER FELT suddenly, stupidly nervous. Maybe because they were standing outside in full view of the house.

"Why don't we take a walk down to the Far South Barn?" Jace suggested, as though divining her thoughts. "I haven't been in there with you since we danced together at Christmas, ten years ago."

She laughed. "We did a little more than dance, if I remember."

"Not much more. Scott always had a sixth sense about that stuff."

"He did, didn't he?"

He held out his hand and she took it. But instead of leading her toward the barn, he pulled her into his arms. Crushed her to him, he kissed her hard. She kissed him right back.

"Thank you for not running." His blue eyes blaze down at her. "For trusting me."

"I kind of did run." She pulled back slightly. "In fact, I thought about flying out to California to visit with the colleagues whose practice I was ninety percent sure I was going to join. But even as angry as I was, I knew I needed to cool off before doing anything stupid. And I knew something else."

"What's that?"

"I knew I loved you."

"I wasn't going to let you go this time." He ran his hands possessively over her back. "If you'd run to California, I was going to come after you, Ember Standish. I always will. All the way to the ends of the earth and back again, if I need to."

"You won't need to." She laid a hand on his face, feeling the smoothness of his clean shave. "It took me a few days to chill out, but when I did, I realized I *did* trust you, no matter what that document said. You'd just spent days showing me who you are, and that person would never betray me or my family. And now, what you've done for us, saving the farm... I'm so sorry, Jace. I know it cost you your job."

"That's no loss. I wouldn't have lasted much longer anyway, not with Terry's philosophy, methods, and ambitions. I only stuck it out this long out of a loyalty to Dad, to try to counter Terry's worst impulses. It'll be a relief to be out of there, to start focusing more on my own projects."

She couldn't help but feel a twinge of fear at the memory of Terry's fury. No one liked to be thwarted, but she had a feeling Terry didn't cope well with being beaten. "Could Terry make things hard for you?"

"He'll probably try to get at me obliquely, but he won't come at me straight-on. He's smart enough to know I spoke the truth when I said I had evidence of ethically questionable if not illegal conduct. He won't risk exposure, for himself or his cronies. And besides, even if I'm out of WRP as an executive, I still own a good chunk of the company's shares, thanks to Wayne. Not enough to command the board, obviously, but enough to merit some deference from them. There's a couple men who'd love to get their hands on my shares—they'll listen to me, if only to court me. Maybe it'll help to keep Terry in check."

She went up on her tiptoes for another kiss, this one achingly tender. "Thank you," she breathed against his lips. "Thank you for having my back."

"That's something I can honestly say I learned here," hanging around the Standish household." His voice was endearingly rough and gravelly. "You guys might have your differences—some pretty fiery differences—but when the chips are down, you've always been there for each other."

"That's what family's all about, right?"

"Right." He brushed an errant strand of hair back behind her ear. "Is that why you're staying in Harkness?"

She heard the unspoken question behind his words. "Family, the people of Harkness, this old house…they were always part of the equation, and yet when I came home, I was almost completely certain I was California-bound. It would have been a dream job. And much as I loved it here, there was something missing. Then Dad sent me out to your father's camp."

He chuckled. "Where you cursed me as soon as you set foot inside."

"I guess I did, didn't I? But we figured it out. We worked it out. And now with you in my life, I've found the missing piece. It all fits together perfectly, and I wouldn't want to practice anywhere else." She cupped his face in both hands. "I love you, Jace. I'm not going anywhere. Not without you."

"That's what I'm talking about." He lifted her off the ground, his arms wrapped around her butt.

Laughing, she looked down at him. "Your turn."

"You had me at *son of a bitch*."

She laughed all the harder. "Come on, you can do better than that. *Say it*."

His face sobered. "I love you, Ember Standish. Madly. To the ends of the earth. For this life and beyond."

He let her slide down his chest, and her breath caught at the delicious friction. "Much better."

"I don't think I ever stopped loving you," he said. "That's why I've avoided you, this place. The idea of seeing you hurt too much. But Terry was right about one thing. My love wasn't—I don't know…mature enough, I guess—to weather the adversity he put in our paths."

Ember's heart squeezed painfully and tears pricked her eyes. "You may be right. We were so young. As heartsick as I was being in Ottawa without you, I think part of me needed to learn that I could do it. Stand on my own."

"You sure did that. And I'm proud of you for it. Watching you with those accident victims… You were amazing." His gaze was serious, the heat in them banked. "In these past few days, I've come to love you so much more. It feels wider, deeper. Worthier."

The tears finally fell, hazing his face. "We got a second chance, Jace. A priceless, precious second chance. Let's make the most of it."

"Marry me," he said.

She blinked at him to clear the blur of tears.

He took her hand and pressed it against his chest so she could feel the wild, pounding proof of it. "We're not kids anymore, Ember. We're fully formed adults, and I, for one, know exactly what I want. I want to marry you. And I want to have kids with you. Kids with a double-barreled Standish-Picard last name, because obviously you're going to keep your name."

Her eyes widened. "Kids?"

"If you want them."

The joy in her chest felt too big to contain. Too effervescent. "Yes."

"Yes what? You'll marry me or you want kids?"

"Yes, I'll marry you. And yes, I want kids. Not right away, but eventually. Two, at least."

"Two, huh? I guess we'd better start looking for a three bedroom house."

"I said *at least*."

He laughed and swept her into another kiss. Inevitably, her elation morphed into desire, liquid and shimmery in her veins.

She pulled back, her hands sliding under that cashmere sweater to explore the warmth of his muscled abdomen. "Didn't you say something about checking out the Far South Barn?"

"I did." He slid his hand over her shoulders, down her arms, sending a frisson of delight through her. "Is Scott going to turn up and bust us?"

"He absolutely will not. Come on."

She took off running toward the barn, getting the drop on him like she used to when they were kids. Jace watched her racing toward the old outbuilding, red hair flying out behind her. If his ankle was a hundred percent, he could have put on a burst of speed and caught up to her, sweeping her off her feet. As it was, he didn't have a hope. But he didn't mind. His bright, beautiful, joyful Ember wasn't running away. She was running toward their future. With her unstoppable energy and zest for life, she'd always been a few steps ahead of him, and probably always would be. But he wouldn't have it any other way.

With a prayer of thanks to Arden for sending Ember to him in that lonely cabin in the woods, he started after her.

— thirty-five —

ARDEN KNEW where Scott had disappeared to.

One minute he'd been sitting there, sipping celebratory champagne with Ember, Jace, Titus, and Ocean; and the next—gone.

He'd be outside, over by the woodshed. That's where he'd often gone when he was younger, to work out any problems on the wood to be chopped. Or just to think things through. The boy wasn't much for talking, but that didn't mean there wasn't a great depth to him.

He and Margaret had done their best to show him a warm and loving home. As far as they were concerned, he truly was their child, as much as Titus or Ember were. But there had always been a loneliness in Scott, despite the embrace of family. It was always there, a sliver of apartness that he couldn't quite drop. Margaret always swore to Arden it would pass in time.

Arden shook his head. Margaret hadn't often been wrong, but she'd been wrong about that.

He closed the screen door quietly behind him. Axl rose stiffly from the rag rug he'd been sleeping on.

"Feel like stretching the old legs?"

Axl's answer was to pad across the porch, down the steps and onto the grass. It was a cool evening, and the dog's nose quivered with the scents of the autumn night. His ears perked to some sound beyond Arden's own hearing.

"Go on, then," he said to the dog. "Go do your perimeter patrol."

With that approval from his master, Axl loped slowly off toward the property line where field met woods. He wouldn't go far, and had long since learned to stay clear of porcupines and skunks.

A roar of laughter came from inside the house as Arden crossed the yard and headed toward the woodshed. He was glad he'd only closed the screen door behind him—the sound of such laughter was long overdue in the Standish house. But hopefully, there'd be lots more now. And if he was really lucky, maybe he'd even hear the laughter of grandchildren before too many more years passed.

When Titus had told Arden that he'd found love with Ocean—a confession liberally peppered with the usual *ums* and *ers* that came with any discussion about emotion among Standish men—Arden couldn't have been happier. Or so he'd thought. But this afternoon, when Ember and Jace announced their engagement, his old heart had practically burst with joy and gratitude. That rat-faced bastard Terry Picard had tried his best to destroy any future for those two, but love had prevailed.

Faye had been there, of course, for supper. She'd even baked a beautiful chocolate cake as her contribution to the celebration. He'd driven her home twenty minutes ago. Now he was free to have a word with Scott.

With the house full of happy lovers, Arden sensed Scott's restlessness. Oh, the boy was genuinely happy for his siblings, but sometimes a body couldn't help but yearn for things they didn't have—or felt they *couldn't* have.

As he walked on, the sounds from the house faded, but they weren't replaced by the *thwack thwack* of wood being chopped.

Just silence.

He quietly rounded the corner of the building to find Scott sitting on the chopping block, looking off toward Harkness Mountain. Back bent, he sat with his elbows resting on his knees. He lifted one hand and Arden saw the glow of a cigarette as he inhaled, smelled the smoke as it drifted by. *Ha. Still sneaking smokes.* As if Arden could still give him hell for it. The boy was twenty-eight, for Pete's sake. Of course, if Margaret were still here, she'd have given him hell, age be damned.

Arden quietly backed up behind the shed. Clearing his throat, he approached again. This time when he stepped around the corner, Scott was on his feet, the butt already ground out beneath his boot.

"Hey, Son," Arden said.

"Hey, Uncle Arden. Have a seat."

The only thing resembling a seat was the chopping block Scott had just vacated. Arden sat, and Scott moved to lean against the faded shingles of the shed. Arden glanced off toward the mountain Scott had been studying. It was little more than a dark smudge against the horizon.

Axl chose that moment to join them. Panting despite the cool evening, he padded over to Scott for the petting he knew he could get. But even Axl had to sense Scott's turmoil, for he gave a lonesome whine.

"That was mighty nice of you to offer to stay a while, let your brother get a rest," Arden said, "but you don't have to. With Ember being around and Faye looking in on me from time to time, I'll be good by myself. Titus and Ocean can still take some time, have a getaway or whatever."

"Are you kidding me? I'm looking forward to it." Scott looked up from petting Axl's greying head. "I think the chimney should be our first project. You game to help?"

So, it was like that. Although he'd managed to sound remarkably convincing, Arden knew Scott would rather be just about anywhere else. Not that Scott would admit it. And not that Arden had really expected anything different. Scott had pledged his time, and he'd put it in, every last day, all the while hiding how it ate at him.

Arden nodded. "Chimney first? That's a good plan," he said. "Titus noticed the liner needed replacing last fall, but we haven't been in much of a hurry to fix it. Not much call for fires in the fireplace with just him and me. But with more folks around, I can see it'll be in demand."

"More love birds who want to curl up in front of a fire, you mean."

"Your mother and I used to spend quite a bit of time in front of that hearth."

Scott grinned. "Yeah. If I remember, you usually dozed off while she read or knitted."

Arden smiled, remembering. After a moment of silence, he said, "You're off to Montreal tomorrow?"

"Yeah." Something flickered in his face. "First thing in the morning."

"That was a pretty long job, huh?"

"Pretty long, I guess. A few months."

"A special one, maybe?"

Scott shot him a look. "Why would you ask that?"

Arden shrugged. "You get this look on your face sometimes when you talk about it. I just wondered."

Scott pushed away from the shed's support. "I made some friends there. One of them's just a kid. She kind of reminds me of me."

"Does this kid have a mother?"

Scott didn't pretend to misunderstand. "She has a very nice mother. A single-parent who's way too busy earning a living and taking care of her kid to mess with any man."

"So the kid's not...?"

Scott frowned. "Not what?"

Arden blushed. Margaret would be so much more delicate with this stuff. "Yours."

"*Mine*? Good Lord, no. I just met the two of them a few months ago." Scott came to stand beside Arden. "There's nothing in Montreal but a job that needs finishing up, okay?"

Arden stood. "Okay, Son." He looked up toward the house and the warm, yellow glow of light spilling from the windows. "Coming in?"

"Not yet, but you go ahead. I think I'll go for a walk, work off some of that chocolate cake."

Arden swallowed an ache of tightness in his throat, wishing like hell he could reach that loneliness. Knowing he couldn't, he settled for laying a hand on Scott's shoulder. "I'll leave the porch light on for you."

"Thanks, Uncle Arden."

message from the author

Thank you for investing that most precious of commodities—your time—in my book! If you enjoyed *Ember's Fire*, please consider helping me buzz it. You can do this by:

Recommending it. Help other readers find this book by recommending it to friends or by sharing about it on social media.

Reviewing it. Nothing carries as much weight as a happy reader's review. Posting a short review at the vendor site where you bought this book, or at readers' sites such as Goodreads, can really help a book gain visibility.

Again, thank you for choosing to read my book!

If you don't want to miss future releases, you can sign up for my newsletter at **www.norahwilsonwrites.com**.

Please turn the page to read about my other books!

Excerpt from

promise me the stars

The Standish Clan, #3
A Hearts of Harkness Novel

SCOTT STANDISH looked at the clock on the wall behind the counter of the truck stop diner. Six twenty. He'd made pretty good time. In less than two hours, he'd be back in Harkness, New Brunswick.

It was a cold, dark, late-October morning, but even at this early hour, he was just one of many patrons. Hands wrapped around a steaming coffee, he leaned over his now empty plate. He'd just finished putting away trucker-sized portions of fried eggs, sausage, home fries and toast. But he'd eaten it because his body needed the fuel, not because he was particularly hungry. Every damned bite had stuck in his throat.

What a crazy few days it had been.

At his brother's behest, he'd gone home for the Thanksgiving weekend, and ended up staying more than a week beyond that. He'd known something was up when Titus had insisted both he and their sister Ember come home for the holiday. He just hadn't known what. Turned out Titus hadn't either. At least not all of it.

Scott balled his paper napkin up and dropped it onto the plate.

The homestead stuff wasn't the only reason that breakfast of champions now felt like lead in his gut.

"More coffee, Sunshine?"

It took him a moment to realize the waitress—a tiny

woman who couldn't have been more than a year out of high school—was speaking to him. The nametag on her pale yellow uniform read *Madonna,* and the hot black coffee waved lazily against the sides of the pot as she swirled it invitingly. He smiled. *Sunshine?* At twenty-eight he was old enough to be Madonna's father. Okay, maybe an older brother. And he sure as hell didn't feel like any kind of sunshine. Especially after yesterday.

"Can I have it to go? Black. And I'll take the bill too, please."

With a snap of pen across the order pad, she handed him the bill, then hustled off to get his coffee for the road. When she returned less than a minute later with his double-cupped joe, he stood and handed her a twenty, waving off the change.

"Wow, thanks."

He knew from Duchess at the diner in Harkness how hard servers worked. And in a rough place like this, he could imagine some of the crap these waitresses had to put up with. Of course, if he ever tried to over-tip Duchess, she'd likely cuff the back of his head. The thought made him smile. "Thanks for the excellent service."

"Have a good day," she called after him as he headed out the door.

Early as it was, the gas pumps were already busy. As he trudged past them, he noticed a display of ice scrapers and snow brushes. They'd soon be in demand. He pulled his jacket closer against the chill as he rounded the building to the parking lot where he'd left Titus's old truck. Two men walked toward the diner, passing a cigarette between them. The air was suddenly pungent as Scott passed them.

Weed.

He was pretty sure that was the least of the drugs that could be found back here. To his left the big trucks parked, the eighteen wheelers. Easy place for an enterprising drug dealer to ply his trade. Drug testing generally kept drivers for the major trucking companies clean, but there would always be drivers working for small companies who didn't employ drug-testing. Having done some short-haul trucking himself, Scott knew some of the latter group would be on their CBs right now, looking for "Lucille". Lucille being the speed or cocaine they wanted to score to help them stay awake longer, or maybe weed to help them unwind and sleep.

He didn't partake himself. Hell, he barely even drank. None of the Standish men were regular drinkers. Although he, Titus and Uncle Arden had tipped a few back the other night. He smiled at the memory.

Scott had left Montreal at eleven o'clock at night, Eastern Time, partly to avoid the traffic he knew he'd encounter if he left the congested city in daylight, and partly because he couldn't stay there another night. Naturally, he'd tell Titus he'd left considerably earlier. Yeah, he'd gotten that whole *not a click over the speed limit* lecture from his brother, and to a lesser extent, from his uncle. But on the Trans-Canada Highway, the old pickup had practically *begged* to be let off leash.

Well, who was he to refuse such a fine old vehicle?

It wasn't like he was in Titus's baby, the new F-250 Super Duty. And strange as it seemed, he swore he could almost feel a kinship with that old truck. Feel the need for speed, the need to break out and run, just to prove it could.

Reaching the truck, he noticed the tarp he'd used to wrap the load—motorcycle parts Titus had asked him to pick up—had come untucked. He flipped it up, checked that the boxes were still there, then tucked it back into place. The lot had security cameras, but one never knew.

Load secured, he climbed in behind the wheel and keyed the ignition. The faithful old truck roared to life, but instead of pulling away, Scott scanned the radio channels. He'd been listening to rock music most of the way home, but the signal had been getting increasingly fuzzy. Now, as he cruised through the stations, he hit upon a piece of classical music. The only "classic" he knew was classic rock, but this piece was...nice. Soothing. Just for a moment, he closed his eyes.

For a few precious seconds his mind was clear, at ease. Sleepy. But then it was once again on *her*. April Morgan. The woman he'd left behind. The one he'd never see again.

Dammit, his leaving had hurt her. He'd seen it in her eyes, right there behind the determination not to show it.

Christ, it wasn't like they were lovers or anything. They'd both been clear about that from the start. Montreal was a temporary stop for him. Like every other place had been. Like every place ever would be.

Then there was April's daughter, Sidney. Or Sid the Kid, as Scott called her. He'd spent nearly every day of the school summer vacation with her at his side. When school started up again, that bright ten-year-old still managed to wriggle out of it from time to time. And when she *did* have school, she'd race from the bus to find him. She'd watched as he'd worked around the Boisvert mansion. She was curious, bright, full of questions. Questions he'd found himself looking forward to answering, or trying to answer. Until she'd asked about the stars.

How do you know the stars will come back? I see them at night, but they're gone in the morning. What if...what if sometime they just go away forever?

But they don't go away at all, he'd explained. *Not really. You just can't see them during the day.*

What if you're wrong, Scott?

He hadn't known how to answer.

Thunk.

His eyes flew open. What the hell was that? A soft but definite noise from the back of the truck.

He turned around in the seat and looked out through the back window. The tarp was still drawn taut over the load. Thank God. He hadn't drifted off. No one had ransacked Titus's parts while he dozed.

A couple passed between his truck and the Nissan Xterra on his passenger side, heading toward the diner. The mother had a toddler on her hip. When they got far enough away, he noticed they had two other kids in tow. Boisterous kids brandishing inflatable bats who ran ahead, whacking car fenders. The father caught up to them, confiscating the blow-up toys.

Mystery solved. One of them must have whacked the truck.

Wide awake now, Scott flipped back the tab on the plastic cup lid and took a cautious sip of his coffee. Then, with stars still dotting the dark sky above, he reversed out of his parking space and made his way back onto the highway.

An hour and forty-five minutes later, Scott pulled into the yard. And as he always did, he breathed a little deeper. He looked over the straw-covered fields. Titus and Ocean had done a good job of getting things ready for winter. Scott would have been happy to help, but Ocean's mother Faye had suddenly needed a ton of work done at her house down the road. Some of those odd jobs could have waited, but Scott knew Faye had just wanted to throw Titus and Ocean together alone. Apparently the strategy had worked. His brother and Ocean Siliker were now pretty much inseparable. It was just a matter of time before Titus popped the question.

Between Titus and Ocean and Ember and Jace, there was so damned much giddy happiness around, it was hard to take sometimes.

He got out of the truck and stood there a moment, his gaze going to the orchard now. They'd done a good job with it too, sanitizing the ground beneath the early-ripening trees, putting vole guards on the younger trees and such. But most of the trees were still heavy with fruit. The crop would be ready to pick soon.

The farm was his responsibility now, at least until after Christmas. He'd volunteered to stay on with Uncle Arden for a few months to give Titus a break. It was the least he could do after all the years Titus had put in. Except his brother hadn't left much for him to do. Thank God there were repairs that needed doing to the old farmhouse. It would be hard enough to stay put here. He couldn't do it and be idle. He needed projects.

A movement to his left caught his eye. He turned to see Titus had come out of the old machine shed. Swinging both doors wide, he waved at Scott. "Might as well back it right in."

Of course. The motorcycle parts. Titus would be anxious to unload them. Probably anxious to check the old truck over too.

Scott hopped behind the wheel again, drove over to the machine shed and backed the truck in.

"Keys?" Titus held his hand out.

Scott grinned and dropped them into Titus's waiting palm. "Good morning to you too."

Titus pocketed the keys. "I didn't expect you till early afternoon."

Scott stretched his back, then his arms. Damn. He'd driven from one end of this country to the other, and the long drives never usually bothered him. He was well used to the rambling life. But as he rubbed a hand over the back of his neck, he felt the tension in his muscles.

"I got an earlier start than planned."

Titus moved to the back of the truck and began untying one corner of the tarp. "How was the drive?"

"Beautiful. I love driving at night. Traffic was light, sky was clear."

"The highway between Edmundston and here?"

"Good. They seem to have filled a lot of potholes this past summer."

Titus nodded. "You must have been able to pick up some time there?"

Ah, yes. Fishing to see how hard he'd pushed the truck.

Knowing a non-answer would drive his brother crazy, he said, "Where's Uncle Arden?"

"Just hitting the shower now. He slept in this morning. First time in years."

Scott felt a chill. "Is he sick?"

"Nah. He was out late. Over at Faye Siliker's."

"Getting out of the house to give you two lovebirds some room, huh?" Scott opened the truck's door again and rescued his cup—less than an inch of cold coffee in the bottom of it.

Titus barely blushed, an indication he was getting used to this girlfriend thing. "Yeah, I think you're right. He goes over to Faye's a lot, but this is the first time he stayed out so late," Titus said. "It was almost midnight when Ocean and I got back to town. When I dropped her home, we found Dad and Faye sitting on Faye's porch swing."

"That's not a bad thing."

"Preaching to the choir, bro. After seeing Dad so depressed for all those years after Mom died, it's great to see him finally doing things with a friend."

Scott smiled, but it was for Titus's benefit. All those years Titus had been stuck here, having put his chosen career on hold to take care of the farm and his parents. Meanwhile, Scott had bailed.

But didn't he always?

"So what kept you out of town until midnight? Were you out on a search and rescue call?" He guessed not. In fact he guessed S&R had been the last thing on Titus's mind when he'd come home so late.

"Nah. Haven't been called out for weeks now." He'd been working on the knots closest to the cab, but his hands stilled. "Ocean and I took a drive up to Rockland Lake."

"Would have been a beautiful night for it."

Titus chuckled. "Did I mention I was with Ocean? Any night would have been a beautiful night for it."

Scott grinned. It looked good on his brother, this love. And no one had been more surprised than Titus to find that the thing he was looking for was right here in Harkness.

Behind him, Scott heard the screen door on the house creak open, then bang shut.

A few seconds later...*woof...woof!*

"Hey there, Axl," Scott bent and patted his thigh in that *come-here* way. The old mutt trotted up to him, tail waving. "Aren't you looking chipper."

"I'm giving him a new joint supplement along with the fish oil. Must be working."

Scott bent to give the dog the good scratching he loved, but Axl ignored him. Moving to the back of the truck, the dog began sniffing, his head bobbing almost comically as he scented the air. Then Axl jumped his front paws up onto the tailgate and strained toward the tarp. He whined.

Clunk.

Scott's adrenaline shot through the roof. Yeah, he'd definitely heard it this time. So had Titus by the way he was pulling the last few ties on the tarp.

Ember appeared around the corner. "Hi, Scott."

"Stay back," Titus commanded.

"What the "

"Just wait by the door, Ember."

Scott had no idea whether she obeyed Titus's command or not. He couldn't take his eyes off the truck. Shit! Had someone crawled under the tarp at the truck stop? Someone dangerous? He and Titus and a geriatric Axl could be the only things standing between some fugitive and their sister.

Dammit, why hadn't he checked that noise out at the truck stop instead of assuming one of those kids had bopped his truck with their toy? How stupid could he be?

Pretty damned stupid, as it turned out.

Titus pulled the tarp away, then jumped back. "What the hell? A *stowaway?*"

Not just any stowaway. *Sidney Morgan.*

She sat up, shivering.

Ember elbowed her way between Scott and Titus to see for herself. "Omigod, it's a *kid.*" She was up on the truck, examining the little girl in a flash. "You poor thing. You're freezing." She looked up. "Titus, grab her. We need to get her in the house and warmed up."

Scott stepped forward. "I'll do it. She trusts me."

Titus's eyes widened even further. "You know her?"

Scott went to the side of the truck and picked Sidney up. She immediately snaked her arms around his neck and clung so tightly, she almost cut off his air supply. "I do."

"Here, wrap her in this." Ember held out a sleeping bag, the one Sid must have huddled in all the way from Montreal. "Now get her inside and I'll see to her," she said with the same doctor-in-charge voice.

He draped the sleeping bag around Sid's trembling form and headed for the house.

Oh, Sid. What have you done?

– other books –

— about the author —

NORAH WILSON is a USA Today bestselling author of romantic suspense, contemporary romance, and paranormal romance. Together with the very talented Heather Doherty, she also writes the hilarious Dix Dodd cozy mysteries, exciting YA paranormal, and even dystopian romance.

The tenth child in a family of eleven children, Norah knew she had to do something to distinguish herself. That something turned out to be writing. She finaled three times in the Romance Writers of America's prestigious Golden Heart ® contest, and went on to win Dorchester Publishing's New Voice in Romance contest in 2004. A hybrid author, she now writes romantic suspense for Montlake Romance and also self-publishes.

She lives in Fredericton, New Brunswick, Canada, with her husband, two adult children, two dogs (Neva and Ruby) and two cats (Ruckus and Milo).

Connect with Norah Online

Twitter http://twitter.com/norah_wilson

Facebook http://www.facebook.com/NorahWilsonWrites

Goodreads
http://www.goodreads.com/author/show/1361508.Norah_Wilson

Norah's Website http://www.norahwilsonwrites.com

Email Norah norahwilsonwrites@gmail.com